A Little Love Story

Roland Merullo

A

Little

Love

Story

a novel

Shaye Areheart Books

NEW YORK

Published in the United States by Shaye Areheart Books, an imprint of the
Crown Publishing Group, a division of Random House, Inc., New York.
www.crownpublishing.com

Shaye Areheart Books and colophon are trademarks of Random House, Inc.

Library of Congress Cataloging-in-Publication Data
Merullo, Roland.
A little love story:
a novel / Roland Merullo.—1st ed.
1. Construction workers—Fiction.   2. Governors—Staff—Fiction.
3. Cystic fibrosis—Fiction.   4. Traffic accidents—Fiction.
5. Massachusetts—Fiction.   6. Artists—Fiction.   I. Title.
PS3563.E748L58 2005
813'.54—dc22   2004024289

ISBN 1-4000-4867-2

Printed in the United States of America

Design by Lynne Amft

10 9 8 7 6 5 4 3 2 1

First Edition

for

Steven Merullo

Kenneth Merullo

Peter Grudin

Dean Crawford

and

in memory of

Gerard X. Sikorski

Love consists in this, that two solitudes
protect and touch and greet each other.

— RAINER MARIA RILKE

Courage is the price that life exacts for
granting peace.

— AMELIA EARHART PUTNAM

A portion of the author's earnings from this book will be donated
to the Cystic Fibrosis Foundation.

Acknowledgments

M Y FORMER MENTOR, Michael Miller, once told me that no one writes a book alone, and in my case at least, that has always been true. I'd like to mention here some people whose names do not appear on the cover but who made contributions, small and large, to this novel.

First thanks, as always, to Amanda for her good faith, spirit of adventure, and steady love.

My gratitude also to: Alexandra and Juliana for the gift of their presence; everyone at the Cystic Fibrosis Foundation, especially Dr. Preston Campbell III and Allison Tobin; Dr. Mark Pian, Dr. Geoffrey Kurland, Dr. James Yankaskas, Dr. Ronald Kahn, and Dr. Marlyn Woo, all of whom generously offered their time and expertise and helped me get the medical details right (any errors here are my own and not theirs); Dr. Janice Abbott, Ph.D., for help with the psychosocial aspects of cystic fibrosis; Dr. Robert Gerstle, Dr. Francis Duda, Dr. Anabel Quizon, and everyone at the Springfield, Massachusetts, CF center for their excellent care; Joe Merullo for his optimism and encouragement, and for suggesting I write a love story; Eileen Keaffer and Senator Stanley Rosenberg for their assistance with the physical details of the Massachusetts State House; my friend, the fine painter John Recco, and Sara Brigham for information about painting techniques and equipment; Maria Recco for help with Greek culture; Avery Rome for two wonderful assignments; Matthew Joyce and his family,

David Manglos, and Fred Phillips for their courage and time—while this is not their story, they were surely an inspiration for it; a thoughtful and helpful group of readers: Amanda Merullo, Craig Nova, Peter Grudin, Dean Crawford, Barbara Cheney, Lisa Ahlstrom, Sydne Didier, Katherine Weinstein, Melissa Preston, and the person who taught me to read and to love books, Eileen Merullo; Cynthia Cannell for placing this novel and for years of support; my editor and friend Shaye Areheart; Jenny Frost, Cindy Berman, Julie Will, Darlene Faster, Tara Gilbride, Debbie Natoli, Kira Stevens, Tina DeGraff, and everyone at Shaye Areheart Books for their tireless efforts; Jeff Foltz, Patrolman Rick Camillo of the Boston University Police, and Coach David Sanderson of the Boston University varsity men's crew for refreshing my memory about the school and the sport; Darra Goldstein for menu advice; Edward Steriti for the way he lives; and Officer Wise of the Dover, Massachusetts, Police Department.

Last, I would like to express my gratitude to and admiration for all the CF patients, doctors, nurses, and family members I have spoken with or interviewed over the past four years. May every blessing come to you.

A Little Love Story

FIVE MILES BELOW I dreamt the blue Pacific, scalloped with whitecaps and looking like it had been frozen in time. In my lap the sleeping black-haired bundle of life stirred and sighed and curled closer against my shirt. I cupped one hand gently against the back of his small head. When he was quiet I turned to the window again and saw four atolls gliding under us, an impossible cluster, four specks of cream-edged green on the immense watery background. I wondered about painting them.

Strange how the demons do their work. With that fragile life sleeping against me, and two more dark-haired creatures close beside, and riding a run of good luck like I'd never known, my mind traveled along the ridges of its flying-fear, bumped and tilted, flipped upside down, and crashed into Brian. It occurred to me for the first time that he might have done some great heroic thing in the last minutes of his life, to make up for the not-so-great things he'd done before that. Alright, a voice in me said, let it go now. Let it be true. Let it go.

The atolls coasted along in their dreamy, improbable still-ness. Beside me I thought I heard a cough. I turned—too quickly—and her dark eyes held an expression that no one could paint. Don't worry, they said. Just an ordinary breath, a good ordinary puff of life, part mine and part yours and part someone else's. Be happy while we can.

Book One

September

1

M Y YEAR OF MOURNING was over, and I decided to mark the anniversary by treating myself to a doughnut.

By my own choice, I had not had sex with anyone during those twelve months. I'm not sure why I did that. Maybe it was out of respect for the woman I had lost, though she wouldn't have wanted anything like that from me. My older brother is a monk, so maybe I was trying to prove I could keep up with him in the abstinence department. Or maybe I was just afraid I would meet someone I liked and sleep with her, then start to think about her all the time, then start to want to have children with her, and then she would be torn away from me and spirited off to some better world—if there is a better world—and that is not the kind of thing you want to go through twice in one year.

So on that wet September night my year of abstinence was finished, and I went out looking for a doughnut as a sort of offbeat celebration. That's all, really. A doughnut says: Listen, for your eighty-five cents I'm going to give you a quick burst of feel-good. No soul connection. No quiet walks. No long foreplay sessions in a warm one-bedroom. No extinction of aloneness. No jealousy. No fights. No troubles. No risk.

On that night, the risk I thought I was willing to take extended only as far as chocolate-glazed. Steaming cup of decaf next to it, little bit of cream, the shabby comfort of my favorite doughnut shop. It seemed a small enough thing to ask, after the year I'd seen.

The steady rain that had been falling during the afternoon and early part of the night had quieted to a light drizzle. The streets were black and wet, streaked with color from storefront neon and traffic lights. I worked my old pickup out of its parking space—foolish move, giving up a parking space in that neighborhood at that late hour—and drove to Betty's.

There is no Betty. Once there might have been, but at that point Betty's was owned by Carmine Asalapolous, a rough-edged, middle-aged man who had told me once that he wished he'd done something heroic in his life so he'd have a piece of high ground to fall back on when the devils of self-doubt were after him. Carmine, I said, just being a decent person, good father, excellent doughnut-maker—that's enough heroism for one life. But he shook his big head sadly and said no, it wasn't, not for him.

Carmine went to a two-hour Orthodox service on Sunday mornings. During the week he liked to make off-color jokes with his regular customers. He had some kind of mindless prejudice against college professors, a scar between his eyebrows that looked like a percent sign, and two young daughters whom he adored and whose pictures and drawings were taped up on every vertical surface in Betty's. He took his work seriously. If you got him going on the subject of doughnut-making, he'd tell you the chain doughnut shops used only the cheapest flour, which is why you left those places with a pasty aftertaste on your tongue.

I parked in front. The roof of Betty's was dripping and one cold droplet caught me on the left ear as I walked in. I remember that odd detail. In line at the counter I held a little debate with myself—how wild a night should it be?—then asked for two chocolate-glazed instead of one, a medium instead of a small decaf. Carmine was counting money in the floury kitchen. I could see him there through a sort of glassless window. He looked up at me from his stack of bills, pointed with his chin at the waitress's back, and made a John Belushi face, pushing his lips to the side and lifting one eyebrow, the expression of a man who had not a millionth of a chance of ever touching the waitress in a way she liked, and knew it.

I carried my paper cup of coffee and paper plate with two doughnuts on it to a stool at a counter that looked out on Betty's wet parking lot. In a minute a trim, balding man sat beside me, with a black coffee and the Sports section of the *New York Times*. "Nice truck," he said.

"Thanks."

"I saw you get out of it," he said.

I could not think of any response to this.

He kept trying. He said: "You don't see many of them still around. Fifty-one Dodge?"

"Forty-nine."

"Gorgeous," he said. "Like you."

I looked away. I was waiting for my coffee to cool, and was not really in the mood to talk, and though I understand sexual loneliness as well as the next person, there was not much I could do about this man's loneliness. Just at that exact moment—it was after midnight—a woman walked out of Betty's carrying a small bag and got into her car and she must have had a slippery shoe or been distracted by something because she put her new Honda in reverse and drove it across about fifteen open feet of parking lot and straight into the back of my truck.

"Whoa!" the man beside me yelled.

I took a good hot sip of coffee. I watched the woman get out, rubbing the back of her neck with one hand and looking as if she wished she had never been born. And then, very calmly, I went outside to talk to her.

2

SHE WAS A NICE-LOOKING woman. Not very tall, thin, with large breasts under a gray cashmere sweater and wide hips and what looked like genuine cowboy boots on, and jeans. She wasn't really dressed to be out in the rain, and she was coughing. I had my coffee cup in one hand and my first instinct was to offer her some because she looked so miserable there, in pain, upset at her bad luck, and sick besides.

"Hi," I said. "I'm Jake. That's my truck you just mashed."

She coughed and coughed and said how sorry she was.

I said it wasn't the end of the world—a phrase I had been using with myself all year. She got out her registration and insurance papers and gave me her business card, and since I don't have a business card, I wrote my name and number on the back of another one of hers and that was the end of it. Carmine had come out and was wielding an old golf club in case there was any trouble, which, of course, there wasn't. Just before the woman ducked into her Honda, she swung her long black hair away from her face and looked at me. Thank you for not making a big deal about it, the look said. But Carmine interpreted it differently.

"You have the phone of this girl?" he asked, when she had driven away.

I said that I did. We were standing there side by side in the drizzle.

"Wait three days for the cold she has to go away, then call."

I finished my coffee right there in the rain, and Carmine took the cup, and I went home and more or less straight to bed.

3

O VER THE NEXT FEW days it wasn't easy to keep from thinking about the young woman in the cowboy boots because I used my truck for work and I liked to look at it from time to time to cheer myself up. It was an official antique, forest green, with a bright chrome grille and a handmade maple rack over the bed for lumber and ladders. Every time I looked at the truck from a certain angle I could see the broken taillights and dented fender and I wondered how hard it would be to get replacement parts and I thought about the black-haired woman coughing in the rain.

I didn't mention her to anyone, not even to Gerard, who works with me and is closer to me than my own brother and sister. I waited three days—for her cold to go away and so as not to seem overly anxious—then dialed the number on her card.

"Hi," I said. It was my lunch hour, I was calling on Gerard's cell phone, because I didn't own a cell phone anymore. I didn't own a TV, either, or a microwave, or a single pneumatic nailing gun, even though I could have afforded those things. I was sitting on a set of exterior steps we'd built as part of a new addition to a professor's house in Cambridge, tuna sandwich on my lap. "I'm Jake Entwhistle," I said into the phone. "You mashed up my truck the other night in front of Betty's."

For a few seconds there was no reply. It sounded to me as though she was still coughing, but trying to stifle it. I pictured her turning her face away from the phone.

"The doughnut shop," I suggested, when she didn't speak.

"My insurance company should have sent you the papers by now."

"I'm not calling about that. I'm calling to ask you out."

"I'm at work," she said.

This didn't seem like a promising answer, but I kept trying: "A restaurant dinner, on me. Maybe a walk around the block afterwards if it's a nice night and we get along."

"Thank you, but I can't," she said. "And I'm very busy right now."

"Alright."

"You should get the insurance forms within a day."

"Alright," I said. "I'm not worried. It's an old truck."

"Good. Good-bye. Thank you anyway."

"'Bye," I said. I set Gerard's phone down on the new stair tread, finished my sandwich, folded the wax paper up into a perfect square, and put it in my back pocket. I looked out at the neighborhood of neat, wood-frame houses with swing sets in their backyards. Eventually I stood up.

Instead of eating, Gerard was using the lunch hour to take a nap on the plywood subfloor of what would someday be the professor's new bedroom. For a while I walked around, checking things that didn't need to be checked, and at twelve-forty-five I went up and woke him. When he opened his eyes and saw me he said, "One more minute, Colonel, I was having the dream of dreams."

Everything was the something of something with my friend. The dream of dreams, the woman of women, the divorce of divorces. He had a rough, honest-looking face, a difficult past, and the two sweetest young daughters in the world. In another minute he stood up, ate a pear, and we spent the afternoon cutting two-by-six studs for the walls of the upstairs rooms and nailing them in place.

"Let's spruce things up, Colonel," Gerard suggested at one point, because the two-by-sixes had been sawn from spruce trees.

"The professor would like that," I said.

"The professor was in my dream. She was asking me to . . . well, I can't say what she was asking me without the risk of offending community standards of decency."

"We're in a school zone, besides," I said.

"The professor had given me a physics problem, I can say that much."

"She's a good professor. We like her particularly much."

"Physics, biology, chemistry. All the sciences were involved. Latin, Spanish."

"Italian?"

"Tongue of tongues."

We went on for a while with this kind of nonsense, driving sixteenpenny nails one after the next through the sole plate and into the ends of the spruce two-by-sixes. When the walls were framed, and the light had softened to an early evening light, we packed our tools away in a safe place upstairs, stood around for a while looking at the work, asked each other what kind of plans we had for that night, shook hands, as we always did, and went home.

At home, I showered, made myself a supper of black beans, brown rice, red wine, and a Fudgsicle, and went into my studio to paint.

"Studio" is probably too fancy a word. I had a three-room, 1,300-square-foot apartment in an old factory building where people had at one time made shoes. There was a small kitchen, a bedroom almost completely filled by the bed and bureau, a bathroom with old-fashioned, six-sided white tiles on the floor, and a very large awkward room with four tall, thirty-two-paned factory windows—my studio. I had two easels set up there, racks for old paintings, and shelves with tubes of paint, cans of gesso, pencils and charcoal and pastel chalks, sketches, brushes, drop cloths to protect a floor that had been gouged and grooved by vibrating shoe machines a hundred years before, then more or less refinished.

In those days I was painting with oil on linen, and I liked to size the linen canvas myself with rabbit-skin glue, and then make a mix of titanium white gesso and a marble-dust filler and apply it in even strokes, all in one direction for the first layer, and then in the cross direction for the second. I liked to make the canvas frames by hand, cutting four pieces of poplar with my miter saw and joining them with mortise and tenon and pin. I painted fairly realistic portraits, of women mostly, but also of children and men. The people were sometimes purely imagined and sometimes based on actual people who had made some mark on my life, and often I stayed up very late working on them. Every eighteen months or so I had a gallery show and sold a few canvases for roughly what I would make in two weeks of carpentry.

I finished—or reached a stopping point—at eleven-thirty, cleaned up, and was in bed by midnight, when the phone rang.

I thought it was Gerard. In those days he often called me late at night to see how things had gone in the nonworking part of my day and to ask what supplies we might need from the lumber-yard to start work the next morning. Another person would have waited until the next morning to talk about how things had gone, and asked about supplies in the afternoon when we were finished for the day. But Gerard could not be held to the standards of another person. He brought Virginia Woolf to work for lunch-hour reading. He liked to recite Latin poetry, by heart, sometimes shouting *Lente, lente currite, noctis equi!* out over the streets of

Cambridge, Allston, or Beacon Hill from a three-story staging. He was addicted to doing research on his computer, and he'd talk for hours about supernovas and scuba equipment, the political situation in Kazakhstan, Tour de France champions, diseases of the beech tree, NASCAR standings. His interests were encyclopedic, his memory photographic, his sense of loyalty and need for affection without bounds. As a boy, his family life had been less than perfectly nurturing. As a young man, he'd dropped out of college—where we'd been friends—and then spent time in a hospital for bipolar problems. I had let him live at my place for a while between college and marriage. And later, I'd hired him to work with me, building additions, fire escapes, three-car garages, tearing out whole sections of houses that had gone rotten or been eaten away, and replacing them with plumb walls and level floors and neat interior woodwork. During the previous year—the Evil Year, I called it—he had paid me back with interest for whatever favors I'd done. So we had complex worlds swirling around in the alleys and avenues of our friendship—gratitude, shame, grief, old childhood wounds, new arguments, a speckled canvas of deep affection that we never talked about.

But it wasn't Gerard's voice in any case. The person on the line had the mother of all colds.

"It's Janet," she said. "Rossi." She turned her mouth away from the phone to cough. "I'm sorry if I was rude today. It's hard for me to talk at work."

"You weren't too rude."

"I hope this isn't too late to call. You were up this late at the doughnut shop, so I guessed you were a night person."

"A night person and a day person," I said. She coughed again and I was going to make a little remark about it, but my sense of humor can get strange sometimes when I'm nervous—I've been told that more than once—so I held back. "Where do you work?" I asked her. What I kept myself from saying was, "In which mine?"

"The governor's office."

"I saw him on the TV at O'Casey's last week."

"He's running again, so things are a little hectic."

He should run, I almost said, because I had some kind of instinctive, bone-and-blood dislike for the man, even though he'd been a decent governor up to that point. *He should start running at the door of the State House and not stop until he gets to Ixtapa,* I had an urge to say. But I was holding on to my comic side with both arms by then.

She said, "I called to see if the dinner invitation is still good."

"Let me check the calendar." I picked up my August *National Geographic* and made the pages flap. "I have a Friday in 2006," I said. "November."

"You're paying me back."

"Or this coming Friday night. Nothing between, I'm sorry to say . . . except this Saturday night. Also good."

There was a long pause then. It wasn't health-related.

"I can be a little goofy this late," I said.

"Are you on something?"

"Paint fumes."

"Oh."

"That was a joke. There's a new Vietnamese restaurant on Newbury Street. Diem Bo. It's a great place if you like that food. Noodles and so on. Shrimp. That coffee they make with all the milk and sugar in it."

"I love Vietnamese coffee."

"Good. Seven o'clock okay?"

"Perfect."

"Friday's better, it's sooner than Saturday. Friday okay? Meet you at Diem Bo?"

"Fine."

"Good. It made me happy that you called."

"I'll see you Friday."

We hung up and I lay awake for a long time, thinking I shouldn't have said it made me happy that she'd called, then thinking it was alright. Thinking I wasn't really ready to go on a date just yet, and then thinking I might be.

4

ON FRIDAY AFTERNOONS Gerard and I quit for the day at four o'clock and went to O'Casey's for a drink. In addition to his other passions and talents, Gerard was a world-class bicyclist, and very careful about what he put into his body, so he usually had tomato juice with a twist of lime. I like beer but beer does not like me, so I usually had a glass of Merlot. Bub, the bartender, made no secret of the fact that he thought our choice of beverages unmanly. He called us "Red One" and "Red Two," though Gerard is dark-haired, going bald, and my hair is the color of old hay.

"Good that you're dating again," Gerard said, when I told him about my plans for that evening. "I've been worried about your mental health . . . which is a subject I know something about."

"Everything is a subject you know something about."

I asked Bub for some Beer Nuts to go with the Merlot. He smirked.

"And Vietnamese is the right choice," Gerard went on. "It's sex food."

"How do you figure?"

"Just is."

"What's love food?"

"Greek, naturally."

I nodded. Gerard's last name was Telesrokis. "What's marriage food?"

"French. Or a steak house."

"What's Thai food, then?"

"Sex food, too. Kinky, though."

"Chinese."

"Chinese is old-fashioned courtship. Szechwan especially."

"Alright."

"Vietnamese is an excellent first date. In time, if things go well, you can progress to Greek or Thai, depending."

"On?"

"The tastes and qualities of the woman involved. What she reads, for instance. How many languages she speaks."

"What's German food?" I asked him, because he had gotten married at a young age to a German woman named Anastasia and had his two beautiful girls—five-year-old twins—by her, and the breakup of that union had been so spectacularly awful for him and for Anastasia and for the twins that it hung around his neck like a great weight of guilt and hurt and he still talked about it too much.

"Heavy," he said, without missing a beat. "Sticks to you."

"Good. I'll remember. Seeing the twins this weekend?"

"You should see your face when you ask about them, Colonel." He looked up at the television screen, but he was not really paying attention to it. "You would be the father of fathers, you know that, don't you?"

"You're kicking my bruise."

"Sometimes a bruise needs a good kick," he said. "I'll call you tonight, either just before midnight or just after."

"Don't."

"I will, though. I know myself."

5

A T FIVE MINUTES to seven I gave a dollar to the valet atten-
dant at Diem Bo and straightened the lapels of my sport
jacket. It was a beautiful September night, clear and warm, with
enough summer still in it to make you believe the world was a
good and happy place, and the couples you saw strolling on Newbury Street were destined for long peaceful lives together.

As I was walking up Diem Bo's brick front steps, I was
greeted by an imaginary messenger from the world of ugly
thoughts. A troll, a goblin, an ugly little creature from the king-
dom of fear. His message went something along the lines of: Why
this again? But I knew why. For the previous twelve months I had
been skating over the surface of things, and I worried that, if I
kept at it too long, I'd end up like some of the guys I knew in the
trades, plumbers and painters and masons—decent enough thir-
tyish and fortyish men who could not really carry on a conversation with a woman, and who skipped along from *Monday Night
Football* to darts at the local pub to long days with the mortar and
cinder blocks, or hammer and two-by-eights, and who were
afraid to ever talk about anything more interesting than what had
gone on last Thursday night in the pocket-billiards league, or the
latest Red Sox game, or the last time they'd had a blow job.

I wasn't like that. Gerard wasn't like that. But Gerard, at
least, had his children to keep him honest. I felt I was drawing

close to that age, that place in life, where you realize one day that what you'd told yourself was a Zen detachment turns out to be naked fear. You'd had one serious love relationship in your life and it had ended in a tragedy, and the tragedy had broken something inside you. But instead of trying to repair the broken place, or at least really stop and look at it, you skated and joked. You had friends, you were a decent citizen. You hurt no one. And your life was somehow just about half what it could be.

I looked up from that pleasant thought, inside the door of Diem Bo now, and saw Janet Rossi at a window table halfway back in the room. There was a tall glass of iced coffee in front of her. I spend a lot of time looking at faces, and her face was not beautiful in the way models' and actresses' faces are supposed to be, but pretty in a way all her own: shining black hair, black eyes, a slightly bent nose, and a wide mouth. There was something—a kind of tough smartness maybe—shining quietly out from her. Instead of walking down the long narrow room, I waited for the hostess to come over and escort me, and I watched in the meantime. Janet put a handkerchief to her mouth and coughed. It was a lousy time of year for a cold.

She was wearing a black dress cut low enough to show the bones on the front of her chest. She smiled when I sat down, a large, even smile that lit up her eyes, one slightly crooked tooth upper left, one freckle beside her nose. I have funny hair, "awkward hair" my girlfriend Giselle used to call it, the kind that stands up too straight, so that if you cut it short like I do, it can look ragged and boyish. I thought Janet might be smiling at my hair but was too polite to say anything.

As I sat down I accidentally knocked a fork off the table. "So, how was your day, honey?" I said, after the noise of the clattering fork had died down in my mind. "Kids okay? Sitter come on time?"

She just looked at me and pushed the long black hair off her right cheekbone. She touched her thumb and middle finger to the iced-coffee glass. "You're a little weird, aren't you," she said, in a tone that had a couple of spoonfuls of regret in it.

I shook my head. "A little nervous, that's all. I'm not exactly Joe Date."

"Joe Date?"

I felt like I had fallen on my knees in a puddle of mud, and now, to make up for it, I was falling on my chest, with a white shirt on. "How are you?" I asked.

"Fine. Are you insinuating you don't go on many dates? Married or something?"

"Never married."

She took a sip of her coffee. "Why? You're what, about twenty-eight? Nice-looking."

"Thirty," I said. I had a glass of water up to my face for protection. I saw Jason or Dominick or Adam-who-will-be-your-serverperson, off at another table, and with all my heart I was willing him to come over and let-me-tell-you-about-tonight's-specials. Janet had me pinned down with the black eyes. She coughed and tried to hold it in. She wanted an answer.

I moved my left foot and felt the fork down there. "I have seven kids out of wedlock," I said. "That's why. I'm up to my forehead in credit-card debt. I'm hyperactive. Women's bodies make me uncomfortable. You're nice-looking and not married either, right? It doesn't necessarily mean you're a bad person."

She almost seemed to be smiling. She hadn't gotten up and walked out, at least, leaving me to pay for her Vietnamese coffee.

"No."

"Hi. I'm Brian and I'll be your server tonight."

"And just in time," I said.

Brian was tall and wide-shouldered, handsome as a shirt model. He blinked twice and started to try to get us to buy drinks before we ate. I could see in his face and hear in his voice that he was the type of person who was nervous around people and pretended not to be. He'd built an elaborate personality over his nervousness. He'd developed an armor, an act, a defensive outgoingness. It was the kind of thing that made me dislike someone right away. And the name was no good, besides. One of God's little jokes.

I said, "We'll both have the special."

"There are two specials tonight."

"We'll have one each." I turned back to Janet. "Would you pick the appetizers and dessert?"

Jason went into one of the speeches he had memorized: "The appetizer special tonight is braised scallops in a lemon butter saffron sauce with shallots and thinly sliced Shiitake mushrooms, finished with a kumquat glaze."

"We'll try one," Janet told him. "Two forks, please."

I could tell by the way she said "forks" that she was a real Bostonian.

"I'll have what she's drinking," I said.

Adam wrote this down and then began to tell us what the two dinner specials were. I put my hand on his arm. "We'll have them," I said. "One each. We've been married eight years, this is our anniversary, we're trying to introduce some unpredictability into the relationship, so we don't really want to know what we're having, if that's okay with you."

Dominick looked at me earnestly. The menus were huge and he was awkward collecting them. "Anything to drink?" he asked.

"What she's having."

"Very good. I'll be right back with the scallops. They're excellent."

"Sorry for giving you a hard time," I said.

When he went away, Janet started to say something, but it turned into a deep, watery cough that sounded like it was shaking her body from bone marrow to skin. She excused herself and walked off to the bathroom carrying her purse. I watched her go.

I put my right hand in the pocket of my sport jacket. They were playing Beethoven quietly from small ceiling speakers, and I heard it as if from a childhood dream: my mother and father home from work and enjoying a drink, asparagus steaming, Beethoven on the tape player. I tried to calm down. I looked around at the other men at other tables. They seemed well groomed, with normal hair and good, white-collar careers, and a regular dating record, or a wife, or a steady girlfriend, or kids. No one else in Diem Bo was nervous. I tried doing a breathing exercise Gerard used before his bicycle races, but it made me dizzy so I stopped and stared out at Newbury Street over the top of my arm. When Janet had been gone twelve or fourteen minutes, Joshua brought the scallops. "And a Vietnamese iced coffee," I said, pointing across the table at the tall glass.

"Very good," he said.

Five or six minutes later he brought it. "How are the scallops?"

"I haven't tried them yet."

"Excellent."

Two more minutes and I understood that Janet Rossi was not coming back. The part of me that had been against going out on a date again had been the correct part, and the little troll reappeared and started in on a not very nice line of I-told-you-so. In compensation, then, I developed a plan: I would eat all the food we had ordered, buy a thirty-dollar bottle of wine on the way home, and then put John Hiatt on my music machine pretty loud and drink and paint until I knew I could fall asleep. Sitting there, formulating that plan, I felt an old sourness rising. I began to feel sorry for myself in the most childish and brutal way, and though I knew from other times that it would pass, that it was only a little half-dry bloodstain on the shirtsleeve of my mind, I wet it and rubbed it and indulged it for a few more minutes until I saw Janet come out of the bathroom. At which point I started spooning scallops onto her dish like Joe Date.

She gave me a wary look, as if I was going to ask her about the coughing. But I had decided not to. Son of a doctor who had made sure my brother and sister and I weren't squeamish about the body and its troubles, I wasn't one of those people who are afraid of catching a cold. Though I'd noticed that several such people were sitting near us.

Before Janet started to eat, she took out a plastic container with several compartments in it, placed six different pills on the tablecloth, and swallowed them with water. It was easy to see that she was waiting for me to ask about them but I didn't ask because I wanted everything to be alright then. I wanted to be with a woman and have no trouble between us, no jealousy, or anything like that, no sickness. Even just for one night I wanted that. She opened her purse again and snapped it closed, and when I didn't mention the pills, she started to eat.

I said, "When I get nervous or when something really upsets me, I make goofy jokes. I've been that way since I was a kid. I would like to officially start over."

She nodded and looked up.

"What kind of a day did you have, really?"

She swallowed. "Awful."

"Why?"

"I'd rather not say. It has to do with the person I work for."

"Which is who?"

"Which is the governor. It was on my card."

"Of Massachusetts?"

Another nod.

"The famous Charlie Valvoline?"

Nod number three, and some little squirrel of bad feeling skittering across her cheekbones. "He hates that nickname. Could we talk about something else?"

"Sure. You start."

The scallops were excellent, and there was something intimate about sharing them that way, and about not knowing what kind of main course Richard was going to bring us. Janet asked what I did for work, but I wasn't really paying attention to the question because by then I was already beginning to get the sense that there was something vast and wrong in her life, some shadow so enormous that it covered her and me and half the tables in Diem Bo. It was in the movement of her eyes and hands, and in her voice—which was on the husky, throaty side, and resonated behind the bones of the middle of her face. The advantage to meeting and dating when you're fifteen or seventeen or twenty is that, except in a few awful cases, there has not yet been too much trouble in your romantic life, or in your date's. You might go through some kind of trouble like that later, together, but at least you start out more or less unscarred. But on dates as a something-less-than-young man, with a something-less-than-young woman, you could start out with someone who had already been through such horror and misery in other relationships that the hope and eagerness in her had been kicked to death before you even had your first kiss.

You could see it in some women's eyes, in their posture. You could hear it in the way they talked: their pain quota had been filled, for life; there was only so far out into that naked middle ground they were ever going to let themselves go again, and who could blame them?

I wondered sometimes if women saw that in me.

But this was different. This trouble was immediate and oversized. It crept around in Janet's voice, in the choreography of her hands—which were long-fingered, strong-looking, beautiful hands. I had just a flicker of a thought then that I should get away from that trouble, protect myself, make things easy. But it was attractive, too, in a strange way. My own troubles stirred and blinked in a bad sleep. They sensed a friend in the room.

"So what kind of work do you do?"

"I make things," I said. "I make houses during the week. At night and on weekends, I make paintings."

Eric was standing by the table. "If I remember this right," he said, "the gentleman had the whole sea bass and the lady had the Duckling Saigon."

"You nailed it," I told him. "We'll have a bottle of wine. The lady will tell you which one."

Jared was happy we were having wine, and Janet ordered a bottle of Sardinian white with what sounded to me like perfect pronunciation and then, when he was gone and we were eating, she said she would give anything to be a person who made things. "I deal in fluff," she said. "Image. Spin." She coughed the wet, two-note cough. "Horseshit."

"I'm totally fulfilled," I said. "My life is superb. Which is why, the first time you saw me, I was out at midnight ordering two doughnuts by myself."

Oscar brought the wine and presented it with a flourish. Janet looked at the label and said it was fine. "Can't smell anything," she said, and he said, "Very good," and opened it like an Olympic champion.

"What hurts in your life?" she asked when we were alone again. I just looked at her. I just wanted Brian to stay away. I wanted the tables at Diem Bo to come with a sign like the ones hotel rooms come with and you can hang on the doorknob. Don't Make Up The Bed.

"You want a joke?" I said. "Or do you want to go there that quick?"

"Alright. I can go there, but let's finish the specials and then go there."

"And in the meantime, what about those Red Sox, huh?"

"No."

"Alright, how about this? In the meantime, what's the shadow over you? What's that pain?"

"A bad day at work." She coughed and massaged the skin over her breastbone with three fingers, and I could tell she wanted off the subject. "What kind of paintings?" she said. "I've always wanted to do that."

"Paintings where I'm trying to say something about life and death, and then at the last minute I chicken out."

"People don't want to hear about life and death," she said.

"Of course not. Why would they?"

"They want to be entertained."

"Which is where your boss comes in. The Wilbur Mills of Lynn Beach, caught with an escort service babe. Eating fried clams, if I remember correctly."

The squirrel ran across her face again. "He'd been in a terrible marriage for years."

"Even so. As a citizen of Massachusetts I felt personally embarrassed. I mean, the guy has to pay for a woman to eat clams with him? What kind of governor is that? Taxpayer money, besides."

"He's done some good things."

"I know it. I just—"

Adam was advancing on our table. With both hands I waved him away. He smiled at me. He winked. Janet and I stopped talking about the governor and shared the food—I wasn't afraid; I never got sick, almost never—and worked our way through the meal and the talk kind of easily. She had somehow taken my natural urge to be too polite—devastating on a first date—and shoved it over the side of the table. She went stretches of several minutes without coughing at all, then started in again. It didn't seem too bad really, just the tail end of a nasty cold.

Instead of asking the usual questions about brothers and sisters and parents, she said, "Everyone has a mess in their family. What's your mess?"

"I'm pretty sure my sister works as a kind of call girl in Reno. She says she does therapeutic massage, but I'm pretty sure she's talking about a certain kind of therapeutic."

"Really? Does she like it?"

"I never asked. She has some methedrine problems and that's made her a little hard to talk to. Unless you talk very fast. My brother is a Trappist monk in northwestern Connecticut. To balance things out."

"Nobody ever married."

"Not yet. What's your mess?"

"My father was working on the Mystic River Bridge and either fell off a staging or jumped. We were never sure. Thirteen years ago today, actually."

"Sorry."

She waved her fork. "He was a good man. I just try to remember the good things."

On that hopeful note, Abraham returned and we ordered dessert from him the same way we had ordered the main courses. Janet said, "Fruit for me, if you have it. Sweet and no chocolate for the gentleman."

With dessert we each had another Vietnamese coffee and the last of the wine and we scooted and slipped through the usual conversational alleys and came out okay. Even though she wanted to split it, I paid the check and put in a forty-dollar tip. I'm old-fashioned there: if you do the inviting, you do the paying. And I was in a mood to spend money outrageously. That happens to me sometimes. Walking away from an ATM machine once in Harvard Square I gave a hundred dollars to a street musician. Five new twenties in his hat. I'd had what people call a comfortable childhood, in what they call the middle class, and I'd built up a thriving little two-man carpentry business, and sold some paintings besides, and I had more money than I knew what to do with and it meant almost exactly nothing to me. During the meal, all the normal insecurities and self-consciousness of a first date had somehow been knocked away and, though I didn't know why that was, I liked it and it made me reckless, nutty. Plus, it wasn't Jeffrey's fault that he was Brian.

When we walked out of Diem Bo I wasn't nervous. It had rained most of that week but the night was unusually warm for September—hot, really—and I felt completely at ease in it, and with Janet, standing on the sidewalk watching women walking dogs, and couples holding hands, and men in suits on cell phones, and taxis and traffic lights, and a moon almost full, and the healthy brick façades of the townhouses there. Gerard and I had gutted a whole floor of one of those townhouses once, tearing out the old and putting in the new, and it had made us feel heroic, in spite of the parking problems.

I believe Janet felt at ease, too. She was standing close to me, and had draped a pretty striped sweater over her bare shoulders. We were looking away from each other, watching the parade of another city night.

Completely without having planned to do it, I said, "Would you want to go out on the river?"

She turned her face toward me and her eyes were slightly wide and it was easy to see that she'd had a little tickle of understanding what I'd meant, or had made a good guess, and the idea was exciting to her.

"I have a key to the BU boathouse. Have you ever been out in a racing shell? Would you want to?'

"Wouldn't we need another seven or eight people to fill it up?"

"They have some that are made for two."

"Are you going to drown me?"

"Not unless one of us makes a huge mistake."

She moved her eyes in small jumps across my face, and I wondered if I'd pushed the elastic edges of our nice easiness too far too fast and it was going to break open and all the good air between and around us was going to rush off up Newbury Street. I stood still and let myself be looked at. In a situation like that, it is the next thing to impossible for a man to imagine the kind of fear a woman is capable of feeling. I knew that, at least. I knew there was no reason for her to be afraid in that way, and knew I couldn't say so.

"How weird are you?" she asked. "Really."

"Weird within normal boundaries."

She looked at me for another five or six seconds.

"The water will be flat on a night like this. The moon's almost full. I rowed four years in college, I even have a Head of the Charles medal, and I can give you a written guarantee you won't fall in."

"Is it hard exercise?"

"Not tonight."

More of the dark eyes on me. I liked it. I was innocent, I was good. I had, for some reason, not even been having indecent thoughts. I wasn't trying to charm her or seduce her or Joe Date her; I was just feeling something different, some freedom I didn't usually feel on first dates, didn't usually feel at all. Had never really felt, in fact.

She said, "Okay then."

We rode in my dented old truck up Commonwealth Avenue, across the Boston University Bridge, and parked in a dirt lot on the other side of Memorial Drive. At the boathouse I used my key in the lock and then turned off the alarm inside and led her down a set of stairs into the concrete-floored, high-ceilinged bays where the long white shells lay on their racks and you could smell sweat and damp concrete and the river. "They used to be made of wood," I said. "They were beautiful."

But even made of carbon fiber, they were creatures to look at: sixty feet long, twenty inches wide, a foot deep, with quarter-inch-thick hulls and V-shaped aluminum riggers, and inside, intricately curved ribs and sleek seats on tracks and pairs of sneakers bolted in.

Janet ran her hands over the bow of a boat named *Leila Sophia*. She flipped the gate of one of the riggers gently back and forth so that it made a *click-clack* sound that echoed in the bays.

"They can go as fast as twelve miles an hour," I told her, "which seems faster on water, much faster, and with eight oarsmen and a coxswain it can be seventeen or eighteen hundred pounds going across the water at that speed, no motor."

We walked around to the other bay where the smaller boats were kept, singles and doubles and fours. She ran her hands over those, too, played with the oarlocks, peered up underneath them to get a sense of the way the ribs and seats were fashioned.

I hadn't yet opened the big red garage door that led out onto the dock. Friend or no, keys or no, alarm code or no, I wasn't supposed to be there at that hour. The head coach then, whose name was Jacques Florent, had been my coach ten years before, and sometimes I came in and helped him organize the two-thousand-meter races on Saturday mornings in May, or did a repair for free on the dock or on one of the weight benches. In exchange for that, he gave me a key and let me take a single out on Sunday afternoons in the warm months. Or let me come in and use the ergometers in the winter when the team wasn't using them and when the streets were too icy for my regular morning run. But the shells were expensive, fragile as the skeleton of a sparrow, and taking them out on the river at night had never been mentioned as part of the deal. Not alone, not with a date you hardly knew. When you rowed in those boats you moved backwards across the surface of the water, so if something was coming downstream in the dark—a tree limb, an old tire—you wouldn't know about it until it crashed through the ten-thousand-dollar bow and the river came pouring in.

But I watched Janet running the palms of her hands across the sleek bottom of a boat, and I watched her fingers—a mechanic's fingers, a pianist's—opening and snapping closed the delicate oar-lock, and I decided it would be a foolish thing to back away from the river now. It called to me, same as always, the wet slide of time. I could smell it in the air that seeped under the big red door. I took off my sport jacket and laid it over one of the shells. She put her sweater over my jacket. When I unhitched the clasp and swung the door open—first one side and then the other—the moldy, silky air washed against my face. "Too bad you can't smell the river," I said.

"What does it smell like?"

"Old."

I slid the scull most of the way out of its rack, told her to go to the other side and rest it on her shoulder. We walked it out and slowly down the dock to the edge of the water. On the dock it felt almost like a summer night. She was thin, as I have mentioned, but strong enough to push the weight of the boat up off her shoulder and straight over her head. She grabbed for a rib inside when I told her to, looked back at me to see if she was doing it right. Beneath the straps of her dark dress I could see the muscles of her shoulders flexing.

"Now roll it over and down against your hip, and hold it . . . You've done this before, haven't you."

"Never."

"Well, you're a natural then."

She coughed. "I played a lot of sports as a girl."

"Just sort of half lean over and half squat down and reach it out so the bottom doesn't bump the edge of the dock."

The hull just patted the flat water. "Perfect."

She held the boat close while I fetched the four carbon fiber oars—works of art in red and white—and then laid their necks in the oarlocks and pushed two oars out over the starboard gunwale. A jet flew over us then, headed out from Logan in the darkness. I showed her how to step in, but something wrong happened. I had been almost completely paying attention, but one small part of me had been distracted by the jet or lost in a little dream. We were upstream, Janet and I, just floating, with the blades of the oars lying flat on the smooth water, somewhere up past the bridge. It was dark there along the bank, the black water glided past. On the opposite shore, cars went up and down Storrow Drive in the street-lights. The city hummed. But we were outside it, close to the breath of the world. We didn't talk. In my little dream I heard the jet. And then I must not have been holding the gunwale firmly enough, or must have forgotten how unstable a scull seems the first time you set your standing weight in one. Or she must have leaned over too far. The boat wobbled, not that much really. But she panicked and tried to catch herself too quickly and the far gunwale slipped out of my fingers and she went over, knocking her shins on the hard edge of the boat, and making a big, loud, awful splash.

I waited about two heartbeats and then dove right across the boat and into the Charles after her, socks on, pants on, dress shirt on, the water dark and raw against my face and shoulders and chest, and then black and silky and unexpectedly warm from the week of rain.

I surfaced to the sound of Janet cursing. She seemed to be able to swim, at least. She wasn't panicking, but her breaths were short little rips of air. The waves we had made were rolling out into the middle of the river, and the streetlights from Memorial Drive wavered on the broken surface. She was breathing hard and then not so hard and in between breaths she was cursing like a plumber. In a minute we were treading water close to each other. Everything below the top two feet was cold.

I said, "The good news is our shoes are on the dock, nice and dry. The bad news is my wallet's in my back pocket."

"Shit, shit, shit," she said. And then: "You promised I wasn't going to get wet."

"I've stepped into boats thousands of times without that happening."

"You wobbled it."

"I had a tiny lapse. You overreacted."

She coughed and spat, swam out away from me a few yards, and then rolled neatly onto her back. I rolled onto my back and floated, too, because it was turning out that I hadn't really been ready to go on a date again after all, and had ruined it, and now there was nothing to do but ride it out and go home, and wait another month or two months or twelve months and try again. I could feel the dark current tugging us slowly downstream, but I let it take me, and I tried not to worry, and it seemed to me then, in spite of everything and everything, that I was rubbing the front of my body against some kind of holy moonlit wonder. I had been dragging myself through the days attached to a burlap sack full of bad history, of mourning, and somewhere in Diem Bo I had cut it loose. It was trying to reattach itself to me at that moment, but I wouldn't let it. I was going to have one night of not feeling bad, no matter what happened with this girl.

I went back to treading water, my body turned away from the boathouse. Janet stopped floating, and treaded water, too. Her hair was slicked down on both sides of her face.

I edged over a bit closer: "I have towels at my place. I'll make tea. You can take a hot shower."

She coughed and coughed and said, "You didn't do that on purpose, did you?"

"Absolutely and completely not."

"Alright. I'm done being angry."

"Good," I said. "I'm sorry. Let me make it up to you with the hot shower and the tea."

"Well, I've never been propositioned before in the middle of a river. It's very romantic."

Blue lights blinked behind us, scampering across the water. Before I could turn around she said, "The good news is the boat hasn't floated away. The bad news is there are two policemen on the dock shining flashlights."

6

THERE WAS NOTHING TO DO but swim back to the dock, climb out, and stand dripping and shivering on the boards.

"Nice night for a dip," one of the officers said sarcastically. He was a BU policeman, portly and jowly, with big fleshy hands, one of which was wrapped around a three-foot-long flashlight. He was looking at Janet's chest. Behind him, also looking at Janet, was a state trooper in his gray Stetson. When she'd been out of the water a minute or so, Janet had a terrible coughing fit, by far the worst of the night. She walked off to the side of the dock and spit loudly there, which only made me feel worse than I already felt. I was showing the officer my somewhat out-of-date, damp, Boston University Alumnus ID and explaining about my key, my very good friend Coach Florent, and our arrangement. But it is not easy to appear respectable when your clothes are dripping. And, to complicate matters, the officer was acting tough and all-business in front of the state trooper—making his mouth stern, glaring at me from beneath his bushy gray eyebrows, and so on.

When Janet came back she put her arm inside my arm and said, in the direction of the trooper, "Allen?"

"It's the governor's girl," he answered, not very nicely. "What's this, a stunt to get votes?"

"No, a first date."

"Another in an endless series," the trooper said.

I looked at him then. The BU cop looked over his shoulder at him, and Janet was looking at him, and for a little empty stretch of seconds no one said anything. There had been a splash of meanness in his voice, and so much naked hurt that I wasn't sure whether to be embarrassed for him or angry. Backlit by the boathouse lights he was still mostly standing in the shadows, his face and the whole front of him in the river darkness, big shoulders, big arms, a big neck, a posture of pure aggression.

I don't like aggressive people. And when I'm even a little upset, I tend to say things without thinking about them first. So I said, "Why don't you do something useful and get her a towel instead of making remarks?"

"What's that?" the trooper demanded, though even with the gentle knock and squeak of the dock hinges and even with the cars humming past on Memorial Drive, there wasn't a chance in a thousand he hadn't heard me.

"There are towels inside. Why don't you get her one instead of making remarks like that?"

It was a very hard look he fixed on me then. I looked back at him. The boathouse lights made a small fuzz at the edges of his shoulders. "Pass that over," he said to the BU cop, and he took my ID and marched up through the bays. We could hear his boots on the steps, then the heavy wooden front door slamming closed.

Janet was shaking slightly, dripping wet, still holding on to my arm. Given what our outing on the river had turned into, that gesture seemed like an act of generosity on her part. "If you go up to the landing and turn right, there's the women's showers," I said to her. "There should be towels in there. No one will mind."

When I was alone with the officer, a motorboat with a bow light went slowly past and I walked back down to where the double scull was floating and held it out at arm's length so the wake wouldn't knock it against the edge of the dock. There was water in the bottom of the boat, three or four inches from when the gunwale had dipped under Janet's weight. When the wake died down I took the oars out and set them aside on the dock and tilted the shell toward me. I splashed out some of the water, but it was still too heavy to lift alone. The college cop came over and squatted down near me. He smelled like cigarettes.

"How'd you feel about helping me get this out of the water?" I said.

"Bad back."

"Alright. Maybe the trooper will help."

"He going to find anything there when he puts your name in the computer?"

"No."

"Kind of a dumb remark, wasn't it?"

"His or mine?"

"Yours."

"Sure. I do that."

"Kind of a dumb stunt, too." He gestured toward the boat.

"You ever been out on the river at night?"

He shook his head. I thought of telling him about when I was a junior and a senior and we had gone out on the Charles in eights in the dark. The captain those years was pre-med, and so was I. We had an organic chemistry lab that went until four o'clock twice a week, so afterwards we'd hurry over to the boat-house and change and go out at four-thirty and by five-thirty it would be black dark. Coach Florent had a spotlight on his launch. He'd ride along next to us and shine the spotlight on you to see how your technique was, to see if you were coasting at all in the middle of the tough pieces. He had a bullhorn. "Entwhistle!" he'd yell in his high squeaky voice. "Down and away with the hands! Come on, John! Down and away. Then stand on the catch! STAND ON IT, GODDAMN IT!"

Sometimes the air temperature would be twenty degrees. A coat of ice would form on the shafts of the oars. But after you'd been rowing hard for a while, everything except the skin of your face would be warm, and sometimes we'd go down into the basin and do thousand-meter pieces there, invisible in the black, cold night. You'd feel like you had skidded off the edge of the predictable world and were just out there where no one and nothing could see you.

But I decided it wasn't a story the officer would appreciate. I splashed some more water out of the boat with one hand and waited.

Soon we could hear the trooper's boots on the stairs, and then on the dock. We stood up. The trooper handed my ID to the BU cop and said, "Do what you want."

"Look," I said, as he was turning away. "She's sick. She was shivering. I wasn't trying to be a wise-ass, you just—"

"She's the governor's slut," he said at me, in a voice that was hard as a punch. "Everybody who's been anywhere near him knows that. Used goods."

He turned and marched toward the light. We heard him trotting up the stairs, and then we heard the door again, and then the sound of the cruiser engine as he accelerated.

7

JANET AND I MANAGED to tip and splash almost all the water out of the boat. Once it was up on our shoulders, the officer gave her a hand with some of the weight, and then helped us set it on the rack. He stood by without saying anything as I locked the bay doors, and then he followed us upstairs and I reset the alarm and turned out the lights. Janet had taken a hot shower but had to put the wet black dress back on, and then her dry sweater over it. She was coughing every fifteen seconds or so, and I worried that the dip in the Charles had taken her bad cold and turned it into pneumonia. Folded up in one hand she was holding her wet black panties and bra, and the officer could not keep his eyes from going there. He asked if we needed a ride. When we said we didn't, he told us to stay out of trouble, and wished us a good night, and, after one last look at Janet and what she was carrying, got into his white and blue college police car and drove back over the bridge.

We walked across the four lanes of Memorial Drive and climbed into the truck. I kept a long-sleeved jersey there for days when Gerard and I got rained on, and for times, after work, when I didn't want to walk into a sandwich shop or a bar all sweat and sawdust. I stepped out of the truck again and changed my shirt, but I didn't put my good sport coat back on. We closed the windows and turned up the heat. It was hard to shake the chill.

"Everything go alright with the state police?" Janet asked, when we were driving over the bridge.

"Fine," I said. "No problem."

"He was on the State House detail a few times."

I was trying hard but I could not think of a good next thing to say. We stopped in a short line of red taillights near the end of the bridge, and it seemed to me that I could feel the roadway trembling. We could have looped around to the left there, back toward Diem Bo, where I supposed Janet had parked, or we could have turned right, toward my apartment. When the light changed I went straight.

"Amazing," I said finally, "how one jerkoff can sour a mood."

Janet watched me across the seat. "And we were having such a nice time," she said. "Swimming and everything."

I laughed. I was just driving aimlessly and she knew it. We were trying to get back to the place we had been in Diem Bo but I wasn't sure anymore how we had gotten there, and my being not sure made her not sure, I could feel that. All the nice liquid easiness that had been swirling between us had somehow hardened up and cracked.

For a few minutes we drove around on the back roads of Brookline in an awkward silence and then I turned, for no particular reason, onto Beacon Street and headed toward Coolidge Corner. She broke the silence: "Did you mean what you said at the restaurant? About being afraid of women's bodies?"

"Terrified."

"Is that something I could help you with?"

Joe Date would have made a cool remark then. "Absolutely," he would have said. Or: "I was hoping you'd offer." Or: "I'm willing to give it another try. It's important not to let your fears rule you." But in order to make remarks like that when you want to make them, your mind has to be focused right on the there and then, and mine wasn't. We were not far from the building—a three-story, redbrick townhouse—where I'd first made love with Giselle, and I was upset at myself for taking that route on that night, for being the kind of person who let the past haunt him, distant and recent, who let the remarks of jerkoffs cut and stick like bits of grit in raw flesh. For an hour there in Diem Bo and afterwards I had slipped free of all that.

We were driving past 1178 Beacon Street and I was smelling the lemon laundry soap on the sheets and Giselle was standing by the half-open Venetian blinds with no clothes on. I had made love with a short list of other women by that point—in college and afterwards—but I had not ever felt anything like what I'd felt with her on that night. I'm not talking just about the physical feelings. I think what happens when you make love is that you communicate with the other person through a thousand secret channels. Every place your skin touches her skin is another little conversation. You can't control those things the way you try to control a regular conversation; you can't decide what to say and what to keep from saying. It's as if the hair on your arms and the skin of your shoulders and the bones of your legs all carry different bits of your whole history there inside the cells. Everything that has happened to you, every thought and feeling and hope and sorrow, it's all stored there. When you put your body against someone else's body the cells can't help but talk to each other, see where they match up and don't, make billions of calculations as to where your histories and dreams speak a common language, what might be the chances of a happy life for the two of you and your as yet unborn child. It's biological, I think, and more than biological, part of the whole mysterious package that makes a pregnancy, or a friendship. That night, with Giselle, all the conversations were carried on without translation—at least it felt that way. In fact, later that same night I dreamt she *had* gotten pregnant, in spite of everything we were doing to prevent it. In time there would be other kinds of lovemaking. Our dreams and visions would veer off into sulky solitudes, but on that night I'd felt, for a while, that we weren't completely separate souls, and that is not a feeling you forget.

I should have forgotten it, though, at least right then, because I almost waited too long before I turned and looked at Janet. I was shaking a little but I didn't think she could see that. On her lap she held the damp pile of cotton.

"I live here near here," I said. Just that clumsy.

And she nodded and watched me, black hair, black eyes, one freckle, very calm. She coughed, barely parting her lips and not bothering to cover her mouth.

"My two ex-wives and my aunt live with me, though, I should warn you. She's a Tibetan Buddhist priest. We'll have to be quiet so we don't scandalize them."

She kept looking at me. I studied the road, glanced over once.

"You're nervous, right?"

"Little bit," I said. "I haven't had sex in over a year."

"You're joking."

I shook my head. "That's not something I would joke about."

8

THERE WAS AN EMPTY parking space in front of my building, a phenomenon roughly as common as a full solar eclipse. On the stoop, hair in dreadlocks, one of the other tenants' boyfriends sat quietly tapping a conga drum between his knees with just his fingertips. He looked up as we approached and said, "Two beautiful raats from de rivah."

"You have no idea," I told him, and then, "Let it go full blast, Eamon. No one in this neighborhood goes to bed before midnight on Friday." So he smacked the drumskin hard for a dozen notes and Janet and I went through the heavy pine-and-glass door and up the stairs to that beat. Three flights, and she was breathing as if she'd run all the way from the boathouse. My hands weren't exactly working perfectly, and my heart was banging around, and I scratched the keys on the face of the lock and deadbolt some before I was able to push them in and open the door.

"Don't turn on the lights," she said, when I started to.

I closed the door and flipped the deadbolt, out of habit. "I'm all river water. I was going to jump in the shower."

"Don't."

She dropped her sweater and wet underwear right there in the uncarpeted hallway. She tugged the jersey out of my pants, and I pulled it up and over my head and dropped it on top of her clothes. She put her hands on my belt buckle, then stopped, then unbuckled it, and stopped again. Faint light from the street pushed

past the window shades in the bedroom and lit the open doorway there. The hallway was dark and so quiet I could hear our
breathing.

"It wasn't true," she said, fixing her eyes on my eyes, "about
the long series of first dates. *He* was a first date, a year ago. I
wouldn't go to bed with him, and he was like a ninth-grader
about it."

"It doesn't matter."

"Really?"

"Really."

"You know what I want," she said.

"What?"

"Brutal honesty. Can we do that?"

"Sure." I pushed the straps of her dress off her shoulders,
but she held the material there, coughing, staring at me through
the semidarkness. "Alright," I said. "It mattered a little."

"It was a lie."

"Good. Can we keep all jerkoffs out of the conversation now?"

She nodded but held the dress against her body. I ran my
fingertips down lightly and just brushed the tops of her breasts
through the damp material.

"I have no diseases you can catch," she said.

"Excellent."

"I won't get pregnant."

"Alright. Information registered. I don't want to talk."

"I want to talk the whole time," she said. "Every second.
Keep the kisses short so I can talk in between, when I'm not
coughing."

I had not forgotten how to kiss. I leaned toward her and
caught her open mouth with my mouth, and my whole body

started in on a fast, small shaking. A few seconds of that sweetness, that thrill, that tremble, and she pulled away and coughed over my shoulder.

"That was nice," she said.

"Shh! My aunt. My two exes."

"Okay, sorry," she whispered in my ear. And then, still whispering: "I want to come in the room where you paint."

"I come in there all the time," I whispered back. "It's no big deal."

She laughed, quietly, as if there were, in fact, relatives and ex-relatives lurking in the dim hallway, all the ghosts from our separate pasts hovering against the high factory ceiling, getting to know each other. We had our chests pressed together, but the damp dress was still glued to her.

"Time to take that off. You're getting me all wet."

"*I'm* getting *you* all wet?" She moved herself a few inches away from me so I could peel the material down off her chest and hips and thighs. I picked up my dry jersey and ran it gently over the skin where her dress had been, over two scars on her belly, shining in the half-light, over the bones at the front of her hips and down the front insides of her thighs. She had a beautiful body and was standing in the almost-darkness with her hands clasped on top of her head, making a soft vibrating noise in the back of her throat. I kept brushing her skin lightly with the balled-up jersey, keeping the buttons and the collar away so that only the softest cloth touched her. She was completely at ease like that, with her clothes off, and it seemed to me that no woman had ever been so naked with me, that it was impossible, almost inhuman, to be as naked as that. I don't know why I felt this with her, it was just the person she was—I'd noticed it in the restaurant, and at the boathouse. The usual defenses weren't there. You felt as though you could reach right inside her chest and explore her whole inner life and she wouldn't fight about it, wouldn't mind, wouldn't worry. She asked me—just above a whisper—if I was afraid, and I told her I had never been so afraid.

"Turn around," I said. "It's an equal-opportunity shirt."

The being afraid part was true. Other than that, I had no idea what I was saying. I had never run my shirt over a woman's legs or the bones of her back in that way, not on my best night. When she coughed I could feel her back muscles clench, as if her whole body were being bent and bent.

"You are the nicest kind of weird," she murmured.

I tossed the shirt backwards over my shoulder but by that time we had somehow moved a little ways down the hall so that the trajectory of the shirt took it right through the kitchen door. It landed on the table and knocked over a cereal box there. You could hear the box fall sideways with a bump and then the cereal spilling out onto the floor, one quick rush at first and then a slow dribble.

The noise made Janet spin around.

"It was just my shirt hitting the cereal," I said. "Quaker Oats Granola. My aunt eats it before she goes to bed."

With both hands she took hold of my head and pulled my face down against her chest. I planted circles of small kisses there, orbiting her nipples. When she began to cough, I wrapped my arms around her and pulled her against me as if I could infect her with my congenital good health.

"Mother of all colds," I said, into her hot flesh. The skin between her breasts was saltier than it should have been, as if she had fallen into the ocean, not the river. As if she had not showered.

"It's not a cold," she said.

"Mother of all bronchitises."

"You can't catch what I have."

"I'm not worried about catching it. I'm stronger than two oxes. I have the immune system of the gods."

"You have your pants still on is what you have."

"You're naked enough for both of us."

"Take them . . . off."

Instead—I don't know what was wrong with me—I picked her up the way firemen do, one forearm behind her legs, her midsection over my right shoulder, and carried her into the painting room. She was not heavy. There was an old backless couch against one wall, canvas green with beaten-up springs. She was laughing as I lay her down there.

"The pants," she said, but then she started coughing again so I put the air conditioner on low to get some of the paint smell out. I unfolded a clean drop cloth and put it over her chest and hips and legs. I climbed in with her as if we were under a sheet.

She pulled my belt out of the loops and threw it on the floor, and then snapped open the button on my wet jeans, pulled the zipper down, and left her hands there. There was a shaft of filtered streetlight slanting in against the wall, and we were used to the dark by then, so I could make out the shape of her face, and see glints of light in her eyes. "Listen," she said, her hands moving around inside my pants, her voice all naked earnestness. "I'm almost a hundred percent sure I can't get pregnant, I mean it. And I can't give you any kind of sickness, nothing. Do you believe me?"

"Yes."

"And you weren't lying about the year?"

"No."

"And it wasn't because there's something wrong with you?"

"There's plenty wrong with me, but no."

She kissed me longer than the other kisses, then coughed over my shoulder again, that wet swampy two-note cough that seemed to echo and rumble in a wet barrel the size of the whole room. I didn't care about the cough. I ran my fingers along her spine and shoulder blades. She had fine soft skin. She pulled away. She tugged my pants down, then brought one leg up, put her toes over the top of them, and pushed down until they were off my ankles. "Your underwear is wet," she said, but I was past talking. It had been 381 days since I had done this and my heart was like a big wet fist slamming against the inside of my ribs. Lines of electricity were skittering across my lips. I moved my right hand down across the side of her hip and down against the wet slick heat between her legs. I could hear her breath change. She rolled half onto her back, half against the wall, and moved her legs apart a little and made the humming noise in the back of her mouth but I could see that her eyes were open. For a few seconds it was awkward. She squirmed and pushed away from the wall to get her back flat on the couch, she kicked at the drop cloth, but she never took her eyes off me. I moved my hand up, fingertips wet. She was yanking down on the elastic of my underwear with one hand. The air conditioner hummed. In the kitchen the phone rang once, went quiet, and then rang again and kept ringing until the machine clicked on. I moved on top of her with my weight on my elbows and I could see her eyes gleaming, fires in the night. In a whisper I wouldn't have heard if her mouth wasn't so close, three little puffs of speech that slipped out of her between the humming moans, I thought she said, "Don't hurt me."

And I thought, before I could no longer think, that there wasn't a chance in a hundred million chances that I would.

9

IT HAS ALWAYS SEEMED to me that all the trouble between people, all the differences that cause trouble, go away with sleep. When you wake up there's a little stretch of time, a few blurry seconds, when you're separated by almost nothing. I fell asleep as soon as we'd finished making love. I woke up after a short while and Janet was on her back and I was on my side, half-leaning against her, and there was no trouble between us.

"You awake, Joe Date?" she asked quietly.

I said that I was. I said, "This is nice. But I have a perfectly good queen-sized bed in the other room and there's not so much bad air from the paint and thinner."

She seemed to have stopped coughing. "I don't want to go in and disturb your exes."

"No exes," I said. "No ghosts in there."

In the small bedroom, under the covers in the dark she said, "I miss the drop cloth, kind of. Propositioned in midriver. Sex under a drop cloth. It's been different."

She started coughing and it went on for more than a minute. I didn't think she was going to stop. She got up and went into the bathroom. I heard her spit, and run the water, and spit again, and I could tell she was trying not to let me hear. When she was back under the sheet she lay quiet for a while. And then she said: "Attractive, isn't it, the spitting girl."

"I don't care. There's a plastic bucket in the kitchen. I'll bring it in here so you don't have to keep getting up all night."

I brought the bucket in, with a dishtowel, and set it next to her side of the bed, wide awake now. She seemed wide awake, too. The clock beside her read 2:11.

We were lying side by side on our backs, a siren wailing blocks away. I put my left hand on the top of her hip bone, trying to signal, not necessarily that I wanted to make love again, but that I wanted to stay down there where we had gone, in that lost nation beyond the reach of words.

But then something came over me and I asked, "What's making you cough like that?" because I believed, by then, that it wouldn't spoil anything for me to ask it. Bad allergies, I thought. Or the tail end of pneumonia. Or some new flu from Thailand or Bali or central Australia.

She waited so long before answering that I thought she'd fallen back to sleep. I would have been perfectly happy not to know. She'd already told me I couldn't catch it, and I trusted her, and I believe people should have their private places if they want them. But at last she said. "You get the prize, then."

"Which?"

"The record for going the longest without asking. Also the record for kissing without asking, and not seeming like you were afraid."

"My mother was a doctor. She dealt with sick people all day and caught a cold about once every twenty years and I'm the same way. Don't answer about the cough if you don't want to."

But after another short silence, she told me the name of the disease she had. The sound of the two words sent a little terrifying thrill down my neck and across the skin of my arms, and I felt two reflexes, almost at the same time. I felt myself recoil away from her, and heard some interior voice trying to convince me there hadn't been anything special about the night, that I didn't really know her, or want to know her. There was a part of me that wanted no more sadness for a while. I didn't know much about the disease but I knew it wasn't good, and I understood then that the coughing and the pills weren't just part of some passing inconvenience. Something inside me pulled away from that. And then something else washed me back. As a boy I had run away from things, from fights, from sadness. When my dad told me my favorite grandfather had passed away unexpectedly, my response was to sprint out the front door of our house and all the way up the street, trying to get away from that truth. When I broke off with my college girlfriend I did it from California, by mail, and only went to see her later, face to face, because she made me. But all that running had left me ashamed of myself, so ashamed that, as an adult, I cultivated the opposite reflex. When Gerard lost his mind for a while in college, I went to the psych ward every other day to visit him. When my father died, I was holding his hand. I helped break up a bad fight in downtown Boston late one night. When things went sour and then tragic with Giselle, I tried, in the most secret part of me, not to run from it but to stand there and face it and deal with it. And so, in the bed with Janet, I could feel the old urge to back away. And then something better, holding me.

She said, "Do you know anything about it?"

"Not much. I've heard the words. My mother would know, I'm sure. Tell me."

So she spent ten minutes telling me. Which is not that easy a thing to do, talk about your terminal disease with someone you barely know, in bed, on your first night together. When she was finishing up, she felt awkward, I could tell from her voice, a little bit worried again that I might hurt her somehow. She rolled over and kissed me, and said she was sorry for running on like that, she had to go to sleep, we could talk about it in the morning if I wanted.

In a minute or two I felt her body relax. I lay awake with the side of my arm against her warm skin, trying to take in what she had told me, to make it more than just words, trying to stay there with the feelings in me. Not to pity, not to run, not to rescue just for the sake of convincing myself I was a good person. Not to lie to myself or to her in any way.

There had been something wonderful and unusual about that night. I tried, for a while, to understand it. Janet didn't have a lot of the ordinary defenses, I said that already. I don't mean she was totally unprotected. No one that smart is totally unprotected after about age four. But, in spite of what she had whispered in my ear, I believed she wasn't really worried about being hurt. I thought then that what I felt in her, what was different about her, was some kind of monumental courage, a courage I could feel as clearly as if another creature lay breathing there between us in the bed. I lay awake for a while, just admiring it. In the middle of the first part of the lovemaking, she had taken my fingers pretty forcefully and run them across the wide, slightly depressed scars on her upper belly. And so while she was sleeping, I put my hand there again, and traced the taut skin, and then I fell asleep, too.

I N T H E M O R N I N G I woke up with no one beside me. I listened for Janet in the bathroom or in the kitchen but after a few seconds I knew the apartment was empty. I do not particularly enjoy the smell of day-old river water on my skin, so I got up. The plastic bucket was not where I had set it, and the dishtowel lay neatly folded on the side table as if it had not been used.

I do not like to stand in the shower a long time. I do not really like to shave, but I have been told I don't look my best with a one- or two-day growth of beard. So I showered and shaved and put on a clean pair of jeans, a clean T-shirt from a road race in which I'd finished eighty-ninth that summer, and sneakers with no socks, and I went and stood in the sunlight in the painting room. The drop cloth had been neatly folded up, and the old green couch looked the way it always looked, as if nothing important had happened there. Light was pouring in through the tall windows, catching a glass jar of brushes just so. On the easel was a canvas I had been working, and though I don't paint perfectly clear and representational paintings, it was easy enough to see that it was a portrait of a pretty blond woman, twenty-five or so, sitting at a table with a vase of lilies beside her left elbow, and a look of ease on her face, as if she had already accomplished the most important part of what she had been put on earth to accomplish, and was proud of that in a quiet way, and at peace with herself. As

if she had learned not to run away from things. As if she believed
those things held, within them, the answers to all the huge questions about how best to live out a human life. On that canvas I was
trying to show that I loved this blond woman, and admired her,
and I think I had accomplished that, or was beginning to accomplish it.

What probably did not show was that the woman was my
mother.

I studied the canvas for some time, then went into the
kitchen intending to clean up the spilled cereal. Janet had cleaned
up the cereal and washed the bucket and leaned it in the sink to
dry, and, behind the faucet, left a note in a precise printed hand.

> *Dear Joe Date. I'm sleeping with the governor.*
> *Safest sex only. My insistence on that makes him angry.*
> *I'll stop if you ask me out again. If not, then thanks for a*
> *kind of weird but nice night. Janet. P.S. The painting is*
> *nice. The woman is beautiful.*

I DON'T HAVE ANY Greek blood that I know of, but I seem to have some mysterious connection to Greek Americans. I don't know why this is. The ones I'm friendly with have a real appreciation for food and friendship and loyalty, which strikes me as a healthy set of appreciations. Gerard was Greek. And Carmine Asalapolous, my doughnut-making friend. And half a block from my apartment was a loud little breakfast place I liked, Flash-in-the-Pan, which was run by Maria and Aristotle Reginidis, who probably had a few drops of Greek blood in them somewhere.

I went there that morning, with Janet's note folded in my back pocket next to my still-damp wallet. For $3.99 you could get two sunny-side eggs with real home fries—the kind with a patchy soft frosting of paprika and oil and browned potato flesh—link sausages you could cut through with the edge of your fork, rye toast with butter, and with marmalade that came, not in plastic packets, but in a glass jar. Good coffee in heavy, thick-lipped cups. The silverware was also heavy, scarred with a million silvery scratches, and if you wanted, you could order a grilled bran muffin on the side, for your health . . . with a quarter-cup of whipped butter on top of it.

I liked the cheap framed photos of Greek temples on the walls, and the clean bathroom with un-painted-over graffiti ("U.S. Out of North America Now!" was my all-time favorite) and the fact that Maria and Ari's beautiful green-eyed nine-year-old girl, Giana, sat at the cash register on days when she didn't have school, making change with a serious face, like an adult. I liked, too, that Maria and Ari weren't afraid to have the occasional little marital spat there behind the counter, as if they didn't need to prove to each other that they had a good thing going on between them. It was the kind of marriage, and the kind of child, I'd hoped to have someday, when I had been planning for a marriage and children.

"The eggshill bucket is full! But why why why can't you tik out the eggshill bucket when is full? Why?"

"See this!" Maria would yell back, decaf pot in one hand, regular in the other. "This is why. What's more important, eggshell bucket or they get their coffee hot when the cup is empty?"

"My other wife could do both!"

Ari had not had any other wife, except in his imagination. They'd shake their heads, mutter in some ancient Kalamata dialect, fuss and fume for a while. Sometimes, rather than sitting there in polite embarrassment, one of the regular customers at the counter would take sides and say something like, "My wife can do both, you know, Maria."

"Good," Maria would say. "Send her in."

Half an hour later she'd squeeze past Aristotle at the grill and lay a hand on his aproned ass.

It was not the kind of food, or the kind of show, you could get in the hotel restaurants, or the chains, where the first commandment was never to seem actually human. Thou shalt not offend the customer's sensibilities under any circumstances. Thou shalt not laugh or shout.

The country was going that way, it seemed to me. Political figures got hundred-dollar haircuts and e-mailed their spin doctors to find out how to say good morning to their children. Our governor, for example, was a clean-faced millionaire with a plastic smile who was trying, that month, to get back the authority to execute criminals because he wanted more than anything to be reelected, and his opponent talked tough on crime, so he had to appear tough on crime, too. He had done some good things, as Janet said, getting poor kids access to better health care, for example, and fixing up some schools. He knew he had the vote of the more compassionate types, and he was trying to steal a few percentage points from his opponent, who would have executed people without benefit of trial if he'd been allowed to. Four years earlier this same man, our governor, had been photographed—by a newspaper reporter—having a nasty argument over fried clams on Lynn Beach with a young woman not his wife, and had made up an absurd story, told a few plastic jokes, posed repeatedly with his two teenage daughters, given blood, gone to church with the cameras on him, and been reelected two months before his wife filed for divorce. His picture was always in the newspaper and on the TV, his voice was everywhere. I had never liked the man.

When I had eaten half my eggs and potatoes and finished my first cup of coffee, I took Janet's note out of my pocket. I unfolded it, smoothed out the wrinkles, and set it on the countertop beside my coffee cup, where I could study the handwriting and the words.

THAT AFTERNOON I put on a summer sport coat over my T-shirt and drove half an hour west to visit my mother. She was living then in one of the leafier suburbs, not far from where I had grown up, in a place called Apple Meadow. People cooked her meals and cleaned her room, and there was a garden with white metal chairs set around a fountain, and manicured lawns, and an activity room with a television and a card table. Doctors, nurses, physical therapists, cleaning women, receptionists—everyone I'd ever spoken with at Apple Meadow seemed competent and caring, and you couldn't find a surface with dust on it if you were paid to, and there was really no other place my mother could have been as happy and safe, or treated as well. But every time I drove up to the guardhouse and gave my name I felt like some kind of traitor, a good enough son wearing a thin suit of selfishness.

She was sitting in an armchair in the sunny visitors' room, gold and diamond earrings my father had given her sparkling at the sides of her face, hands resting in her lap. She might have been waiting for me or she might not have been. At sixty-seven, she was the youngest person there. Probably the healthiest, too, except for the fact that her mind—which had been a wonderful mind— had started to travel down roads that were closed off to most other minds. She recognized me when I came through the door, though; her neatly trimmed eyebrows lifted a quarter of an inch and she flashed her small, pretty smile, one corner of one top front tooth chipped away from when she had tried to bite the flip top off a can of Pepsi. "Ellory!" she said, holding out her arms. "Doctor Entwhistle!"

A year before, just about the time when everything had changed for me, she had started calling me by my brother's name. She had also started talking to me as though I were a physician— which is what she had been, which is what I'd been expected to be. It was as if she somehow understood that my happy enough little world had just been blown up, and her response to that was to make me into someone else, as if that might let me slip free of the pain. After trying various other strategies, I had finally decided to play along. As a pretend-doctor, I could at least accompany her a short way down some of the roads she traveled. I could do a better job of bringing that light to her face when I walked into the visitors' room. Somehow, by some interior mechanism I did not understand, my being a doctor partly rebuilt the connection that had been broken by her illness. I could sit again in a skewed version of the warmth and generosity I'd grown up with, and once you've had that kind of affection in your life, you are marked by it forever. What my mother had given me, given us, was exactly what Gerard had not been given enough of as a boy. He and I talked about that sometimes.

That day, Mum and I walked the neat grounds of Apple Meadow, around and around, back and forth. It was the new pattern: sometimes she held my arm and was quiet. Other times she said things like this: "It's not a question of money, Ellory. Money just represents something else, an agreement to value one thing over another. Only children don't have this value put on them because children have one foot in the ocean and pay no attention. It terrifies us, this ocean. But the fear of drowning is absurd. We already *are* drowned."

"Exactly," I'd say, and we'd stroll along like intellectuals on holiday in Baden-Baden.

And then, at some point after it had circled and circled and spun off in a series of nonsensical eddies, the conversation would drift back to her old world, the world of medicine, the world of being paid to care about other people's pain and fear. It was very strange because, in that world, whole sectors of my mother's memory and thought processes had been left undamaged, and it always sent a happy jolt through me when the conversation went there and we were actually almost making sense again.

"How is your practice?" she would ask, with so much pride in her voice that it made me wish I'd stayed in med school. "What interesting cases have you seen recently, Doctor Entwhistle?"

Sometimes, before visiting her, I'd go on Gerard's computer and spend an hour researching exotic illnesses. One Saturday we'd talked at length about intestinal parasites in children, and the strange variety of symptoms they could cause. The Ebola virus fascinated her, and had led us to leeching and leukemia. Her mind was a library in which certain floors and sections of stacks had no electricity, and others were still well lighted enough for reading.

"I have a patient with cystic fibrosis now," I told her on that day, because I had not been able to stop hearing Janet's voice as she lay in the darkness.

"Horrible," my mother said. "A ghastly disease. A torturer. A killer of children."

"Young adults now, mostly," I said. "They've made some advances."

"You're more in touch with these things than I am."

"She's twenty-seven, my patient. Almost the statistical mean age of death now."

"Ah," my mother said, sounding surprised. She spent a little while searching around in her interior darkness. *"Pseudomonas bacterium?"*

"Yes."

"Constant coughing? Digestive troubles?"

"Pancreatic enzymes," I said, and with that, I came to the end of what I knew.

"Horrible, horrible."

We walked another few paces. "What causes it, Mum?"

She turned her stone-blue eyes up at me. "What causes it? You must have slept through the lecture that day, Ellory. Are you asking seriously?"

I nodded.

"A gene. A defective gene."

"I know *that,*" I said, and gave a little fake chuckle. "But at the cellular level. What is the exact . . . what is going on?"

"Salt and water don't pass between the cells easily enough, the mucus is thick, the skin is salty, haven't you noticed? It's one tiny mistake. A glitch."

"There are new drugs being developed," I ad-libbed. "There's talk of a cure in the not-too-distant future. I wanted to ask you what you'd recommend in the way of treatment."

"Not my area of expertise." She swung her hands out, palms up, her ring finger wobbling slightly as I had seen it do a thousand times. "But they have identified the gene, as you know."

"Yes."

"Done some work with new antibiotics."

"Yes, that's right."

"What I would suggest is that you go and speak with Doctor . . . at the Beth Israel. With Doctor . . . Doctor . . ."

I could feel the change sweeping through her. It was as if

she'd managed to escape from a great heavy demon and run a few
steps back toward sanity, and then the demon had caught her
from behind, wrapped itself around her, and was now in the
process of dragging her back into the darkness. Her muscles stiff-
ened. Her face puckered, turning up the fine light hair on her
cheeks. Four, five, six times she tried for the doctor's name: "You
really must consult with Doctor . . . Doctor . . . Ellory, it's Doctor . . ." At last she surrendered and let herself be dragged back.
When she spoke again we were miles apart. "Gwendolyn Mitchell
and her brood of six went to the minister's house for Sunday dinner, you know, and once the squash was served you couldn't find a
place to sit at the table, can you imagine?"

There was a connection somewhere, I knew that. I had
some understanding of the ways her mind worked now. Maybe
one of the Mitchells had suffered from cystic fibrosis. Maybe the
doctor's name at Beth Israel was Mitchell or his wife or assistant
was Gwendolyn. Sometimes the word my mother was searching
for would pop up again an hour later, in the midst of another conversation, or as we were saying good-bye, or when I spoke with
her on the phone in the middle of the week.

"Nothing is harder to imagine, Mum," I said.

"They weren't always that way, the Mitchells."

"No."

"In fact, we liked them. Out of pity, I sometimes thought,
but we liked them."

"Never a good motivation," I said.

I turned her back toward the main building and when we
were inside I spent a little time with her in front of the communal
TV, watching football—her latest passion. When I was ready to
say good-bye she kissed me and held me in her strong arms as if

she were still living in the two-hundred-year-old blue saltbox in Concord, and my father was still alive, beside her, smiling and puffing on his pipe, and my brother Ellory was still a hell-raiser who had not yet shocked the neighborhood by turning Catholic and becoming a monk, and my sister Lizbeth was just a pretty teenager who had not yet made her life into a constant search for drugs and the money to buy drugs. For those few seconds my mother squeezed the guilt and sorrow out of me and we traveled back to a place where we had been happy, unusually happy, unscarred, suburban, American, bubbling over with health and brains and energy, convinced the future would be kind and good. Our embrace was a kind of code. "I'm still me," she was signaling. And I was answering, "I know. I know."

But I left Apple Meadow wondering how many years she would live like that, and what it felt like inside, and whether it really made any difference at all to her if I visited or stayed away.

You called at a key moment," I told Gerard on Monday
morning, when he asked why I hadn't answered the phone to
tell him about my date with Janet at Diem Bo.

"There are three key moments."

"It was the second."

"That's it? No details?"

"Have I ever provided details about my love life?"

"Not in a year or more, no. I was only giving you the
opportunity to enjoy the experience a second time by telling the
story to your closest friend."

"Thanks. I'll pass."

"I'm hurt."

"We went to Diem Bo for supper. How's that?"

"What did you have?"

"Scallops and sea bass and duck."

"*La frutta di mare.* Good. And where did you go afterwards?"

"For a swim."

"Skinny-dip?"

"Fully clothed."

"Alright, stop there," he said. "For an imagination like
mine, that's enough. The possibilities from that point are endless."

"In the Charles River," I said.

"No no, don't spoil it, Colonel. Let the imagination run

free. Let it run wild! The Charles's fetid waters lapping against her tight bodice. You in your Sunday best, your trousers wet and your manhood surging against the material. No, leave me to my imaginings. Please."

I left him to his imaginings.

We had finished framing the professor's addition and were involved in the monotonous nailing of half-inch plywood onto the second-floor walls. The professor's name was Jacqueline Levarkian and she taught theoretical physics at Harvard. She was an attractive and obviously brilliant single woman, and from the day we'd started working there, in midsummer, Gerard had been trying various stunts to get her to pay attention to him. Once, when he knew she was home, he pretended to slip off the staging and dangled there, holding on with one hand and screaming out over the sedate Cambridge neighborhood for me to rescue him, pedaling his legs and gesticulating wildly with his free hand, three feet above the ground, like a circus clown. Two or three times during the workday he'd flip his thirty-two-ounce hammer into the air, end-over-end, three full revolutions, catch it expertly by its blue handle, and pretend to be making up physics formulas to describe the hammer's movement ("You take the cosign of s, where s represents the centrifugal force of the atomic weight of steel . . ."). He'd sing snatches from operas he liked. He'd bring books of poetry—Latin, Russian, Italian, Greek—to the work site to impress her. Once, when Jacqueline had an afternoon off, she brought us out homemade oatmeal cookies and iced tea and Gerard engaged her in a complicated discussion of something called string theory, then kissed her hand afterwards.

I knew this about my friend: early in his life he had not been given some quality of motherly or fatherly attention that says: I see you. You are fine as you are, flaws and all. You are accepted, you are beloved. And ever since then he had tried to fill up that empty place by getting attention, especially from women. Which had not made marriage an easy thing for him. Or for his former wife. With me, he talked too much and joked too much and laughed too loudly and called at all hours. But he could work like a pair of oxes, and I had never seen him be mean, and when Giselle died, he made sure I never sank below a certain level of rock-bottom misery and I did not expect I would ever forget that.

I picked up a sheet of plywood, leaned it sideways against my hip and shoulder and the side of my head, and then passed it up to him on the staging.

"Huddy! Queek!" he screamed as I was climbing the ladder. "Eeet eez sleeping from my grahsp!"

When we had worked it into place and were driving the galvanized eightpenny nails at six-inch intervals, I asked him if he knew anything about cystic fibrosis.

"Jerry's kids," he said, going into a terrible imitation of Jerry Lewis's honking, bighearted goofiness.

"That's muscular dystrophy. I'm asking about cystic fibrosis. CF."

"All the alphabet diseases are awful, Colonel, I know that much. AIDS, ALS, MS, Ph.D."

"Is this something we want to be joking about?"

"If it is what I think it is, then one of the only things we can do is joke about it, Colonel. You should understand that."

"Right. The woman I went out with on Friday night has CF."

"Sorry."

"Don't worry about it. You need a governor on your mouth, though, sometimes."

Governor on your mouth. Amazing how things like that just slip out. Gerard, naturally, would not let it go.

"Actually, if I had incarnated into a woman's body, I wouldn't mind the governor on my mouth. Our governor is one cute governor compared to, say, the governor of New Mexico . . ." and so on until I finally told him to stop, twice, and he did.

When we finished the nailing and were putting our tools away, I asked him if I could come over and do a little research on his computer, and I did that, then went home and painted for a while on a fresh canvas. But the work was timid work, uninspired, unsurprising, no good. As if they were marching on a parade ground behind my eyes, I could feel whole battalions of jealous soldiers in new uniforms. And I could hear a lying old self trying to convince me that Janet was a one-night type of woman. Skate on, skate on, the voice said. Too much trouble. Skate on. I gave up on the painting, cleaned the brushes, turned the easel around so I wouldn't have to look at what I had done. After thinking about it for another little while I picked up the phone and called Janet to ask her out again, and we didn't talk about the governor, or the alphabet diseases, or any kind of subject like that.

Book Two

October

1

I̶N BOSTON, OCTOBER is the month when you have to stop
pretending to yourself that the good weather will go on and on.
The leaves catch fire and swirl out gold and lemon patterns at the
bases of maple trees, but it's just a last show meant to take your
mind away from the fact that things are dying all around. If you
work outside, you can feel this dying very plainly in late October
in the afternoon. The cold Halloween air has an unsympathetic
quality to it. Lights blaze out from storefronts and third-floor
apartments, but the darkness seems to swallow them after they've
traveled only a few feet so that they feel cut off from each other,
isolated pockets of warmth that offer themselves happily and opti-
mistically but really are only hoping to make it through another
night.

I like October—early October, especially—in spite of the
slow death of things. Janet, it turned out, was a big October fan.
And it turned out that we matched up in other ways, too. Drives
in the country, Middle Eastern food, art museums, music that ran
the spectrum from Bach to Pearl Jam, weekend nights in bed,
weekend mornings in bed, spontaneous bursts of harmless adven-
turing, long rides on Friday nights (it took a while for the replacement parts to come in, but I'd gotten the truck fixed up finally),
people who were quirky and generous—we had an appreciation
for a lot of the same types of things.

We did not talk about the governor, or Giselle. And we talked only in short, rare bursts about cystic fibrosis—those were the unspoken rules for us. She was getting sicker; it did not take a pulmonologist to see that. And, by the time we'd been going out for a few weeks, I had done so much reading on the disease that I knew where the getting sicker would take her, and along what routes, and about how fast.

I had learned that there are certain kinds of bacteria with pretty names like *Burkholderia cepacia* and *Pseudomonas aeruginosa* that thrive in the thick mucus in the lungs of cystic fibrosis people. These bacteria are everywhere—in the skin of onions, in the moist air of a shower stall, in Jacuzzis, in river water—but they move into and out of normal lungs without anyone ever noticing. If they visit the lungs of a person with CF, though, they stay there and form colonies, and the colonies throw up dense films that act as shields against the assault of antibiotics. The delicate tissue of the inside of the lung tries to protect itself against these colonies and becomes inflamed. Over time, the inflammation breaks the cells down so that the complicated system of blood and breath doesn't work anymore the way it was designed to work. Over time, over almost thirty years in her case, enough lung tissue has starved and rotted so that you can't walk up three flights of stairs to your boyfriend's bedroom without sounding like you've just been on the treadmill for an hour at the gym.

Near the end of September, Janet's pulmonologist, whose name was Eric Wilbraham, sent her into the hospital for five days of intravenous antibiotics to try to control the bacteria, and I went there every day after work to make her laugh. One night I caught Doctor Wilbraham in the hallway. I have the bad habit of forming solid impressions about people on first meeting, and I didn't like him. But we had a pretty good conversation about spirometers, and pseudomonas, and cepacia, and chest physical therapy, and inhaled steroids and Pulmozyme, and things like that. My mother would have been proud. I had become semiknowledgeable on the subject, which was not necessarily a good thing because I could see, beyond the doctor's pleasant and hopeful science-talk, the outlines of what was happening, and it was like a small, sharp-toothed animal in my gut, gnawing away. In the week before she went into the hospital, Janet had started to use oxygen at night sometimes. Usually she had to stop twice to rest on the way up to my apartment. She was twenty-seven.

After that hospital stay, though—a "tune-up" she called it—she had a good week. The movement into her blood of the most powerful antibiotics in the medical arsenal had beaten back the bacteria. She coughed less, she had more energy, a healthier color returned to her face. She was pretty and hopeful again, the way she had been when I'd first seen her.

By then, Gerard and I had the professor's addition all closed in and we were nailing up the long, rust-colored rows of cedar clapboard, a job I loved. On the second Friday in October, the start of the holiday weekend, I finished work, went home and showered, and drove down to the State House to pick Janet up. On two other occasions I had been to her office, and had met a couple of her friends there, and I could tell she had been talking to them about me, and that they were examining me to see if I was worthy, which is what friends always do. That night I found a parking space two blocks from the side entrance and went in that entrance, through the security checkpoint and up two flights of stairs. The Massachusetts State House is really a spectacularly beautiful building—murals on the walls, mosaic tile floors, stained glass, carved wood. Someone named Bulfinch designed it, and he went all out to impress people with the authority and importance of government. But for some reason I had never felt comfortable there. Years before, I'd been inside the State House for an Arts Council ceremony. I had won a grant, and though I was glad and honored to have won the grant, the air in the building seemed to press on me from four sides with that history—all golden and flashy on the surface, all dirty and smoky underneath. It was a strange thing: I felt that if I stayed in there too long, I'd never be able to paint again.

And that was before Governor Valvelsais had taken office, and before Janet and I never talked about him.

We could have set a time and I could have met her outside. It would have been easier not to have to look for a parking space on Beacon Hill. But Janet said she couldn't always be sure she'd be able to leave right at seven o'clock or whatever time we set, and she didn't want to keep me waiting outside like that. And I had the feeling she liked to be seen walking down the corridors with her arm hooked through someone's arm, liked the security guards and senators' aides and the people she worked with to know she had a semblance of a social life, an actual boyfriend, a date. One of the bad parts of her disease, along with the physical suffering, was the way the persistent coughing and sickliness made people want to push you away. Once, after three glasses of wine, Janet spewed out a whole list of things people had said to her as a girl—in movie theaters, in classrooms, at parties. "Go home if you're sick." "Stay away from me with that cough." "Doesn't your mother feed you?" "You've had that cold for, what, about a year now?" And so on.

Complete strangers and acquaintances alike would say such things, even though they were infinitely more dangerous to

her than she was to them. She told me it made her want to just
hang around other people with CF, but this was the twist of the
knife: she wasn't allowed to hang around other people with CF.
She couldn't be in a closed car with another person with CF,
couldn't come within three arms' lengths for fear that one of them
would give the other some lethal new germ they hadn't yet been
introduced to. She'd found out about that the hard way, she said,
but wouldn't elaborate.

I walked down a long hallway, past a dozen closed doors,
and then toward the front center of the building, where the governor and his closest aides have their offices. A state trooper stood
guard at the entrance to the executive suite. Janet had given him
my name, and while he looked over my ID, I studied the portraits
on the walls, all the recent governors, captured in oil, larger than
life. As election day approached, more people stayed late in the
offices there—strategizing, maybe, or proving to the taxpayers
that, under the current administration, they were getting their dollar's worth. Still, the doors were thick old doors, and it was usually
quiet in the suite at that hour, so I was surprised, as the trooper
handed back my license, to hear voices. Two people arguing, it
sounded like. Syllables muffled. The trooper didn't seem to notice.

As I walked on, making a right turn past the governor's
door, then a left, I was even more surprised to realize that the
voices were coming from Janet's office. And then that one of the
voices was hers. I was about to turn around and make another lap
of the corridor when the other person roared out: "I don't *give* half
a shit about him, alright?" It sounded like our governor, not on
his best behavior. I hesitated for one breath. And then, because
there was a note of what might be called distress in Janet's muffled
answer, I took hold of the doorknob, turned it, and pushed.

The scene inside was not a highly original one. The office was small. Janet's desk faced the doorway, an old green-upholstered armchair in front of it. Behind the desk, with one large window as background, was the chair she sat at when she worked, and she was standing to the side of that chair, holding the top front of her dress together with one hand. Her hair hung messily over one side of her face and it was easy enough to see, in her eyes and the muscles around her mouth, that she was angry and upset. There was a wash of fear there, too. Before that moment, I had never seen fear on Janet's face. I'd seen her cough until she almost lost consciousness, and I'd heard her talk about having her stomach cut open when she was twelve years old, and how she had become infected and sparked a fever of a hundred and five and almost died. But I had never heard the bruise of real fear in those stories, or seen it where I saw it now.

On the opposite side of her chair was the splendid governor of Massachusetts, the Honorable Charles S. Valvelsais, who had been elected in part by promising to make sure the legislature funded preschool and after-school programs for children from poor families—a promise he'd made good on. He was wearing a white shirt and a loosened tie. He also looked upset. There was a multitude of reasons why he could have been upset, but in the second or two seconds before I did what I did, it seemed to me that there weren't many reasons why Janet would be standing the way she was standing with a button ripped off her dress and that look in her eyes. Governors sometimes yell at the people who work for them. Fair enough. But most governors don't yell at the people who work for them *and* tear buttons off those people's dresses. I was bothered to begin with, being in that building. And I had been a jealous person in a past incarnation, I admit that, and probably hadn't yet completely reformed.

And so I sort of made a run at all that, without stopping to consider. A straight sprint. Except that the green-upholstered arm-chair and the heavy oak desk were in the way. So I ran over them, one step up on the chair, one step across the desk, and I leaped over Janet's computer and onto Governor Valvoline. In mid-leap I remembered that he'd been some kind of judo champion in college. But college was a long time ago for the governor. And probably, whatever the other demands of the political life might have been, he hadn't spent the past nine years carrying two-by-tens across job sites or walking half-inch sheets of wallboard up two flights of stairs.

We crashed to the floor, two nuts, arms and legs entangled, papers and statues of the Commonwealth and small electrical appliances banging down around us. Someone screamed, Janet probably. The governor was grunting, "I'll fix . . . I'll fix you," in his most governoresque voice. He tried some kind of judo move on me, taking hold of my arm and using it as a lever to flip me out of the way, but we were on the floor, and the move only partly worked, and then it was all confusion and he was scraping at my face with his fingernails and we were wrestling and grunting and one of my hands flew free and so I punched him at close range, just a little awkward jab, and his nose started to bleed. One of Janet's cowboy-booted ankles came between us where we struggled on the carpet. She was yelling at us and making small kicks with her foot. We scuttled away from each other and stood up.

I was breathing hard and feeling like a boy. Between breaths I could sense a putrid disgust seeping up from the floor and all around me. The governor was leaning over from the waist, trying to catch the blood in his cupped right hand so it didn't fall onto his shirt. A very small white-haired woman came through the door with a security guard—not the trooper—right behind her. I had never had much to do with security guards before meeting Janet. He had a gun out and was pointing it, sensibly enough, at me.

The governor pulled a handkerchief out of his back pocket and put it up to his face. Through the material he said, in a weird voice, a public phony voice, "No, no. Get him out. I fell. I tripped and fell. It's not broken." He actually tried to laugh then. The sound came out from under the handkerchief like the chuffing of some animal trying to force its way up through the skin of a human being. "Out," he commanded. "Everybody but Janet out."

"Not a chance," she said, in a shaking voice. She had been standing between us while we calmed down, but had now moved to the other side of her chair. The state trooper appeared at the door. The security guard put his gun back where it belonged, and when he did that I felt as though everything behind my navel— the mucus and blood and half-digested food—settled a few inches lower in a heavy soup. "Out!" the governor said loudly. "I just tripped and fell, that's all. Everybody out."

We made a not very graceful exit, me with my clothes all rumpled, and Janet breathing hard and having some trouble getting her sweater off the back of her chair, and Charlie Valvoline putting on a stern, manly face for whoever the older woman was—his secretary, I suppose—and the trooper asking the governor if he was sure he was all right, and the security guard eyeing me all the way out the door, as if, after all those years of just sitting around reading golf magazines, he had wanted more than anything to have been allowed to pull the trigger.

Janet and I walked out of the executive suite and down the long corridor, not touching and not talking. I had been an idiot, I understood that in the most visceral way. A dirty wave was washing over me, a bad mix of feelings from my worst days with Giselle. I shook my head, hard.

We walked down the steps. Before turning with me toward my truck, Janet seemed to waver a moment. We went the two blocks in silence and I realized I had parked near the little Catholic church where Ellory had liked to go after his conversion. I unlocked the passenger door for Janet and she climbed in. When we were pulling out of the parking space she started to cry. I wanted to touch her or find something to say, but wrestling with governors—with anyone, in fact—was not exactly a specialty of mine, and having a gun pointed at me was also not a specialty of mine, and I was not exactly in a state of mind where I could comfort someone else. My ribs and hands were sore, my left cheek was scratched, my left shoulder hurt where Valvoline had done the judo move, and my mind was replaying the scene again and again. So I just pulled out into the smoky madness of Friday-night traffic and listened to Janet cry.

Before the bad scene in the State House, I'd had an idea where we might go that night—we took turns deciding, surprising each other, seeing who could be more inventive. She loved New York City, and that's where I had been planning to take her. In the fog of bad feelings I thought it would be best to basically stick to the plan, and just take things a minute at a time.

It was stop-and-go all the way down Beacon Street to Clarendon, and then not much better once we reached the entrance to the Mass Turnpike and headed west.

My body stopped shaking. Janet didn't cry for very long. She coughed, looked out the side window for a while, and then said, "I hate things like that. I hate that you did that."

"What did he do to you?"

"Nothing."

"Here we are with brutal honesty."

She kept looking out the window. We were stopped in holiday traffic in a long line of cars and trucks near the first tollbooth, still in Boston. Close enough to turn back.

"He was talking to me. I was trying to get something for him out of my files and I turned around and he was pressing his face close to me, telling me he loved me. I pulled away. I told him he didn't love me and I didn't love him, that I was going out with someone now. He reached out for me, not to hurt me but kind of to get me to listen, and he accidentally caught the top of my dress and I pulled away. He started to yell . . . And then you came through the door like a wild gorilla. I don't like that kind of thing *at all*."

"I came through the door ordinary. Then I went to wild gorilla."

She didn't smile.

"He deserved it," I said. "I'm only seventy-five percent sorry."

"I'm not asking you to be sorry. *I'm* the one who's sorry . . . that I ever let him touch me. You can't imagine the depth and range of my sorrow right now."

"Why did you?"

She shrugged.

"Why did you let him touch you?" I said again, but I was just talking, filling up air. I was feeling less sorry by the second. By the time Janet spoke again I was down to thirty-five percent.

"Sometimes you just want a little pleasure, that's all. Some connection with somebody. Some, I don't know—"

"A doughnut."

"What?"

"A doughnut, you want a doughnut. You want your share of sweetness to make up for all the shit you have to go through. You deserve the two doughnuts, or the kiss, or the cocaine, or the new car, or the new earrings, or the new fishing rod."

"What in the name of God are you talking about, Jake? What fishing rod? I don't—"

"Now you're going to lose your job," I said, to reel myself in.

She laughed then, a small laugh with a hem of bitterness along its edges. "Not before the election anyway. You heard him. 'I fell! It's nothing! Everyone out!' When he goes to buy underwear he worries which brand will get him more votes. He's the epitome of the political animal."

"Why'd you sleep with him, then?"

It had slipped out, and I couldn't pretend to myself anymore that I was just filling air. Janet looked at me, then looked forward again. An oily silence floated between us in the cab of the truck. Until that minute I'd done an excellent job of not being jealous. From the time I'd read the note she left on my sink, jealousy had been whispering in my ear night and day. I'd see the governor on TV and I'd look at his hands and wonder where and how those hands had touched her. I'd look at his mouth. I'd hear a radio talk show host—this was rare—say he was handsome, or dignified, or that his plan to execute criminals meant he was the first governor we'd had in years with any *cojones*; I'd wonder if she'd ever touched his *cojones*; I'd notice that *Boston* magazine had named him one of the city's top ten eligible bachelors. I'd see news clips of the governor with his daughters, or on his morning run, or lining up to donate blood for the hundred and twenty-seventh time with a big sappy smile on his face. And so on. It's one thing for your lover to have had lovers before—who doesn't have to deal with that, high-school sophomores? It's something else to have that other person's face and voice and picture and name ricocheting around every bar you step into, every newsstand you walk past, every radio station you listen to on your way to work. Jealousy fun house mirrors.

Still, in the months before I met Janet, I'd had a lot of practice turning my mind away from certain types of thoughts, and, in the time I'd known her, whenever jealousy made one of its runs, I'd just stepped aside and let it crash past. Who knows why my little sidestep move wasn't working that night? Because I'd actually wrestled around on the floor with the governor, maybe? Because he was still reaching into a part of my life with his pathetic I-love-yous long after he should have bowed gracefully out? Because the part of my life with Janet in it was becoming more important to me every day? Who knows?

The traffic softened up slightly. We headed west at a slow pace.

After a while Janet said, "I don't ask you things like that."

"I know it."

"I don't ask you who you've been with or anything about Giselle, or why you didn't date for a year after you broke up with her, or even if you're sleeping with someone else now."

"I'm not."

"Good. I'm not either."

A mile or so of edgy silence, not so bad now. This was the weird complicated tango of modern relationshipping. This was as ancient as dust and sweat.

She said, "I was lonely. I got just very lonely. Of the four other men I work with, one is gay, two are married, and the other one has egg on his face when he comes to work."

"Literal egg?"

She didn't laugh. "I'm not exactly . . . I don't exactly have attractive guys lined up at my door, no offense."

"You're beautiful, you're smart, you're sexy. What are you talking about?"

I could feel her looking at me across the cab of the truck, but I was afraid to look back.

She said, "Come on, Jake. I cough. I spit. I ply myself with pills before every meal when I'm out on dates in restaurants. I'm a fun time, but not exactly what you'd call a good long-term investment."

"Not if I can help it," I said, without thinking.

"Meaning what?"

"Meaning I'm going to keep you alive."

"By the force of your heroic masculine will?"

"Don't insult the force of my heroic masculine will," I said. "I have a perfectly solidly average-sized heroic masculine will, maybe slightly larger."

She didn't laugh then, either, but I glanced across the seat and caught something in her eyes, one flash of good light. We drove along. "Where are you taking me?"

"Sanctum sanctorum," I said. It was Gerard's term for a woman's body. It had just slipped out—like everything else I had been saying on that blessed night.

"You are an odd soul, Joe Date."

"To New York or by bus," I said. One of my mother's jokes.

"You are essentially odd. If you ran for office, you'd never make it past the primary."

"Thank you. I consider that a high compliment. But could we keep all references to running for office out of the conversation? All jerkoffs?"

"Okay."

"I have the blood of jerkoffs on my hands."

"You're going goofy on me," she said.

"I'm on a crime spree. I've assaulted an elected public offi-cial and now I'm going to trespass on monastery grounds."

"He won't press charges," Janet said. "What monastery?"

"We're going to see my brother. The monk. Then we're going to New York or by bus."

2

M Y BROTHER ELLORY is eight years and two months older than I am. After a brilliant teenage career of rebelling against what he called "our upper-middle-class subterranean upbringing"—including one glorious night in which he drove my father's new Mercedes convertible off the road, between two pine trees and down the third fairway at the Wannakin River Golf Club— he decided to really hit my parents where they lived, and he'd converted to Catholicism. In the beginning, this conversion had everything to do with a college girlfriend named Renée St. Cyr (who believed that premarital intercourse was approved of by the Good Lord, in her particular case, as long as the other intercoursee was also Catholic), but soon it took on a life of its own.

My brother started to attend mass at the radical church near the State House that let homeless people sleep between its pews. He started to talk about "the Lord" all the time. He stopped driving cars onto golf courses. A year into this our father died, and my brother felt so guilty that he decided to leave his old life behind entirely and become a monk. After a decade or more of monkhood, he'd persuaded the abbot to let him live as a hermit in a one-room cottage on the monastery grounds (he told me there was some precedent for this in Church history), and he spent his days there praying and chopping wood, growing vegetables to give away to the local food pantry, and, three or four times a week, walking up to the main monastery buildings to teach and counsel novices. After the initial shock, my mother was not really unhappy about all this. If nothing else, it meant that Ellory would never again get his name in the paper under POLICE BLOTTER, and embarrass her at the hospital. It didn't matter very much to me one way or the other, except that I saw him less. He was still my brother. He still smoked, still gave the abbot some trouble the way he'd given his parents trouble, and his teachers, his scoutmaster, his golf coach, and so on.

In the first blush of monastic infatuation, Ellory had been in the habit of sending me letters that always ended with a kind of eager encouragement. "The Lord's gifts come in strange wrapping," he'd write. Or "Pain is a blessing." Or "Pray every second." Things like that. It got so bad that, whenever Gerard or I banged a finger with the hammer, or dropped a crowbar on a toe, or tripped over a sole plate and went crashing into a wall, the other person would immediately say, "Pain is a blessing."

But Ellory and I had always been close, in spite of the age difference, and his godly enthusiasms didn't really put much distance between us. It seemed to me that he was at least as happy and well balanced as most of the non-monks I knew. On the four days a year when he was allowed visitors, I took my mother down there—it was less than three hours from Boston—and we had a meal with him and some of the other monks, his friends. Since a piece of her mind had been carted away, my mother had come up with the idea that my brother's name was my name—John—and that he was, for some reason, an airline pilot, always in uniform, living in a mansion with all his pilot friends.

With time, Ellory had evolved an individualistic interpretation of the monastery rules. He was still celibate, as far as I could tell, though he told me he missed the company of women more than anything else. He observed a strict fasting regimen during Lent, and said formal prayers either six or ten times a day, I could never remember. But every few months I went down and visited him, in an unofficial way, sneaking through the woods to his hermitage, and he always broke the rules a little bit then. He always wanted me to smuggle onto the monastery grounds exactly one pack of Marlboro cigarettes. If it wasn't Lent, I might bring him a bottle of red wine and some Jarlsberg cheese and good bread. Or a few cigars. Or some copies of *Sports Illustrated* (not the swimsuit issue). Once, on his thirty-third birthday, we arranged to meet at the side of the nearest road and I brought a change of clothes and spirited him off to a golf course for nine holes.

He was a good, devoted monk, and a good man. These were things he did, little things, ten times in a year maybe, to maintain some sort of interior balance. Even the pope, he pointed out to me, had sneaked away from Vatican City to go skiing once or twice when he was younger. "God doesn't want machines, Jake," he liked to say, after he'd been there awhile and had stopped ending his letters with "All the good Lord asks of us is that we think of Him."

I said I didn't know what God wanted anymore.

And he said, not in a preachy way, "You know right from wrong, Jake. God is just the part of you that knows right from wrong."

"Sure," I said. "Stalin had that part, too. Hitler. Mussolini. Idi Amin. They were all sure they knew right from wrong. So were nineteen assholes with box cutters."

But by the time I took Janet there, Ellory and I had stopped having conversations like that. We just did what we did. He was a monk, I was a painter. I banged nails, I punched governors. His part of my father's inheritance had gone to the monastery. My part had gone to buy the apartment I lived in. My sister's part had gone into pharmaceuticals and roulette. We knew what was right and wrong and we wanted to serve our own little selfish demons, and balancing those things was called life.

I didn't usually sneak up to the hermitage at night, though, unannounced. And I had never taken a girlfriend there.

For dinner, Janet and I stopped at a sub shop in Sturbridge—still a bit of bad air between us—and I had the pierced, beringed, and bespectacled young man make an Italian with everything on it, to go, for Ellory, and then bought the cigarettes at a convenience store in the same little strip mall, where another pierced and tattooed young fellow asked me to show my ID.

3

On a quiet, two-lane highway not far from the monastery there was an unmarked dirt parking area large enough for two cars, nothing but woods all around. Hunters used it in fall and spring. Teenagers probably used it as a lovers' lane. I had used it a dozen times to make my clandestine visits to my brother. I pulled the truck off the road there and killed the lights. Janet and I locked the doors and walked up the highway to the spot where I had met Ellory on the day we'd gone golfing. From there we stepped off onto an old logging road that had almost been reclaimed by the forest, an old wound, mostly healed. I kept a cigar-sized flashlight in the glove compartment, and had remembered to bring it, so we had a little light to work by, and a three-quarters moon, and, for Janet, even in sneakers and a partly buttonless dress, the going wasn't too bad.

She'd been out of the hospital only a week and wasn't coughing very much at all, but even so her lungs were functioning at only about thirty-five percent of capacity, so I went along at a slow pace. The visit was foolish in several ways, but I had mentioned Janet to Ellory in a letter, and he'd written back saying I should bring her to the next family day, which was scheduled for the start of January. But I knew that when Janet's lung capacity dropped into the mid-twenties, which it would the next time she caught a cold, it would not be very easy to take her walking in the woods, or on a ride to the monastery, or much of anywhere else.

It was about half a mile on the trail. We stopped twice to rest. Janet did not like me to see how out of breath she was, so when we stopped she stayed a couple of steps away from me and turned her back. I pretended I'd found some interesting mushroom or something to study in the beam of my little flashlight. From things that had happened in my own life during the previous year, I knew about pity and what it ruined. My promise to myself, from the night I'd first typed the words "cystic fibrosis" into Gerard's computer, had been that, no matter what else I did, I was going to steer my feelings for her a hundred and fifty miles wide of pity.

So I waited for her to say she couldn't do something—couldn't make love, couldn't come into my studio because of the fumes, couldn't walk a flat half-mile in the woods—but she never said that. I sometimes thought of her toughness as an iron bar running up her spine. Other times I thought of it as a fire in her chest. Once in a while, on my three-times-a-week morning runs, I'd find a long steep hill and sprint up it as hard as I could, just to feel the pain of wanting breath, and to realize she felt some version of that pain for most of her waking hours.

Soon enough the woods ended and there were open, almost-flat hayfields coated in silvery light, and an old rail fence with signs every thirty feet: MONASTIC ENCLOSURE. PLEASE KEEP OUT.

We ducked under the top rail. Crossing the hayfield, I took her hand. By then we had left the State House behind, it seemed to me, though my face hurt where the governor had scratched it, and my ribs and shoulder where he had practiced his judo on me. Janet's hand felt hot against my palm and I had an urge to stop and lay her down in the sweet grass and make peace that way. I put the flashlight in my front pocket, then took it out and put it in my back pocket. We crossed a low rise and could see Ellory's cabin ahead another eighty yards. The only window was an ocher rectangle, but as we got closer the light went out.

"He's just going to bed," I told Janet quietly. "It's good, he'll be done with his prayers, he'll be hungry."

We walked up to the cabin and I tapped on the door three times, two quick, soft knocks then a pause, then one sharp knock. In a minute the light came back on. Another minute and Ellory opened the door, any ordinary, nice-looking thirty-eight-year-old in a bathrobe, little spark of devil in the eyes.

"Hi," I said. "Sorry to bother you, but have you noticed lately how much trouble there is in the world? Have you ever wondered why?"

4

Ellory took a step out of his hermitage and squeezed me so hard I thought the rib the governor had bruised was going to snap. Before I could breathe well enough again to introduce Janet, he said, "Either you've brought a beautiful woman with you or Brother Theodorus is playing dress-up again."

"I'm Janet Rossi," she said, holding out her hand.

"Sorry. I'm not allowed to shake hands with women." Ellory stepped farther out from the hermitage and embraced her, too, though not as hard. "Come in, before the night watchman sees us and they turn me back into a Protestant."

The hut was sixteen feet by sixteen feet with one chair, one table, one bed, one lamp, one three-shelf bookcase on the wall, a woodstove, a small sink with a hot plate to one side of it, a half-sized refrigerator, and a door that led to a closet with a flush toilet and a shower stall. I took the flashlight out of my pocket and Janet and I sat on the plain gray blanket on the bed. Ellory pulled his chair over. On his feet he was wearing a pair of no-heel leather slippers, color of a peanut shell, that my mother had given him when she was still, as we liked to say, "sharp." They were in tatters, the tops and soles barely holding together, a toe showing through. Everything else in the room was perfectly neat—no cobwebs, no clutter, no excess—as if the monks had convinced my brother that the condition of his living space had some influence on the condition of his soul.

"Would you guys like me to call out for a pizza?" my brother offered. He paused one beat for effect, then went to the door, opened it, and, in a not very loud voice, sang out, "Pizza! Pizza!" He came back in and sat down, smiling like a kid in a swimming pool.

I could tell he was nervous.

Janet was watching him. "You have your brother's sense of humor," she said after a few seconds.

"It's our dad's, actually. He was an investment banker and then a financial counselor—did Jake tell you? White shirt and tie all week. Big serious meetings at which big serious men talked about large sums of money."

"Big serious money," I said.

"And at night, or on the weekends, or when we went someplace on vacation, he could be as foolish as a four-year-old." He turned to me. His eyes were steady and clear. He was happy we'd come. "Remember Bastille Day?"

"We were on vacation in Paris," I said to Janet, "and we were all sitting at a sidewalk table getting ready to have dinner."

"Rue Mouffetard," Ellory said. "No cars, you know. Little shops. Cobblestones."

"And some guy with an accordion started playing lively French tunes. So my father grabbed my mother by the arm and pulled her out into the street and started dancing with her there, spinning her around, bending her backwards like Fred with Ginger.

"Which would have been fine, except he couldn't dance to save his soul. He improvised. Mum improvised with him. It went on and on. The food was served, Mum came back to the table eventually, but Dad just kept going, solo. We started to eat and he just kept dancing, twirling around, flailing his arms up in the air.

It really wasn't that unusual a sight for us, him making a spectacle of himself. The people at the other tables loved it, though."

"Mum loved it, too," I said.

"Of course she did. She dealt with sick and dying kids all day, he was her relaxation . . . How is she anyway?"

"Okay. The same. Last time you saw her she was asking for me."

Ellory almost smiled. "She's not in any pain," he said, and I could see the suit of guilt on him, too.

"She mixes us up," I explained to Janet.

"You told me."

We didn't talk for a moment. Janet fussed with the top of her dress and pushed herself back on the bed so she was against the wall. She let her eyes wander over the sparse furnishings. Those sparse furnishings, I noticed for the first time, included a framed picture of a young woman, which sat on the top of Ellory's bookcase, above a row of lentil soup cans and next to framed pictures of my sister, me, and our parents. I looked at it once, and then just focused on a corner of the room where my brother had set up a little shrine—crucifix, votive candle, a vase with a few stalks of some kind of wild berry in it.

I knew Janet well enough by then to see that she was at ease with Ellory and in his little house, the way she had been at ease in my apartment almost from the first minute. Families are like countries. They have their own language and jokes and secrets and assumptions about the right and wrong ways of doing things, and some of that always shows in the children, the way something of Germany or Australia always shows in a German or an Australian, no matter where they go. Outsiders like it or they don't, they feel at home there or they don't. It's like the taste of cilantro. Giselle had never liked cilantro.

I had been thinking about the photograph and holding the bag with the sub sandwich and cigarettes in it. I was somehow not paying attention. After she'd finished looking at the pictures and the soup cans and reading the titles on the spines of Ellory's books, Janet touched my arm and pointed to the oil stain on my pants. I handed the bag to my brother and told him what it was. He insisted we share the sandwich with him. We said no. He insisted again and we said no again, we'd just eaten, we were fine. And then he said okay but he would save half of it for the next day's lunch. And then he ate the first half of the sub from a plate on his lap, with his bathrobe on and his hairy shins showing, in about three seconds. My eyes wandered up to the bookcase again, and I could not keep myself from thinking about something he had told me: that the monks in his order weren't supposed to talk and so they learned sign language and there was a certain sign they used for greeting each other and it meant *memento mori,* remember death. When he'd first told that to me and for years afterwards I thought it was one of the worst things I'd heard about the monastery, right there in line with *Pain is a blessing.* "Remember life," I thought they should be saying to each other. "Remember fun."

But I'd gotten older and certain things had happened to me and to people close to me, and the monks' little hand signal had started to make more sense. All of Ellory had started to make more sense.

I took the pack of cigarettes out of my shirt pocket and handed it over. He placed it on his desk, just so.

Janet pulled the top of her dress together again and asked him what it was like, living alone all the time.

In his early monastic days, Ellory would have said, "I'm not alone, I have the Lord's presence," or some special thing like that. But he'd grown up, finally, after thirteen years of no sex and no carousing and no sleeping later than four a.m. He looked up at her and said, "Oh, shit. You've been here all this time and I haven't asked about you at all."

"My life is an open book," she said.

He smiled. He was still holding the dripping oily sandwich in both hands an inch above his plate. "Mine, too, but . . . What kind of work do you do?"

"I work for the governor of Massachusetts."

"Doing what?'

"Reading and interpreting polls, deflecting and entertaining lobbyists, working on his travel itinerary in campaign years, advising on speeches, being a liaison with the press. Getting him reelected. My title is Special Assistant for Public Relations."

"He must be a good man, then, if you work for him."

"He's a jerkoff," I said. My hand was hurting more now; there was about two percent of being sorry left in me.

Janet had a particular way of pursing her lips when she was bothered by something I did or said. It made small ridges of skin at the outside edges of her mouth, and made the freckle almost disappear. When she pursed her lips like that in my direction, I knew everything was more or less alright between us. Ellory looked from me to her and she said, "No, he's . . . flawed. I thought he might be someone special when I first went to work for him. He's charismatic, in a politician's way. He seems to care about children, really, and he's good with his own daughters. When I first saw him—I went to work for him during his first campaign when I was right out of grad school—I thought he might turn into a great governor someday. I thought he might even run for president—he still wants to. But I've been there almost four years now and he's squeezed three-quarters of the idealism out of me." She coughed her deep wet cough and I watched my brother watching her. "I wanted to do something good for the world. Now I want to keep my health insurance and have someplace to go on rainy weekday mornings in February."

"I was more idealistic at first, too," Ellory said when she was finished. "The routine here breaks it out of you. That's good, I think, or natural. Every life does that. Marriage does it, work does it. The trick is to somehow keep the gates open in the fences at the edge of your mind and not get hard and bitter. You don't strike me as hard and bitter. Jake doesn't strike me that way either, in spite of everything that's happened to him."

Janet looked at me when Ellory said that. It was as if I'd just taken off a pair of dark glasses and she was seeing my eyes for the first time. She looked back at Ellory, who was taking the opportunity to gulp down the second half of his sandwich, and whose eyes slipped once to the cigarettes on the desk.

"Don't you miss sex?" she asked abruptly. "Don't you miss being close to someone that way?"

"Sure." Ellory got up to put his dish in the sink, and toss the waxed paper in the wastebasket. He washed the oil from his fingers, dried his hands, and looked at the cigarettes again, then came back and sat in his chair. "When I first started living here I used to masturbate every Monday night, right on schedule, once a week. It was something to look forward to."

It did not sound like he was talking about sex. All the dirtiness and sweet spark had been taken out of it.

"I miss women," he went on. "I miss that kind of intimacy. But I think whatever people do, they do in search of pleasure. Or trying to get rid of pain or fear, which is the same thing, basically. Everything, everything is really about that. Everything is about bringing your mind to a place where it's at peace. There are just different routes. Some of them seem to lead there, and lead there for a while, and then don't. Some things work for one person and don't work at all for another person. Our sister takes a lot of drugs. Jake told you that, I'm sure. She just wants to put her mind in a pleasurable place or she just wants to get rid of the pain that's there. It's not a sin. It's not something God despises her for. It doesn't work, that's all. And it just leads to her doing things, to herself and other people, that drive her farther away from the peace she's looking for. That's hell."

Janet was staring at him. I was looking at the bookcase on the wall, measuring everything Ellory said against the photograph there.

"Bro," I said, when he stopped for a breath.

"What?"

"You're, you know, preaching a little."

Janet said, "No he isn't, Jake." Then, to Ellory, "And this works for you, living like this?"

"It's a good setup for someone like me, it wasn't always."

"Jake said you were wild."

"I was afraid of dying, that's all."

"And now you're not."

"I might be, when the time comes. I imagine I will be, but maybe less than I would have been if I hadn't come here. I'm curious about it some days."

"Me, too," Janet said.

I got up off the bed a little too suddenly, stepped out through the front door, and closed it most of the way. I went just far enough to be out of the window light, partway around the corner of Ellory's little house. I looked across the dark fields. By then the moon was well up in the sky and the night was clear and we were far out in the countryside so that, even with the moon, there were about three times as many stars as I was used to seeing. You could feel the first bite of winter in the air. And in the darkness the monastery grounds and the dark shapes of buildings on a little rise half a mile away seemed to be giving off the scent of desolation.

My hand and my rib and one side of my face throbbed every time a pulse of blood went through them. I knew we weren't going to New York then. I suspected I had never really been planning to take Janet to New York on that trip. Something moved up through me when I admitted that to myself, a twist of old anguish twirling up the bones of my back. Riding along with the anguish, or right behind the anguish, came a beautiful sense of relief, something like what I had felt at Diem Bo on our first date. It was a kind of fearlessness, I understood that then, a way of just standing in the moment of time I was standing in and knowing I could probably survive whatever was going to follow that moment. I understood, too, that, in their own ways, Janet and Ellory had both learned to do that, live in the present like that, gobbling up their fears.

After a time I went back into the cabin and they were looking at me. "Thought I'd pee outside," I told them, and when Janet pursed her lips again, I said, "The neighborhood has gotten lousy here, I thought I heard somebody stealing the golf clubs out of my truck." And when she kept her eyes on me and that expression on her mouth, I said, "I just needed a few seconds. All is well."

But she kept looking.

We stayed another ten minutes. We talked about plans to bring my mother there for the January visiting day, and about the season the Red Sox were having, and a little bit about Janet's mother, a devout Catholic herself. Over the course of the time we'd been dating, Janet had told me how her mother had taken care of her as a girl and as a young woman, doing her chest PT every night, taking her to doctors, sleeping on a cot beside her hospital bed, cooking special meals. A little overprotective at times, Janet said, but kind and tough and fond of men who worked with their hands. Janet kept saying how much I'd like her and how much she'd like me. I'd seen pictures of the woman. But, though she lived only ten minutes from Boston, I noticed that Janet made no move to actually introduce us.

My brother gets up at 4:15 every morning to pray, and Janet and I were supposedly on our way to New York City, so we said our good-byes, exchanging embraces like explorers getting ready to set off across different oceans. Janet and I stepped out into the night. When we were a few dozen steps from the cabin, I looked back and saw that the light was still on, the door still open, Ellory standing there in his bathrobe, watching us. Just before we crossed the rise, I looked back again and saw that the door was closed and the light still showing in the window and I knew he was praying for us then, asking whatever saints and spirits might be out there to watch over us, help us not to turn bitter and hard, not to be afraid.

I did not feel any of those things as we made our way across the monastery hayfield in the moonlight—not bitter, not afraid. I felt then, for some reason, that life was larger and more complicated than I'd ever thought. You couldn't always be sure where bad luck ended and good luck began. You had to just endure certain things, and let time pass, and try to keep the gates open at the edges of your mind.

5

JANET AND I didn't say a word as we made our way across the field and onto the logging road. We didn't say anything walking back along the two-lane highway toward where the truck was parked, either. No cars passed, and the moon had swung behind the trees, but there were small breaths of cool October wind against the skin of our faces, and the woods were black and trembling on both sides of us, and we walked through a feeling you can't find in the city. The whole human drama seemed like just a crazy sideshow, a circus ring of glitter and anger set against some enormous dark background, little wisps of hope here and there.

When we were sitting in the truck with the heater on, I said to her, "New York or by bus?" because I couldn't yet bring myself to tell her where I was actually planning to go.

And she said, "A decent motel. New York tomorrow, okay?"

There was something strained and unfigurable in her voice. I thought maybe she was in a hurry then, or tired out, that she wanted to get to a motel room with enough time and energy to make love. But when we found a place, and checked in, and had gone into the room and closed the door without turning on the lights—which had become a little ritual for us—she said, "I want to do something different tonight, will you, Jake?"

I said that I would be happy to, depending on what kind of different she had in mind, but probably I'd be happy to.

"I want us to take off all our clothes and sleep next to each other and not make love."

"Not make love, or not make love and not indulge in any variations on the same theme?"

"Nothing. I just want to talk a little, and then sleep. We'll make love when we get to New York."

"Why?"

"Because I've never done that before."

"I have," I said. "I did it lots of times when I was fifteen and sixteen, except the girl wasn't completely naked and neither was I and it didn't go on all night."

"And you remember it fondly," she said.

"Vividly."

"It's one night, Jake. I'd like to try it."

We tried it. We took off every particle of clothing and climbed into the motel bed where so many other souls had made love and had sex and been angry and hopeful and afraid and alone. We just lay there in the darkness holding hands. It wasn't too bad until she hooked her left ankle over my right ankle, and I could feel her thigh against my thigh, and the heat of her all down the length of my leg.

"Is this supposed to be in sympathy with Ellory or something?"

"He's a kind man. I liked him. I liked what he said about pleasure and dying."

"Are you paying me back for being a gorilla with the governor?"

She pushed me with her elbow, not too gently. "It's not a punishment, it's an experiment. It's just something I want to do. I want to feel what there is between us if we don't have sex."

"You can feel what there is between us. Let me turn on my side."

Another strong elbow. "Stop," she said. "I mean it. If you can't handle it I'll just crawl into the other bed. It's one night."

"Alright."

"I have something important to tell you."

"Alright," I said, but in the course of three seconds the air in the room had changed. I breathed in and out. I said, "Is this because of what happened in your office?"

"It has nothing to do with that, and it has nothing to do with meeting your brother. I had already made up my mind before those things."

"You're going to become a nun," I said, because I was nervous then. *Memento mori.* I was worrying about what Ellory might have said to her when I went outside. I was thinking there are all kinds of deaths and you'd have to be half-machine in order not to remember that.

"Jake. Stop."

"I'm stopped. I'm ready," I said, but naturally I wasn't. All my beautiful thoughts about being in the moment and not being afraid just lifted up and flew out through the cheap drapes and I was left lying there in the body of my actual self.

"I'm going to put my name on the list for a double lung transplant," Janet said, up into the darkness of the room. "I thought, before, that I'd never want to do that, but now I'm going to."

6

WHEN SHE WAS ASLEEP I tried to time her breaths against my own. Three to one—quick short inhales and slower exhales, as if her body didn't quite have the strength to push all the old air out. I wondered how she could even sleep, breathing that way, and why it didn't exhaust her by about eleven o'clock in the morning.

I heard trucks going by on the highway next to the motel, and I thought constantly about what she had said. From the hours I'd spent in front of Gerard's computer I knew what it meant to sign up for a double lung transplant: it was the last miracle a CF person reached for before giving up. Even if she made it to the top of the list of people waiting for new lungs, and even if the operation worked, she'd be condemning herself to a life of even more medication and even more side effects. Tremors, bone loss, sleep problems, high blood pressure, high cholesterol, muscle cramps, increased susceptibility to diabetes and to opportunistic infection. She'd still have cystic fibrosis, but for a year or five years or eighteen years, she'd breathe, and for a while at least the breaths would come easy.

I took her left hand and lay it palm-down on top of my thigh, and put my own hand over it. I tried to calm myself by breathing with her, concentrating hard on that awkward rhythm and the feeling of her hand and nothing else.

But it is hard to keep the mind still like that. I went from the rhythm of our breathing to thinking about what Ellory had said about his wild years. From there I tried to imagine, for the ten thousandth time, what Giselle must have gone through in the hour before she died, and then what dying really was.

Air stopped going into and out of a pair of lungs, that was all. Your heart stopped squeezing and relaxing. Millions of cells stopped doing the kinds of things they had been doing for ten or twenty-seven or ninety years. Clear enough. But if you tried to ask what happened to the part of the person you couldn't see or measure, the part you envied or argued with or loved, then you sounded like a ninth-grader on marijuana.

It seemed to me, lying there with Janet, skin against skin, that Ellory had come to understand something I didn't understand—not about death or God as much as about minute-to-minute living. In the sterile room, with the whine of tires and truck engines beyond the windows, I felt that some absolutely essential fact was right there for me to take hold of, right there. I went to sleep reaching for it.

7

A T BREAKFAST THE next morning I told Janet I had changed my mind about where we were going. "I'll take you to New York next time it's my turn to pick," I said, and she nodded and said that was fine. But there was a strain in my voice, a weight, a bad nervousness. And I knew her well enough by then to see in her eyes that she wanted to talk about it.

When we were in the truck again, I asked if she could deal with four more hours of riding.

"I love riding," she said. "It's moving without having to get out of breath."

"We're going to Pennsylvania."

"Fine, Jake. Just go," she said, but there was something unspoken between us, wisps of warm smoky fear in the air of the cab.

She sat with her bare feet up on the dashboard, one arm dangling out the window, the wind blowing strands of hair around her face. To make it so we didn't have to talk, I put good music on the CD—John Hiatt, Mary Chapin Carpenter, Springsteen, Chopin, Saw Doctors, Dave Matthews, a little-known Cajun outfit called Doctor Romo.

To someone used to the Rhode Islands and New Hampshires of this world, Pennsylvania seems like an enormous state, the Montana of the east. I remember Gerard saying, after his cross-country bike trip the summer of his divorce, that Wyoming and Idaho were nothing compared to Pennsylvania, where, instead of one long climb and one long descent, you had an endless series of exertions and exhilarations, pain and freedom, pain and freedom, sweat and pain and then wind in your face and pure effortless speed.

From time to time I would feel Janet looking at me in a way she had not looked at me before our monastery visit. But we said almost nothing and did not touch. We drove and drove.

The place where we finally stopped was a humble little city in the middle of the Alleghenies. A few months earlier, nine miners had been trapped in a coal shaft there for three days before being pulled out. They had gone through something unforgettable, horrible. And the people who rescued them had been smart and brave, and all kinds of other people had given food and help. But something about it sickened me: the news anchors with their manufactured earnestness, the way the reporters seemed almost to enjoy it, locals enjoying the attention, too; the way, after a certain critical point, you could smell the book deals and movie deals, as if all of it had been nothing more than food for a ravenous entertainment machine. Not long after the miners' ordeal, I gave my television set away to one of the local homeless shelters. I did not know how you were supposed to tell about that kind of terror, that kind of worry that someone you loved might slowly suffocate underground while you wanted to help them and couldn't. But I knew a sour note when I heard it, and the TV, it seemed to me, had been full of sour notes all that year.

The pickings were a bit slim thereabouts, but I found the nicest hotel I could. We walked the streets for a while to work off the dullness of the drive, then ate at a steak house, went back to the room, and left the lights out.

"Are we there yet?" Janet asked. We were on the fourth

floor and she was standing at a half-open window looking down at the lazy traffic.

"Almost."

The day had been warm for October—low seventies—and at lunch she'd changed into the other dress she'd brought, a summery dress with small yellow flowers everywhere on a sky-blue background. I stood behind her, unzipping it. When I had unzipped it as far as her hips, I tugged it down off her shoulders, and when she took her arms away from the windowsill, the dress fell around her feet. Carefully, as if we had all of time in front of us, I picked up the dress and lay it on one of the beds. I put my hands on her bare shoulders and we stood that way, front to back, looking out. "The kids are asleep," I said. "I checked."

"You're nervous again. I could feel it at dinner."

"Calm is my middle name."

"You're going goofy."

"Highway hypnosis," I said. "Hydroplaning. Driver's side air bags. My other truck is a Cadillac."

"Jake."

"What."

"Take off the rest of my clothes."

I did that. Still, she did not turn around. Our breathing was more similar now.

"Is there something here you want me to see?"

"Tomorrow there is."

"Alright. Are your clothes off?"

"No."

"Is my body exciting to you? I'm not fishing for . . . my hips seem wide to me, my feet seem large. I don't think that would be exciting. This body doesn't work right in so many ways I just want it to be right in one way."

Instead of answering I lifted up her hair and kissed the back of her neck. Which was saltier than any normal back of the neck should have been. Which was the whole problem. I kissed the back of her neck and then I kissed the back of where her lungs were, and then kissed down bit by bit to her heels. She turned around and I kissed slowly back up, not touching the usual sex places but spending time on the bones at the top of her hips, the insides of her elbows, her collarbone, her throat. She stood still and didn't touch me, but the tightness came out of her muscles almost as it had when she'd fallen asleep against me the night before.

"Cells singing," she said, at one point.

I kissed her mouth, and because she could go a fairly long time that week without coughing, it was a long kiss, something new for us.

For some reason then, I bent down and licked the surgery scars on her belly, which she'd thought were so ugly that she'd stopped ever wearing a two-piece bathing suit, thirteen years old. I kissed the soft fleshiness of her breasts as if I could heal what lay beneath them, as if the pure force of my wanting pleasure for her could pass through skin and flesh and blood and cauterize the colonies of bacteria. Cells singing. In fact, the bad bacteria communicated with each other—researchers had just discovered that—and different ones had different assignments, like bees in a hive, like terrorists on an airliner. The tiny tubes through which her life ran were being choked off in minuscule increments every day, every instant. I kissed and licked her and I believed I could feel all that going on inside her and I wanted to burn down into her with what was in the middle of me, with the good in me, the good-wanting. I did not want any more death and suffering now, in my little world, not for years and years. Sometimes I could feel the force of that not-wanting as it scraped up against something larger. My own power, my own small will, against the huge merciless spinning-out of time. I had made a year of trying to yield to that something larger, and be understanding, mellow, resilient. But I wasn't in a mood to do that anymore.

The song of Janet's cells lifted up through her throat and murmured in the back of her mouth, echoing there, as her voice always did, soft flute notes tapping against the sides of a wet barrel. As I kissed her I unbuckled my pants. I pulled the zipper down and let them drop and stepped out of them and she pulled my underwear down, letting her soft hair brush the insides of my legs. I started to move her toward the bed but she brought her face up so that I was looking into her black eyes and she said, "I want it to be not just sex."

"You're talking to the right man."

She turned around and put her hands on the windowsill and I stood very close behind her, with the shadows of the room on us, and the tinny bell of an elevator beyond the door, and then two or three people walking along the corridor, laughing loudly. I had my fingers on the tops of her hip bones and I could feel my pulse in every square centimeter of skin, but I knew exactly what she meant. I wanted a connectedness that was not just about lust, not just about orgasms. I wanted to pull it back from the world of gossipy magazines and television, the seen world, the talked-about and written-about world, the world of pretending life went on forever. Janet wanted that, too, I was sure of it. We were both all full of want on that night.

8

T HE NEXT MORNING we slept in later than usual, and made
love again when we woke up. Something had changed in the
lovemaking, I don't know how to say it. It was not driven by anything. There was nothing watching us. We could not have talked
during it, or about it.

The diner where we had our late breakfast was busy with
lunch customers, so instead of sitting in a booth we sat on stools at
the counter. We didn't talk about our feelings for each other, but
those feelings had changed, had moved from blossom to fruit. In
some strange way, going to visit my brother had been a kind of
public statement for us—though a hermit's house might seem
like an odd place for public statements. I wasn't a sacrilegious person. Ellory knew I wouldn't take just any date onto the monastery
grounds. And, once we'd been there, Janet understood that, too.

The food was oily and real and served on big oval plates—
eggs and link sausages and potatoes. Janet liked raspberry jam on
buttered wheat toast, almost burned. We drank coffee and grape-
fruit juice and ice water and afterwards shared one piece of warm
apple pie because the pie was sitting in a glass case just in our line
of vision. By then I did not want to find the place I had driven all
that way to see.

When Janet went to the bathroom I started talking to the
man on the stool to my left. He was wearing a Pittsburgh Steelers

cap, and the skin of his cheeks was pitted, and he was eating pancakes, and he told me his name was Peter. There was something wounded and friendly about him. We got onto the subject of children, and he told me he had three of them, two almost-grown boys and a girl. They had lived with their mother for a long time now, but everyone still got along pretty well. I asked him what he liked best about having children, and he thought for a few seconds and said, "It's the closest you can come to being the other person." And then, after another couple of seconds, "A lot of times, if you try, you can be who you really should be with them, who you want to be."

I thought about that. I said I thought there was always a distance between who you are and who you want to be. And then, because it was hurting me to think about those things just then, I tried to make a joke. I said, "I have an appointment with disappointment every day." It was foolish. I was nervous. I waited for the stupid words to drift away. I asked him how to get to the place we were headed for and he gave very careful directions. When I asked him what it looked like he said, "I've never gone out there. I've seen enough of things like that. I never wanted to go."

"Where did you see things like that?"

"I flew fixed-wing propeller planes off carriers, in Vietnam."

I asked if I could buy him breakfast. It wasn't because of the Vietnam part, but just because I liked him. He said, "Why?"

"I'm just in a mood to."

"Alright," he said, after he'd considered the offer a moment. When I got up to go to the bathroom he took hold of the sleeve of my shirt and held me there. "I don't talk about this with a lot of people, but if you get *Life* magazine and look at the issue for April 1970, you'll see my picture."

He was perfectly sane and normal, but I had the feeling that if the waitress had been just slightly rude to him one day, by accident even, he might never come back there. April 1970 had made a mark on his life that could not be erased. He seemed to me to be filled to the eyes with all the awful things he had seen, all the friends he had lost, to be swimming along on a sea of suffering that was invisible to everyone else. I liked him.

The bathroom was very small and clean, but the tiles were broken here and there, and powdered soap poured out of the dispenser if you barely touched it. I turned on the water too hard and it splashed right out of the sink and all over the front of my pants. Coming out of the little room, I took a right instead of a left and walked into the kitchen.

When I made it back to the counter at last, Peter thanked me for the breakfast, and when Janet came back he thanked her, too. He reminded me about the *Life* magazine, and I said I'd be sure to check it out, but I have never done that.

"This town has some odd energy," Janet said, on the sunny sidewalk. She had been in the bathroom a long time and I worried she was getting sick again already.

"This is the town where the miners were rescued. Over the summer."

"I saw the 'God Bless Our Heroes' sign. I was wondering. That's not where we're going, though, is it?"

"Not those heroes, no."

"Your voice is different today, Jake."

We drove out of town on a two-lane country highway, past an airport and a two-truck volunteer fire station and a man in a checkered shirt with his hands in his pants pockets, staring at a ten-foot-tall pile of gravel. The land there was woods and farm-land, hilly but hard-edged, and you could see the marks of the severe winters on the roof shingles and clapboards. At one point we passed a sign that said:

WELCOME TO SHANKSVILLE

HOME OF THE VIKINGS

A FRIENDLY LITTLE TOWN

ESTABLISHED 1803

Shortly after that we passed a wire fence where someone had tacked up a piece of one-by-ten with FLIGHT 93 MEMORIAL and an arrow painted on it. But I did not think Janet noticed.

Following my friend Peter's directions, I turned off the highway and we wound along a smaller road lined with fluttering flags. There were streaks of sweat on the steering wheel. We made a right turn onto a steep gravel road called Skyline Drive. Next to that road, outside a house decorated everywhere with stars and stripes, some enterprising folks had set up a gift shop where you could buy souvenirs. We rolled on, over the crest of the hill, and I pulled the truck into a lot where a few other cars had parked and where people had covered the aluminum guardrail with a kind of worshipful graffiti. The land in front of us was desolate land, slanting down and away in stony, weedy slopes with a lot of Queen Anne's lace growing there, and with sharp-winged brown birds darting back and forth and making shrill cries. I remembered that the site was in fact a filled-in strip mine, but it looked to me like an abandoned cattle ranch where the soil had been too stony and poor to grow meat. Far off to our left, on another hill, sat a rusty strip-mining crane, impossibly big, and there were fences, a farmhouse, the birds squealing, but your eye was drawn straight down the slope to a new chain-link fence that enclosed a more or less rectangular area, several hundred yards long, with a treeline behind. There was an American flag tied to the fence. Janet was looking in that direction.

"You can still see where the trees were burned," I told her, but it came out in an even newer version of the new voice so that she started looking at me instead of the woods behind the fenced-in area. I tried again. I said, "Let's go up on this little hill." But I should have just kept quiet.

You could not get anywhere close to the actual fenced-in site with the burned trees behind it, but on a little rise near the parking lot there was a piece of chain-link, maybe ten feet by twenty feet, that had been erected as a sort of public billboard. Hundreds of people had left things on that scrap of metal, an odd assortment of things: baseball and football caps, rosary beads and medals of saints, Stars of David, crucifixes, a couple of Buddhas, real and plastic flowers, stuffed animals, children's toys, a T-shirt from a Las Vegas plumbers' union, flags and flags and flags and not just American, drawings, notes encased in plastic wrap so the rain wouldn't spoil them—"Let's Roll" and "God Bless You All" and "For the children who lost a parent, friend, or loved one." Dollar bills.

I hadn't wanted to ever come here because I had wanted my own grief and confusion to be private. I did not want anyone making assumptions about what I felt for Giselle, or what she had felt for me. I did not want the newspapers and television to touch even the smallest part of that, not because I believed it was more important or more special or even different from what other men and women and children had felt on that day and afterwards, but because I did not want my feelings cheapened, and the entertainment machine was all about cheapening feelings, about making complicated things simple. That was the whole purpose of it, after making money: to dull the edge of things. Scenes of blown-up discothèques in Haifa one second, and racy commercials for lite beer the next. How could we tolerate it?

Not far from me, a little girl was standing with her father and she said, "These people were good people, Daddy, weren't they?" But even that was somehow a wrong note.

Janet had drifted away from me. I saw her standing in front of an unofficial plaque that showed the names of the dead. The flags there were fluttering loudly in the wind. I stared past her, down the slope, to the fenced-in area near the line of the woods. One of the things I'd read—when I had started to let myself read about that day—said that, at the very end of the ordeal, the plane's engines were no longer functioning and it had been coasting along in silence, upside down, as it came over the houses near Shanksville. I had thought about that many times.

Many times, times beyond counting, I had imagined Giselle's fear, and the feelings of the rest of the people in that plane, and in those other planes, and in those buildings. Every sane soul in the world, it seemed to me, had imagined that.

Janet walked over to another memorial someone had made, with small photographs of the passengers glued onto it, their names and ages. Hours and hours some person had spent doing that. I did not want to see it. I could feel myself starting to cry. Not cry, exactly. I could feel myself starting to weep. So I walked past the chain-link billboard, past a sheriff's car, over a second small rise, and I stood there where no one could see me, with my back to the filled-in strip mine. I put my hands in the pockets of my jeans and I let my head droop down so that a steady salty stream worked into the corners of my mouth and onto my T-shirt, and though I tried to be very quiet, I could not. I walked a little farther away, over another stony rise, and I stayed there a long time, weeping until it was all out of me, and then I wiped my face with the bottom of my T-shirt and looked up into a perfectly empty sky and breathed and breathed.

It seemed to me then that the whole problem with the way the world was designed came from the fact that we lived in separate packages. You could not ever really reach out of your miniature world and into someone else's and feel what they were feeling. Not really. Not enough. Maybe making love, or maybe during short flashes of conversation with a friend, or maybe, maybe, for a few hours after the world had witnessed something horrifying. Gerard had said to me that when your children were young you could do that. And when my mother had talked to me about her parents' deaths—which had been slow, hard deaths— she'd said there came a point when you felt something like that. All the dying person's protection had been burned away, she told me; it seemed as if they opened themselves up to you, cut themselves open and allowed you in.

I breathed and breathed, wiped my face. After a long time, when I was more or less calm again, I turned and walked back toward my truck. From the top of the second rise, I could see, over the white roof of the sheriff's SUV, that Janet had put down the tailgate of my pickup and was sitting there in her summer dress, dangling her legs over, watching for me. I looked away. Another few steps and I looked back and when I was up close to her she put a hand on my shoulder, leaned forward, and licked the salt from my face.

9

THE TRUTH IS that Janet and I did not talk about Shanksville on the first part of the long ride home. The silence was uncomfortable. At the same time, there was a way in which we were at peace with that discomfort. The distance between us felt like an honest distance, unthreatening.

I could not help thinking that, with Giselle, if things had happened differently, we would have talked and talked, about the memorial, about America, about former lovers and families, and God and pain and death and mysteries. We would have filled the cab of the truck with words because that was the territory we had gone to in order to try to escape the loneliness we felt with each other, the vague, nagging, secret disappointment. If she had not been on that particular plane on that particular day, if we had been able to work out the trouble between us, then Giselle and I would have grown old together sitting on a porch somewhere, reading aloud to each other from sections of the Sunday newspaper, waiting for the grandchildren to call.

The road away from Shanksville lifted and dipped, curling along high slopes over wide red and gold valleys, with sparking rivers slicing through them, and the long rich hills rising on either side like blanket-covered bodies sleeping at some distance to one another. Janet and I listened to one CD—Derek and the Dominos, made before either of us was born—then just rode quietly.

She had started coughing again, intermittently. The sound of it stabbed at me like a dull blade.

We stopped for lunch, and for a gas fill-up for the old machine, and afterwards Janet asked if she could drive for a while and I said, "Of course." She was an intent, careful driver, speed limit minus five. I closed my eyes and moved in and out of a half-sleep infested with smoky dreams.

Somewhere in eastern Pennsylvania she pulled over. We switched places, but still didn't say much. Darkness fell when we were in New York State, on 684. The highway was a necklace of white and red lights looping toward home.

In Connecticut she said, "I went to prep school near here. My mother thought it would be good for me to go away after my father died. We argued about it. I wanted to stay with her and I was really private about taking medicines and so on. The last thing on earth I wanted was to have a roommate watching me use the inhalers and the vest and so on. She's sweet, my Ma—you'll see when you meet her—but she has this drill-sergeant/kung-fu master side that comes out when she's worried about me. So I applied, got a scholarship, ended up with a bulimic genius roommate and some great friends. Senior year I had a boyfriend named Alonzo. From this fabulously wealthy family in Venezuela. He invited me to go home with him for Christmas, and my mother said I could go—his family was paying—but I didn't want to."

"Were you sick?"

"Not that sick then, no. I just wanted to be home at Christmas. I knew my mother was having a hard time and trying to pretend otherwise for my sake, and I wanted to be around her. Anyway, Alonzo and I used to go out for walks in the woods near the campus and just kiss and hold hands. We never did make love. The summer after graduation we wrote a lot of letters. And then every year I was in college he'd write to me in November and ask if I wanted to come to Caracas for the Christmas holidays. I always said no. Senior year, for some reason or another, I went. I was really starting to feel not so good by then, maybe that's why. Maybe I was starting to understand that no one would ever marry me, and I knew that Alonzo had always had a special thing for me. Plus, a friend of mine I'd been in the hospital with a few times had already died . . . Anyway, I went. It was about like you'd expect: the family lived in a twenty-room house with servants and they were very gracious with me and we had a feast on Christmas Eve and went to church the next day and had another feast after church. I had my inhaler and my pills and my vest, and I was feeling okay, but I could see it made Alonzo uncomfortable, you know, how much sicker I'd gotten since high school, the progression of things, the medications. I think, since then, I've always been sensitive about that, on dates especially. One of the things I liked about you in Diem Bo was that you didn't seem bothered.

"Anyway, they were a very kind family. I went horseback riding with his sisters. I'd never been on a horse. The next day Alonzo and I drove to a beach house they had near a place called Puerto La Cruz, which was a beautiful little city with pastel houses and a stony beach. It was warm, we took a swim, we had crab legs and this delicious white wine for dinner, I remember. We went back to the house and went to bed together for the first time and we kissed and everything and it was just like before except that I was coughing a lot and when it came time to . . . he was, he couldn't . . . he was impotent. He felt horrible. Eventually we went to sleep, but in the morning it was the same. It didn't matter to me very much, but to him it was terrible. For the rest of the time I was there he could barely look at me. All the way back to Caracas he talked and talked, but he could barely look at me. Has that ever happened to you, Jake?"

"Once."

"I've always believed it was because my being sick turned him off so much."

"The woman I was with that night wasn't sick," I said.

"Was it Giselle?"

It was the first time either of us had spoken that name. I shook my head.

We rode on. After a few minutes I asked Janet why she had told me the Venezuela story just then, and she said she didn't know.

"Was he the great love of your life?"

"No, you are," she said, just straight and plain and serious like that, without any drama. And then, "Was Giselle the love of your life?"

I shook my head without looking at her, and then looked. She was almost smiling and seemed very calm. I drove along. We were past the little knot of Hartford by then. "We met in a bar on Boylston Street," I said. "Three and a half years ago. We had a good time at first. I had my first show, sold a couple of paintings. We went to Mexico. We went up to Quebec City a couple of times. Everything was nice. We fought a lot—stupid little fights—but everything was going along pretty well. She was selling mobile phones and she was good at it, and then she got promoted to regional sales manager and, I don't know, things started to go sour. She wanted to start having children and I was fine with that idea. But she had a whole plan—three children, a certain kind of house in the suburbs—and I kept saying I'd grown up in a family with three children in a nice house in the suburbs, and there was nothing wrong with it, I just didn't really want to do it all over again exactly that way. She was pushing me to go back to med school. I kept saying I didn't want to go back to med school, I wanted to paint. It got to be a regular thing for us—"

"I didn't know you went to medical school."

"I quit after the first year. I . . . we'd go along fine for a few days or a week, sometimes two weeks, then we'd get into the med school discussion, the suburbs discussion."

"Ellory said you were planning to get married."

I looked over at her. In that quick glance across the shadowy cab I couldn't read her face, but there had been a kind of sad, bending note in her voice when she said "married." It surprised me.

"I thought he might have said something."

"I asked about the picture on his bookshelf. He said she'd died, he didn't say how, but he told me you'd been engaged."

"No," I said. "We'd talked about it, but no."

"No ring?"

When she said "ring," I heard the bending note a second time.

"No."

"I interrupted you. I'm jealous, I'm sorry. Keep going now, and then after this we never have to talk about it again, alright?"

"Alright. Giselle had grown up poor—her parents were from Brazil, actually. After she met me, she started to make a lot of money and then she started to worry that if she stopped to have kids she'd be poor again. But she didn't want to leave the kids and fly all over the place every few weeks. It was a big confusion for her. I have plenty of money, you know. I make a good amount from carpentry. I sell a few paintings every year, the apartment is paid for and worth a lot. She knew all that. But . . . I don't know . . . everything got tense. She started to travel more. She started to talk about this guy she worked with. They traveled to sales conferences once or twice together. I met him once. I knew there was nothing going on. But then some more time went by and I wasn't sure there was nothing going on. I asked her. She got upset. Nothing was going on, nothing. Then the next day she told me they'd gone out for a drink at the last conference and they'd kissed afterwards and made out a little, but she hadn't gone to bed with him. So I didn't like that, naturally . . . She said it was wrong, she was sorry, she would never do anything like that again. From there, somehow, we got into another three-kids-in-the-suburbs fight. A few days went by. We made up. It was rocky for a month or so—this was the summer before this one, a year ago, a little more than a year . . . She had a meeting in New York and then a conference in San Francisco, and, I don't know, we were talking on the phone when she was in New York and I had a bad moment—I thought I was done being angry and jealous but I wasn't—and I asked her if this guy—Brian, his name was—if he was going on the trip with her the next day and she said he wasn't, and we left it there . . . And then, afterwards, you know, after the day and the funeral services and everything, I went about three months without checking and then I had another bad moment and I looked up the list of the people who'd been on the plane and Brian's name was there."

"She could have just wanted you not to be jealous and that's why she didn't tell you."

"I know that."

"But you still didn't go out with anyone else for a year?"

I nodded. I promised myself not to say anything else about it, and then I immediately said, "I did that for myself, for my own guilt. I wasn't in good shape. Gerard used to take me places like I was a little kid—to his daughters' dance recitals, to museums, to scuba classes. I was a little zombie-ish for a while. There was so much talk about it, naturally, in the papers every day, on TV every night. People who had lost husbands and wives and children. I stopped reading the papers, stopped watching TV. I banged nails and painted and got through the winter, and in the spring I started driving into the country alone on weekends and sleeping out in the woods in a sleeping bag, or going for long hikes, or going to see Ellory. It was rough for a while and then not so rough, and then I was starting to feel semi-alright again. I remember calling you that first afternoon, from work. Just sort of peeking my nose back into the dating world."

"And I responded so nicely," Janet said.

"I was almost better by then. I knew when I put the phone down, after you said no, that I was most of the way better."

B<small>Y THE TIME</small> we got back to Boston it was eight-thirty at night. We stopped for takeout at Fez and set the warm paper bags between us in the cab of the truck on the way to my apartment. While I was getting out plates and glasses, Janet called the governor on his private line and I heard her leaving a message in a don't-mess-with-me-you're-lucky-to-have-me voice: "Charlie, Janet. I'm taking the holiday tomorrow. I'll be in the office Tuesday morning as usual."

We sat at the small kitchen table I had made from some tiger maple I'd found at a mill in western Massachusetts on my way home from visiting Ellory one time. Maple is a nice-looking wood anyway, but tiger maple has shimmering bands of light and dark running down the grain, so that even a board that's been planed and sanded perfectly smooth seems to have ripples in its surface. In certain kinds of light, the ripples seem almost to be moving. During the first breakfast we ate together at that table—it was the morning after the third time she slept over—Janet noticed the wood and said how much she liked it. I'd been starting to feel something with her that I didn't think I was going to be able to let myself feel again, and I was nervous, and in a little spasm of nervousness I started to tell her all about the different woods: how poplar had an olive-green or brownish tint to it and how well it held paint and how it was more stable than pine for

interior trim; how southern yellow pine was as hard as some hard-
woods, even though it wasn't one, technically, and so it made good
flooring if you didn't mind the heavy, wavy grain; how the archi-
tect I liked to work with ordered screen doors from a tiny company in Maine that made them from South American cedar,
which was not really cedar at all but a species of mahogany that
was used on the decks of ships because it was resistant to insects
and rot and didn't swell or warp when it got wet. Interesting stuff.
I went on and on and she watched and listened and started to
smile and finally I stopped and smiled, too. It became a joke with
us. We'd be at a bar downtown and she'd say, with a perfectly serious expression, "Jake, what kind of wood is this?"

"Siberian chestnut," I'd say. "Very rare." And I'd go off on
some made-up spiel about how the chestnuts themselves were
considered to have aphrodisiac qualities, or how the black Siberian squirrel gnawed the twigs to survive in bad winters. Some
elaborate mishmash like that, just to hear her laugh.

She'd taken her pills and she'd done her chest PT with the
vibrating vest, and while I was putting together the food, she sat
running her hands over the tabletop. We'd bought lamb kebabs
with hummus, pieces of warm pita bread that the people at Fez
baked themselves, a spicy yogurt dip—and there were Fudgsicles
in the freezer for dessert. I opened a bottle of white wine—
Sardinian, the same Argiolas we'd had on our first date at Diem
Bo. Janet was coughing more already. Just as I sat down she
coughed and got up and went to the bathroom. I heard the toilet
flush. When she came out she had one very small droplet of blood
on her lower lip. I started to eat.

"So how did you ever end up working for this guy?" I
asked her after a while.

She looked up, searching for jealousy in my face, but there was not much jealousy there anymore. No jealousy at all, really. Almost none.

She said, "I was having a conversation with some friends in my college dorm and I was saying how rotten the world was, how the politicians were corrupt, how the system was all twisted and skewed. One of my friends said, 'Why don't you do something about it, then, instead of just whining?' So I decided to. I went to the Kennedy School and got my master's and Charlie was running and he was promising to fund children's programs and completely eliminate poverty in Massachusetts—not cut it down, completely eradicate it."

"I remember."

"Nobody says that. Most politicians don't even mention the poor."

"The poor don't fund-raise," I said.

"So I thought it would be perfect. I was still fairly healthy. I thought I'd do that for a while and then, if they came up with a cure, I'd try something radical like running for Congress. I was twenty-three, a bit on the naïve side."

"You'd make a good congresswoman."

She waved a lamb kebab and coughed. A little flash of pain cut across her face.

"I mean it. You care about people. You're tough, you're smart."

"One," she said, "I'm not a millionaire. Two, I'd go crazy saying the same thing over and over and over again during a campaign. Three, Americans don't vote for sick people. Four, I'm not that great a compromiser. Even if I got elected somehow, I'd just alienate everyone. I have crazy ideas. I think we should put a lot of money into desalination plants, for example, because the key commodity of the future will be water, not oil. I think each little town and neighborhood should have its own high school again and that the buildings themselves shouldn't hold more than about twenty classrooms, and that the healthy kids should spend some time every week tutoring the special-needs kids, and that nursing homes should be built right there against the school in the same complex—they do that already in some places, but not with high schools, usually. I think everyone should do six months of volunteer work between high school and college—not just grunt work, painting bandstands and bleachers, but hospice work or environmental work or . . ." She coughed and coughed and made another trip to the bathroom. When she came back the drop of blood was gone and she went on talking as though she'd never left. ". . . or military service. Everyone. Every single kid, even the ones in wheelchairs. I think women should have six months' paid vacation after they have a baby."

"I'll write you in," I said. "You can run as the Idealist Party candidate."

"It's just smart," she said. "It's all just really practical."

"Or you could run on the electrocute criminals, cut-art-in-the-schools, hate-your-gay-neighbor platform like the guy Valvoline's running against."

"Right."

"Makes your boss look good."

"He changed, Jake. Power changes people. The fear of losing power changes people most of all. His wife left him—because he'd changed so much—and then he panicked and changed some more. He's not a bad man."

"Just small," I said, without thinking. But almost all the ugliness in me had been washed out during that day. It was as if

I'd finally decided that I'd had enough jealousy for one lifetime. It must have showed in my voice because Janet was watching me, and after a few seconds she smiled her pretty smile, and it was like forgiveness.

AFTER THE MEAL I said I wanted to paint her and she said she didn't mind, but that she was tired, and could probably only stay up another hour or so.

In the warm months Janet liked to sleep naked. But it was getting colder by then, and she had a pair of sea-green silk pajamas she kept at my apartment in a drawer with a change or two of clothes and some medicines. I turned on the air purifier I had bought after the second week we were together. She put the pajamas on and sat in a chair with her legs crossed at the knee and her arms crossed at the wrist, looking straight at me. I paint in oil on linen, as I said. Linen is expensive, but I like it because, even though most people say it doesn't make any difference, I think it makes the edges of things not perfectly sharp and if you don't lay the paint on too thick, it can give everything a smooth quality. I had a canvas already gessoed. In the center of it, I painted just the sea green with its light and shadows, and worked for some time getting the arms and legs right. Then I painted Janet's face and hair, and then I used a #16 brush and almost a whole tube of Paynes gray to make a background. When I had it roughed in enough so that I thought I could finish it without her being there, I stopped and cleaned up and we went to bed.

I lay on my back in the bed and she lay half-leaning against me with her face on my shoulder and one arm across my chest. When she coughed she brought her right hand up to her mouth and trapped the cough between her palm and the skin of my bare shoulder. Between coughs I could hear her breath rattling around. We lay like that for a long time without saying anything.

"What is the waiting list looking like?" I asked her finally.

"I'm eighteenth. In Massachusetts they've been averaging about two a month."

"So next summer."

She coughed, then nodded her head against my shoulder, but I listened to her breathing and I knew she wouldn't live until the next summer. I was sure she knew it, too.

She wrapped herself tight against me, one arm over my chest, right thigh on top of my thighs, face against my neck, and we fell asleep that way.

THE NEXT DAY, Columbus Day, there were tremendous winds in Boston during the morning hours, winds like I had never seen except in the edge of Hurricane Belle. The tops of the trees whipped back and forth. Leaves and newspapers and people's hats went skidding down the sidewalks like exuberant children. Janet and I slept late, then she sat for another little while and I worked some more on the painting. Afterwards, we took a trolley to the North End and had pasta and salad in a place with six tables, where, before you ordered, they brought you small bowls of olive oil and a basket of hard-crusted bread that was soft as cotton inside.

After the meal I said I wanted to walk to the Back Bay, my favorite part of Boston. In the 1800s it was just marshy tidal flats, but as the city grew, the area became more valuable and the marshes were filled in with thousands of tons of granite from quarries in Needham. Something about the flat straight avenues lined with four- and five-story brownstones, something about the particular mix of buildings on Boylston Street—clothing stores, churches, skyscrapers, little take-out Thai and Szechwan eateries—something about the beggars and businessmen, something about it just felt to me the way a city is supposed to feel—edgy, busy, a visual feast. The winds had mostly died down. Janet said she was feeling strong enough to walk, but by the time we'd gone as far as the Public Garden—maybe a mile and a half—she was having a hard time. When I glanced at her once I could see that the muscles of her forehead were pinched tight, as if she were working out some complicated math formula, when all she was trying to do was breathe.

I said how nice the gardens looked, with the trees so bright, and the more muted colors in the flower beds. I pretended I wanted to sit on one of the benches there and watch kids feed the ducks.

"I hate this," she said when we sat down and she caught her breath. A hard little wind blew her hair up around her face. She was quiet for a minute, then, softly, almost as if she were talking to herself, "Being dead, I think I can deal with. Being alive and not able to do things, not be able to walk, for God's sake . . ."

I put my hand on the top of her leg. In a minute she turned her face away, and started crying. I took my hand from her leg and put it around her shoulders, and pulled her against me.

"Some days I want to scream. I want to stand out in the middle of the street and look up at the sky and just scream and smash things. I want to ride a horse or jog on a beach or go bowling. Anything. I used to be so physical. I played field hockey at school. I loved to swim, to skate. Everything I tried, I loved—hiking, cross-country skiing." She stopped. She swiped at her right eye with the bottom of her palm. She took a breath and blew it out. We stared at the Public Garden for a long while and then she said, "Alright. I'm finished with that."

"All you do is complain."

"Right," she said. "I'm sorry. Do you want children, really?"

I heard the bending note again.

"Most of the time. You?"

"I'd have eight if I were strong enough. I'd fill a huge house with them. I have dreams about having children. Two or three times a week now I have a dream like that."

"Are you sure you can't?"

She turned her face away.

Not far in front of us, in the direction Janet had been looking when she asked the question about children, a little towheaded boy and a little towheaded girl were throwing something into the pond. Potato chips, it looked like, tossed up and wobbling in the breeze. The ducks weren't interested in that particular brand of potato chips, and the girl was getting more and more upset about it and trying to stamp both her feet at once and yelling in a lispy, weepy, aggravated voice: "Duckies! Duck-IES!" The boy seemed to think the problem was that he wasn't throwing the chips out far enough, so he'd rear back and fling them mightily and then stand with his fists at his sides as the ducks made their quick turns back toward the middle of the pond. There were adults, alone and in pairs, sitting nearby on the other benches, and on the grassy bank, but whoever the parents were, they were of the school of parenting that said, Let your kids play right on the edge of a dirty pond deep enough for them to drown in and let them get really frustrated there and don't say anything to them or do anything about it.

After a few minutes an older woman walked over to them. She reminded me of my mother, the same erect posture and sureness about her. The boy and girl didn't seem to know her, but the woman gave each of them a slice of white bread, and showed them how to tear up the bread into pieces. When the ducks saw this turn of events, they came gliding toward the towheaded twins, a white fleet of expectation, and the girl started jumping up

and down again, her shoes lifting all of an inch into the air. Duck-
ies! Duckies!

Janet and I were both watching. For some reason the little
drama made me think of something I had seen in Mexico, years
before. I had sold a painting—my first—and to celebrate, Giselle
and I had flown to Puerto Vallarta on a whim. We didn't even
make hotel reservations, just took a taxi from the airport into town,
asked around with our high-school Spanish, and found a very
clean *casa de huespedes* with pastel-colored tile floors three blocks
from the beach. We stayed ten days. In the mornings I would get
up early and go for a run before the sun had come up over the
mountains. Then I'd go back and shower and we'd walk to a
breakfast place we liked, where there weren't any other tourists.
One morning we were sitting there with our *huevos rancheros* and
café con leche and a small skinny boy walked in and began going
from table to table with his hand out. The boy was six or seven. He
had sores on his face and arms, and a threadbare T-shirt. We gave
him what amounted to three dollars or so and he managed to get to
one more table before the owner came and roughly ushered him
out. At the next table, behind Giselle's back and directly in my line
of vision, sat a man in a fine gray silk suit and a white shirt open at
the collar—I will always remember this man—and when the boy
had been chased out unceremoniously into the happy seaside
morning, this man started doing strange things with his food. He
took one of the fresh breakfast rolls that eggs were served with in
that place and he opened it down the middle with his thumbs. He
picked up the juicy browned slice of ham with his fork and folded
it into the roll, then he lay a piece of avocado in there, then some
fried egg. I watched him over Giselle's right shoulder. The owner
watched him, too. The man worked with a surgeon's grace, with

careful movements, without dropping any food on the material of his expensive suit. When he was finished he wrapped the sandwich carefully in two napkins, stood up, and hurried out the door, and I watched him trotting down the sidewalk in the same direction the boy had gone. In a few minutes he came back and finished what was left of his breakfast.

Book Three

November

1

B Y EARLY N OVEMBER in Boston the trees have lost most of their leaves. On wet days the branches and trunks are black and slick-looking. In the afternoons a damp hard wind blows off the harbor, and then darkness swells up out of the tar streets, and the traffic lights shine like jewels. It is not winter but no longer truly fall, and the tourists are gone, and the city is stripped down to a tight rhythm of moneymaking: the mouths of subways suck in clots of workers and breathe them out again across town; the streets are full of taxis and delivery trucks and touched with a kind of coldness and sadness I have always secretly liked.

I like it right through Thanksgiving, and the first snow, and Christmas, and then, near the middle of January, I begin to hate it. The days will never be warm again, I'll never wear a T-shirt and running shorts again, or see women walking down Massachusetts Avenue with their legs bare and happiness on their faces. There is ice on the river, or the water is purple and raw. Why would anyone want to live here?

But November is fine. Smart carpenters have gotten their outside work finished by then—Gerard and I learned that the hard way one year—so, by Election Day, we had Jacqueline's addition closed in and clapboarded.

Once we had the outside work done, we cut open the tight pink rolls of fiberglass insulation and stapled them into the stud bays, a miserable job that makes your wrists and neck itch for hours afterwards. On top of the insulation we stapled sheets of clear plastic, to keep the water vapor that's inside the house from penetrating the walls and making the insulation damp and ineffective. And when that was done we began to put up the wallboard—Sheetrock, it's usually called.

Hanging "rock" is not a particularly enjoyable job. The board itself is made of pressed gypsum, heavy and awkward, and the cuts and joints have to be done just right. Most carpenters used screws and drills by then, but I have a crazy need to do some things the out-of-date way, so Gerard and I used hammer and nail. The trick to nailing up Sheetrock is to press the board tight against the studs with one hand and hit each nail hard enough so that you make a "dimple," but not so hard that you cut through the gray paper that holds the pressed gypsum in place. Later, you fill the dimple with joint compound and sand it smooth, and if you do it right, when the wall is painted, the nail and the dimple don't show. The best old carpenters have a feel for it, and, high or low, swing so that the business end of the hammer strikes the wallboard flat-on.

Gerard was a past master at dimpling. That Election Day morning—it was sunny and nice, low fifties—I heard him in what would be Jacqueline's guest bedroom giving her a lecture on Sheetrock. "The Greeks discovered gypsum, you know," he said. "*Gypsos,* they called it. In America, factories started mass-producing this stuff right around World War Two, which put a lot of plasterers out of business. My dad was a plasterer. He went to school at night to become an environmental engineer, but then he became a barber. He was one of the first unisex barbers in Greater Boston. He actually invented the disposable razor for women, but had the patent stolen from him by a big corporation I won't name."

"Really?" Jacqueline said. She was too savvy to be buying much of it, but she liked him anyway, liked us both. From what she'd told us, there weren't that many laughs to be had in the hallways of the Harvard Physics Department. Sometimes when Gerard would be thirty feet up on a ladder reciting Ovid, or we would be bored with nailing subfloor and were going back and forth with lines from movies ("Chollie! Chollie! They took my thumb, Chollie!"), I'd look over my shoulder and catch her watching us, and she'd smile and turn away.

My friend Gerard could be a goofy soul. But he was a good carpenter, one of the truly superb dimplers of all time, a natural teacher, too. I listened to him trying to persuade Jacqueline to take his hammer in her hand.

"I'll ruin something," I heard her say.

"What could you possibly ruin? Here, try it where the baseboard will go. That way if you make a little mistake you'll never see it. Go ahead. Dimple away."

At lunch, after Jacqueline had gone off to work and Gerard had calmed down a bit, I asked him if he was going to vote for Governor Valvoline, who had been good enough to keep Janet on the payroll after her boyfriend went gorilla, and decent enough to cease and desist from saying he loved her at close range. In the weeks leading up to the election she had been working twelve-hour days.

"Not," Gerard said, "in two million years."

"Who then? Captain Privatize?"

"Privatize your aunt," he said.

"Who then?"

"Nader. I want to send a message to the big multilingual corporations."

"Nader's not on the ballot."

"Sure he is. You hit the button for Buchanan, Patrick J., and it counts for Nader. Everybody knows that."

"Buchanan's not on the ballot either," I said. "It's Valvoline, Captain Privatize, or the Libertarians."

"The Librarians, then. I'm bookish on libraries."

"Be serious a minute," I said.

"Alright. Valvoline is the boss of the love of your life, correct?"

"Correct."

"But there's just something about him we don't like, am I right?"

"Right."

"We don't know exactly what it is, but he's, you know, kind of a mook. And we don't vote for mooks even if good people work for them. Alright, Captain Privatize is as rich as an Arabian prince and wants to bust unions and strap the bad guys down and jolt them. The Librarians want the government to leave everyone alone, rely on people's natural good-heartedness, and hope everything works out. Where does that leave us?"

"Up the well-known creek."

"Exactly."

"But not voting is un-American."

"Precisely," he said. "Which is why yours truly is going hanging chad."

"It's a kind of dimple."

"Dimple gone wrong."

I took a sip of root beer and watched an ambulance go past, lights blinking, siren off.

Gerard said, "I'm glad we had this talk," and stood up to go back to work.

2

I WAITED IN LINE at the polling place in my work clothes—boots, jeans, and an old Boston University Varsity Rowing sweatshirt with gypsum dust on it.

I get sentimental when I go to vote. My precinct includes a neighborhood that's mixed in every direction: white lesbians in business suits, Honduran maids just finished with a day's work at the hotel, Russian Jews who remember Stalin's voice on the radio, black ironworkers with their AB hardhats in one hand, Waspy white guys with gypsum dust in their hair. Looking at an improbable mixture like that when I'm in line to do my democratic duty, I think: There's no country on earth anywhere near this good. And then, later, that it *is* a great country, and we *have* welcomed people from everywhere on earth, but that we somehow never really live up to our own grand rhetoric; that if we were half what we claimed to be, we'd long ago have cured every illness on the planet, and wouldn't have hungry kids in Kansas or the Bronx, and a million or two million people in prison. And so on. I think about the whole mad, spiritless rush we call the working week. I sink and sink.

In the end, that day, after wandering the moral maze for five or six minutes in the little booth, and feeling the usual election-day depression creeping up my leg, I cast my vote for the Idealist Party candidate, a write-in ballot: Rossi, Janet, S. And then I went home to get ready for the victory bash.

3

THE ELECTION-NIGHT party for Charles S. Valvelsais, a.k.a Charlie Valvoline, was held at the third most expensive hotel in Boston, a twenty-two-story palace with a lobby so heavy on mirrors, brass, and oriental carpet that you felt as though you were in an Ashkabad hookah joint where the lights had accidentally been turned on. Janet had been asked to help make some of the arrangements—a kind of demotion for her, Valvoline's idea of payback—and as I walked down the carpeted corridor toward the noise of the ballroom, I couldn't keep a bad thought from attaching itself to me. It was a thought I'd had before, and it went something along these lines: Janet had compromised herself and I had not.

Hoping to change the world, she'd aligned herself with a man who was mixed-up inside, decayed, corrupt, false, whereas I hadn't aligned myself with anyone and had stayed pure. I knew this kind of thinking was distilled bullshit, 180 proof, and I knew it came from the bad soil of a feeling that I hadn't done as much with my life as I could have—I'd been given a good brain, a good education, a healthy body, and hadn't helped anyone who really needed help, hadn't given much back to the world besides a few dozen well-built additions scattered around Greater Boston, two small houses, eight garages, a hundred little repair jobs. I'd started medical school with the intention of doing what my mother had done—spending a life making sick people feel better—and then

I'd somehow gotten tired of cramming scientific facts into my brain. I'd made an invisible turn, inward, thinking I'd be better off healing myself first, before I went after anyone else. Some days that seemed like a good decision, important, humble, mature; other days it seemed like escape. I had a room full of paintings, a short string of failed romances, no wife, no prospects for children. And in a certain kind of light, all that could take on the mean glint of failure, and that failure could make me start to tear down people who had done something more valuable. In that light, even Chuck Valvoline had led a more useful life, and I wondered if Janet ever compared us that way, if she had bad little thoughts about me that stuck to her, if those were the kinds of thoughts that ate away at the tissue of love, year by year, until you went looking for a replacement.

But once I turned into the noisy ballroom—a happy, comical scene—it wasn't too hard to shake those thoughts. The interior world, the world of art and musing, the world of working with your hands—those places had their value. And I was more or less satisfied with the man I had become, stupidities and all. On that night, I was almost at peace.

The huge room was filled with men and women who believed that Valvoline was as good as we could do just then, a well-meaning guy in a tough profession. His supporters stood around in funny hats and shirts with his name written on them. They glanced up expectantly at the TV screen above the stage. They sipped drinks and laughed and leaned placards in the corners. They hugged and shook hands and their voices bounced in a crazy speckled roar against the walls. Valvelsais. Valvelsais. Vahlv-sai, Vahlv-sai. The name flashed everywhere you looked, but the man himself was sweating it out in a suite somewhere above us, surrounded by his closest aides, TV on, phones in constant use, paper plates with pizza slices and Styrofoam coffee cups strewn across every horizontal surface.

Janet was up there, and all of a sudden I wondered if I should just go to O'Casey's, watch the returns on TV, and call her the next day. I hadn't seen her in a while, though, and I missed her. And she'd told me there was a chance she could slip away from Command Central sometime after 8:00 p.m. when the polls closed and the first numbers were announced and there was nothing left for her to do. We'd had a two-minute phone conversation at noontime, and she'd told me the exit polls were saying what all the other polls had said: too close to call. There had been a happy spark in her voice, the thrill of battle maybe, or the end of a long stretch of work. Or even just the anticipation of seeing me.

I helped myself to a plastic cup of Pepsi and a celery stick, and I stood in front of one of the large screens and watched Johanna Imbesalacqua, my favorite news anchor (because I liked her name and because she had announced the events of September 11 with tears streaming down her face), filling airtime until the first results could be posted.

A pleasantly plump, partly drunk woman came over and stood beside me. She had a drink in one hand, and beautiful brown hair with reddish highlights in it, and little silver crucifix-earrings. After a minute she asked how I thought it would go, and I tried to sound worried and said it was too close to call.

"You really think so?"

"What I really think is he's going to win in a landslide."

"Really?"

"Sure. Look who he's up against."

"Isn't it odd?" she said. "How could anyone vote for that man?"

She moved half a step closer. Her eyes wavered when she spoke and I guessed she had been drinking since the first bottles were set out. "I mean, what are his qualifications?"

"He has money. He talks tough."

"I think he has a lot of unresolved anger," she said.

We looked up at the screen. Johanna's face had been replaced by an advertisement that showed a blond model driving an SUV through deep mud.

"What's the message there?" the woman asked.

"Any stupid thing a man can do, a woman can do just as well," I said, and she laughed with her head thrown back.

"What do you do for work?"

"I'm a carpenter."

It was loud there in the ballroom, and I have the typical Boston accent, and she didn't, and she misheard. "Boston's finest," she said. "Are you undercover tonight?"

"No," I said.

"You sure?"

"Positive."

"My ex was a fireman," she said. "One election night we had sex while we were watching the returns. It was Reagan and Mondale. Every time another state was announced for Reagan, I made him just stop and be absolutely still. I wouldn't let him move until I said so."

"Republicanus interruptus," I said, and she threw back her head again, gleam of gold in her mouth.

"He was hot and bothered *that* night, I'll tell you."

"No wonder."

There was a little pause in the conversation, another flashy commercial—one of the fast-food chains pretending its hamburgers were fat and juicy—then the woman tapped me on the arm and said, "You wouldn't want to get a room upstairs and celebrate in private, would you?"

I looked at her. She seemed lively and happy. Under the happiness I thought I could see old hurts running, old disappointments, things she had hoped life would give her, and was still hoping life would give her. I thought of those hopes as little toys with batteries, only the batteries had almost all run down. This kind of thing—a proposition from a nice-looking woman after a few minutes' conversation—had happened to me only once before. It was New Year's Eve at a ski resort, and I'd been so surprised I hadn't handled it the way I should have. This time I put my hand on her upper arm and squeezed gently and said, "My fiancée's meeting me here in a little while. Otherwise I'd be at the desk with my credit card in two seconds."

She nodded. A smile went wobbling across her mouth. She said, "Well, in some other life, then," and drifted away.

When she was gone I watched the TV screens for another little while, watched the crowd, sipped my Pepsi. It wasn't the place for me. I walked out of the ballroom and back down the corridor. In the glassy, brassy lobby I went up to the reservation desk and paid for a room, then rode up in the elevator with a man, a woman, and three small children. One of the children leaned against my leg without looking because he thought I was his dad. His mother smiled down at him, and then at me.

In the room, I dialed Janet's cell and, when she answered, a huge loud cheer went up where she was. We had to wait for it to die down. "This is Doctor Entwhistle," I said, when she could hear me. "I'm in Room 876."

And she said, "Good news from all directions. Ten minutes."

4

A T FIRST, WAITING for her, I turned on the TV, which was hidden in a fairly well-built oak-veneer cabinet at the foot of the king-sized bed. But by then I had slipped all the way down my usual Election Day slope from sentimental to cynical, so after a few seconds I turned it off and closed the cabinet and lay flat on the bedspread, looking up. I had always loved the feel of a nice hotel room, the order and anonymity. Before my brother and sister and I grew too old for it, my parents had liked to take us to New York or Montreal for special weekends. Once, we'd spent two nights at the Gramercy Park Hotel, in two rooms. I remembered the big beds and musty curtains, the way the boards in the hallways squeaked as you went across the carpet, and I remembered my father pointing out a man in the breakfast room, and telling my brother and sister and me that this hotel was the man's home. "Nothing to hammer or paint," my father said. "No trash to take out. No meals to prepare."

In some odd way, Ellory and Lizzie and I had been marked by that moment. We'd become more up-to-date versions of that man in the breakfast room: solitary lives, not a lawn to mow among us. It was strange, my parents had been so perfectly professional and so politely suburban, and their offspring had gone methedrine-Reno and monk on them, gone carpenter-artist. Two of us more or less happy in our own oddball ways, and the third . . . I promised myself to call Lizzie, soon. She'd try to make me feel guilty, because that's what she felt. She'd end up yelling at me when I refused to send money. She'd hang up in a righteous addict's huff. I'd call her anyway. It was good to get yelled at every once in a while. It might keep me from turning out like some of the well-off young couples in my neighborhood—fretting over what flavor of fair-trade coffee to buy and cutting into line at the checkout when you looked the other way.

"You want to have kids of your own," I said aloud in that room. "That's all. You want a love like that, close against your life. You want that to be your contribution." And then there was the sound of knocking.

I hadn't seen Janet in nine days. She'd been flying all over the state with our glorious governor and his team on a last-hour vote-getting polka. I opened the door all expectation. She was dressed up for the big night in a dark purple spaghetti-strap dress and her hair was brushed and beautiful, but her cheeks were sunken and her eyes large and the muscles above her collarbones and around her shoulders looked like they'd shrunk by half. In nine days. She watched my eyes as if she knew what she looked like and was hoping something on my face would show her she was wrong, that the mirror lied and the scale lied and the breathing gauges lied. Pity made another run at me then, but I had already made up my mind about pity.

"Hi," I said, holding out my hand. "Doctor Entwhistle. Come in, you're right on time."

After a small hesitation, she shook my hand and smiled. "Hello, Doctor. I have forty-five minutes, tops."

"Forty-five minutes will do. Come in, take off your dress and your shoes, please, and sit on the edge of the bed."

When she was undressed and sitting there, I checked the reflexes of her knees with an imaginary rubber hammer and said,

"Excellent." I examined her toes and fingers, running my own fingers along them and feeling the way they were rounded because the blood vessels there had been starved for oxygen for years and years and had grown thick with overwork. She was the perfect patient, and I was a considerate doctor, and, at first, it was just a cute little love game we were playing to keep the conversation away from other things. It was a minute or two before I realized what kind of trouble we were in. But I couldn't think of anything else to do, so I kept going. I wrapped my thumb and middle finger around her left bicep—thinner than my wrist—and pretended it was a blood pressure cuff. "One-forty over ninety-one. Are you agitated?"

"I ran all the way up here," she said. She coughed.

I took her pulse—eighty-one—pretended to flash a light in her eyes, poke an otoscope in her ears, check her tonsils with an imaginary tongue depressor.

At last she said, "I'm having sexual problems, Doctor. It's embarrassing to talk about."

"Ah."

There was some kind of warning siren going off inside me. I ignored it. I asked her to stand up and remove her brassiere and I spent a long time examining her breasts and nipples, and then the scars on her belly. "Trouble digesting?"

"Only when I eat."

"Ah."

I turned her around and tapped gently on the bones of her spine. I worked down from the back of her neck, feeling my way lightly along the rounded trail of bones between her shoulder blades, then along the lower curve. I folded down the elastic top of her underwear and pressed my thumbs in against the dimples there, expertly. An expert failure. Standing close behind her, I ran my palms down the outsides of her upper arms and she shivered. And then, because pity made another run at me, I wavered for two seconds, and then just plunged in. Pretending to hold a stethoscope to the back of her lungs and pretending to steady her with my left arm around the front of her chest, I said, "Have you ever had a bronchoscopy?"

"A hundred and eleven times."

I could hear what I wanted to hear in her voice then, a will toward humor, toward grace, a courage so enormous it seemed to radiate around her like a second body. I felt small beside it. I said, "Deep breath for me now, Ms. Ross."

"Rossi."

She took a shallow breath, all wet trouble.

"Again, please." I was running my hand across her nipples.

"Cough now, please," I said, and she started coughing and could not stop. She coughed and coughed and sucked in air, her back muscles tight as iron. I panicked inside myself. I reached back on the bed and balled up my T-shirt and held it to her mouth and she spit into it. I felt a change in her then, an anger or a frustration or a bitterness rising. She wiped her mouth and threw the T-shirt hard at the TV cabinet and turned to me, but before she could say anything I was kissing her mouth, the kiss of kisses, and then turning her onto the bed on her back.

And then I was trying, with everything inside me, with all my own pain and understanding of pain, with my own small supply of courage and strength, with everything the world of work and musing had taught me about being alive, I was trying to show Janet what I felt about her. I did not want to try to squeeze it into words because words cannot hold certain things, any more than a painting or a photograph can.

Beneath me on the bed she was weaker than I remembered, her skin warmer, the arms around my back sharper-edged. I wanted to put my whole self inside her, muscles, bones, breath. I timed my breath to her breathing. I slid my right hand underneath her and lifted her off the sheets with me and I wanted to have pity on her and have no pity at all. I wanted her to feel like she was running but without having to run. I wanted her to escape the pain of breathing hard and be lifted out of her body and into a warm sea of pleasure. My face was pressed into her neck and she was humming a quiet song, coughing once, taking quick breaths and then making a string of sounds like the sound of someone working, pushing toward something, more and more urgently, and then all the urgency was gone and she was breaking open against me, a breaking apart, a death, two deaths, and for a little blessed while we weren't two packages of bone and blood, but one package, every pain erased, every protection gone. I had never felt anything like that.

5

LATER, GOING DOWN to the ballroom in an empty elevator, Janet held my arm in a way that seemed to me a gesture of pure love. She had called the governor's suite, and when she got off the phone she told me they could tell now—from returns in certain precincts in the western part of the state—that Valvoline was going to win by four percentage points or so. "He calls them 'manure-rakers,'" she said. "It's shorthand for rural people. 'Spuds' is shorthand for Irish, 'Garlics' for Italians. 'Twiddles' for gay people. As in: 'Nettie, get me a meeting with some voices in the Twiddle vote, but make sure it's not on TV.'"

"We should be glad then, Nettie. The manure-rakers have come through for our guy."

"We should be glad," she said, "because Nettie still has her health insurance."

But we weren't glad then, in spite of the feeling we'd had on the big hotel bed upstairs. I remember the warmth of her arm against my body as we came out of the elevator, and I remember walking down the corridor and hearing a burst of wild happy yelling pour out of the open ballroom doors, and I remember feeling that we were being sucked away from the mysterious and the real, and back tight against something toxic, a Superfund site of the soul. It wasn't only Valvoline. It was just all of us, shit-rakers, Twiddles, Spuds, stuck in our individual skin-packages, afraid of our dying and our demons, always clawing for more—a breath, a break, an orgasm, a corner office. Janet and I moved into the ballroom as if wading into a hot bubbling tidal pool.

We sipped from plastic glasses of wine. Janet introduced me to people she knew, mostly State House types who had played some small role in the campaign. I watched the way her friends looked at her, and I could see, in their faces, beneath the happy gleam of victory, a species of fear, of love.

At quarter past ten, when Valvoline came down for his speech, the room exploded with cheering and applause. He worked his way up onto the stage. Women were hugging him. Men were shaking his hand and looking into his eyes and clapping him on the back as he squeezed past them toward the podium. For a little while, Janet went up on stage with the crew, and when the governor was introduced I clapped right along with everyone else, and even flashed him the thumbs-up sign once, when I thought he looked my way.

6

JANET WAS TOO TIRED to drive herself home, and she needed her vest and inhaler, so after the party we left the hotel and I drove her to her apartment on Beacon Hill. She put her arms through the holes in the vest and pressed the Velcro straps together and did her half-hour of chest PT, spitting mucus into a little bowl, her body shaking and her mouth twisting down, as if she were a kid on a funhouse ride she was tired of. While she did that I wandered around the room. I'd been there a few times, but had never really looked at the pictures—Janet in a soccer uniform, her tough-looking dad in work overalls, her mother beside a small new car. She sucked on her inhaler, popped a pile of pills into her mouth, had a hit of oxygen, and we went to bed. In her small bed, with the lights out, she rolled over against me. Her breaths were short strips of wet cloth being torn out of her, one by one.

"I'm taking a week off to see if I can get back some strength," she said quietly near my ear.

"Good."

"I've moved up three slots on the transplant list."

"Double good."

For a few minutes I listened to the traffic on Beacon Street and to the building's old pipes knocking. I thought she had fallen asleep—she was tired enough, but the oxygen always kept her awake for a while. Her right foot twitched twice. She ran the sole of it over my calf. She swallowed.

"You know I'll never last long enough to get new lungs, right, Jake?"

"No, I don't know that."

"I'm about half a step away from going back into the hospital. The last lung function test was twenty-seven percent. I've been around enough CF people to know what twenty-seven percent means. I've seen enough of my friends die, and I remember what they looked and acted like a couple of months before they died. It doesn't make it any easier for me if you pretend it isn't there. I don't want that from you."

"Alright."

"I'd like to make it to Christmas. I'd like to buy you a motorcycle and give it to you on Christmas Eve, and buy you a leather jacket to go with it, and make love to you with you wearing the leather jacket and nothing else."

"Okay."

"Don't sound so excited."

I had two minutes then of not being able to get any words out. She was running the sole of her foot over my instep. During those two minutes my mind, my strange mind, was absolutely consumed with an image of her father, balanced on a staging 150 feet above the Mystic River, patching concrete and obsessing about his daughter. I had spent a little time with Giselle's mother and dad after her service, and had some idea what the grief of a parent felt like. I thought about them, too. In the warm room—so warm we had only a sheet over us—I was buried under the idea of what it might feel like to know your child was going to die before you died, and how she was going to die, and having to watch that as it happened, to live those days and those hours and those minutes, one after another, year by year.

"Earth to Jake," Janet said tiredly. "Jake, come in. Over."

I tried to talk but it was like trying to pull myself out of myself.

"Begin reentry." She coughed and kept coughing and climbed tiredly out of bed and went into the bathroom for a while, then came back. "Coast straight down through the gloom cloud, it's clear here on Beacon Hill."

"Coasting down," I finally managed to say. I felt tiny beside her then. Tiny and not brave. There had been a time when I thought her father was a coward for doing what he'd probably done, but his picture was so close on the night table that I could have reached out and held it and I had nothing bad to think about him then. Nothing. Not one bad thought.

"Mum Rossi wants you for Thanksgiving dinner."

I had my eyes closed. My arm was around her. I could feel her ribs.

"RSVP ASAP." She nudged me with her knee.

I couldn't say anything. I could not squeeze out one sound.

"You can bring a date, if you want. A marathon runner. A triathlete. An oarswoman from your college days."

She pushed me, hard. I said, "I'd like to bring Helen."

"Who is Helen?"

I coughed. I took two breaths. "Remember the blond in the painting I was working on the first night you slept over?"

"Who is she?"

"Helen."

"Right. Don't be an ass. Who is she to you?"

"My mother."

7

A MELIA ROSSI, IT turned out, was one of those people who get their satisfaction in life from having guests in the house, cooking for them and watching them eat, making a fuss over them, making them happy. I remember reading that in some places, in ages past, opening your house to strangers had been considered an essential part of being human, an acknowledgment of some kind of invisible link. I like that kind of thing. I like warmth and uncalled-for kindness, the small unnoticed generosities that speckle the meanness of the world. Often, over the years, customers would make Gerard and me a bowl of hot soup at lunch, or bring out iced tea and cookies. Once, when Gerard was having a tough time just after his divorce and the woman whose garage we were rebuilding was a psychotherapist, she'd taken him into her office for a half-hour session, gratis. Those small gestures always lifted us out of the work routine and put a kind of polish on the day.

Janet's mother wanted me there for Thanksgiving, then she wanted me and my mother. Then me, my mother, and Gerard. Then me, my mother, Gerard, and Patricia and Alicia, his twins. I was afraid that, next time Janet talked to her mother, Gerard's ex-wife, Anastasia, would get an invite, too, and though Anastasia is a fine woman and a good mother and an excellent dinner companion, it probably would have meant trouble, having her and Gerard looking at each other over a turkey carcass. But Anastasia was visiting her dad in a nursing home in Carlsbad, California. So, on Thanksgiving Day we had a two-pickup caravan heading out to the blue-collar suburb where Amelia Rossi lived and where Janet had grown up: Mum and I in front; Gerard, Patricia and Alicia bringing up the rear.

My mother was having a fairly lucid day. I'd told her we were going to my girlfriend's mother's house for Thanksgiving, and that seemed to make her happy. I'd been having a peculiar feeling all that morning, though, even before I'd driven to Apple Meadow to pick her up. Something was haunting me, some bad breeze from a forgotten dream, some premonition. I thought it might be because one of my favorite uncles had died on Thanksgiving Day, years before, so the holiday was always ringed in black for me.

The sky was low and gray, the winds wirling, and the truck felt less than perfectly stable on the road. To make things stranger, on the way over the Mystic River Bridge, as I was thinking about Janet's father again, my mother said, "We forgot to pick up Dad at work."

"Dad's gone, Mum."

"Gone where?"

"He died."

"Of what?"

"Two strokes."

She fell silent for a while, as if the shock and sadness of this fact had knocked her back down into a world of feelings that wrapped themselves around her like wet sheets. She sat there, wrists crossed in her lap, bouncing on the truck's old seat, making her way all wrapped up and with great concentration along one dim interior alleyway after the next. Her husband was dead. Why had that happened? What did it mean?

On the north side of the bridge we left the highway and stopped at a traffic light, and in the mirror I could see one balding head and two blond ones. That cheered me up.

8

AMELIA ROSSI'S house was a one-and-a-half-story box with
an attached garage, set behind a swimming-pool-sized patch
of lawn. Janet had parked at the curb, leaving a driveway just big
enough for one caravan. Gerard and I worried we were making
too much work for Mrs. Rossi, so to compensate for that we'd
brought along half a supermarket aisle worth of here-we-are gifts:
wine, cider, eggnog, chestnuts, two cheesecakes from a famous
Jewish deli in Brookline, a bouquet of flowers. We climbed out
into the driveway and unloaded the cargo. I was nervous, for
twelve different reasons, buffeted by cold winds and demons.
Handing a package of chestnuts and a half-gallon of eggnog to
Patricia and Alicia, respectively, I said, "And all the guests were
amazed that the father of the bride had saved his best eggnog for
last." Even my mother looked at me as if I were crazy.

The house had been built into the slope of a hillside, so that
from out front the first floor seemed like a second floor. I looked
up. Janet's mother stood in the picture window there, a vision of
what her daughter would have been with thirty more years and
one different gene: plump, pretty, happy, shining a little beam of
good feeling down on people she had never seen.

Patricia dropped the bag of chestnuts. They spilled out and
rolled off lopsidedly in five directions, and by the time we col-
lected them and made our way to the front door, Janet's mother

was standing there. She greeted the twins by getting down on one knee. "But who, who are these two perfect creatures at my front door?"

They said their names at the same time. By then, Amelia had a hand on each shoulder. "I can tell you apart already. Patricia has a pink dress on, and Alicia's dress is pink!"

The girls squealed, showed her their offerings, made an attempt at the curtsies Gerard had been ridiculously trying to teach them. Squeezed into the six-foot-square entranceway, we made our introductions. Gerard kissed Amelia's hand and spoke a rehearsed phrase in Italian, even though I'd told him three times that Janet's mother did not speak the language of languages and had never spoken it. Amelia took my mother's hands in both of hers, said something about having heard so many good things about her, and about her son.

My mother said, "Yes, Ellory's chief of surgery now."

Amelia had been briefed on the situation. "Oh, how wonderful," she said. "You must be very proud."

"I am."

When it was my turn, she thanked me for the cheesecakes then reached up on her tiptoes, kissed me on the mouth, and gave me the kind of hard squeeze that surprises you and makes you smile. Above us, I could smell the turkey cooking, and I said what you usually say, that it was nice to meet her, and nice of her to invite us, that I'd heard wonderful things about her, too. And then I said, "Your daughter is a precious gemstone in my life."

This was not the kind of thing I was known for saying. And it was spoken, naturally, into one of those moments when everyone else has gone quiet—just a little pocket of accidental silence, so that the precious gemstone part went up the stairwell and thumped around in the small house like a pigeon with a broken wing. Gerard was halfway up the stairs by then. He stopped and looked back at me, lifted his eyebrows and held them up there in one of his comic faces. Janet's mother started to cry, and wiped at her eyes with her fingers, smearing a little bit of makeup. The silence stretched out. I rushed to think of something else I could say, but from the top of the stairway Janet called down, "Pay no attention, Ma. He says dumb things when he's nervous, that's all."

Amelia couldn't quite get everything back together, though. We were standing looking at each other, a background song playing "Precious Gemstone." The tears kept squirting out. "Go up, go up," she said at last, taking hold of my elbow and turning me, and when I started up the carpeted stairs she ducked outside for a breath.

Janet had met everyone and was leaning against the top of the railing, looking gaunt and breathing very badly. "Nice going, Romeo," she said hoarsely before I kissed her.

In three minutes, Amelia was back in the kitchen, dry-eyed. We heard the hinges on the oven door, and she was prodding the turkey with a long fork. Janet made a fuss over the girls the way her mother had, getting down on one knee and holding her hands behind her back, then bringing the hands out one by one and giving each girl a certain kind of doll Gerard had told her they liked: soft, long-legged creatures with their hair in dreadlocks, the fashion of the season. She set them up with *The Sound of Music* on the bedroom VCR, then came back and poured wine for my mother and me and a glass of orange juice for Gerard. I was looking at her and pretending not to, a new trick of mine, and I did not like what I was pretending not to see.

Gerard told Amelia he enjoyed watching people cook—
which was true—so we all ended up standing at the kitchen door
in a knot, taking turns setting our glasses down and carrying out
dishes of sweet potatoes and lasagna. There were good smells
everywhere, plates and forks and butter knives shining on a gold
embroidered white tablecloth, Tony Bennett on the stereo. I kept
sneaking looks at Janet. Just before Gerard volunteered to start
carving the turkey, she disappeared into one of the bedrooms and
I heard the sound of the oxygen machine, food for the starving
rest of her, its dull bubbling hum already standing next to something else in my mind.

In the room where the girls were watching their movie, I
heard the Mother Superior singing "Climb Every Mountain."
Gerard went in to fetch them. My mother was fingering a photo
of Janet's dad, naturally, of all the pictures on the side table.
Amelia called us in to eat. I had little lines, little hot currents running in my legs and hands, the universe sparking bad messages
through me. I went into the bedroom to call Janet to the table, and
she was sucking in a last few breaths. Before she knew I was there,
I saw what I had seen before, a strange thing to see: she was holding the oxygen tube in place under her nose and pricking her finger for a blood-sugar level at the same time, and it was as if she
were somehow outside her body, tending to it as if it were a
machine, an appliance, without being annoyed or affectionate, as
casual and unperturbed as if she were cleaning crumbs out of a
toaster oven. People had jumped off bridges because they couldn't
deal with this, and stepped outside to cry on a holiday because
they couldn't deal with this, and lay awake on a couch in a room
filled with paint fumes, trying to deal with this. She was cleaning crumbs.

She saw me, checked her number, set the tube back in its clip and the blood-sugar meter back in its neat leatherette holder, and turned the tank dial to Off.

I said, "I came to ask if this would be a good time for a quick roll in the so-called hay."

9

I T LOOKED TO ME, when we first sat down, as though Janet's
mother had cooked for the seven people at the table, and also
for another seventeen or twenty people who were standing
patiently in the leaf-strewn driveway and who would be allowed
in for a second seating once we had eaten ourselves into uncon-
sciousness. In my family we had always made a good meal of the
bird itself surrounded by various species of root crop under gravy,
and something green for good measure. But to describe the Amelia
Rossi table you'd have to add lasagna, cheese balls, meatballs, and
hot sausage in tomato sauce, grilled green peppers stuffed with
spiced bread crumbs, mushroom caps stuffed with the same bread
crumbs, broiled mashed pumpkin with about a stick of butter
melting on it, baked beans, white beans, green beans. The middle
of the table was covered with dishes, the counters were covered
with dishes. If we'd all sat there eating until there were two shop-
ping days left until Christmas, we'd still have had three or four
different kinds of pie, cake, ice cream, and the deli desserts to
work on.

Janet had warned me: "It's a ritual offering to the god of
excess. Don't have any breakfast and go light on dinner the night
before. Tell Gerard, too."

Mrs. Rossi managed to give the clear impression that she
would be permanently offended if we left so much as two cheese

balls on a plate, uneaten. This was conveyed via pleasant little remarks—"Oh, no, a big man like you? Who works so hard? That's all you want?"—followed by insistent spoonfuls of meatballs, mashed potato, pumpkin, white beans. I don't even like white beans and I ate a cup and a half or so.

We teased the girls, made a big fuss over them, then left them alone to torment each other and try to eat. The conversation tripped and puttered for a while, settling eventually, for no particular reason, on the Big Dig, a gigantic construction project that was sucking money out of the state budget and would do so for years to come.

"I say this," Gerard proclaimed. "I say whoever it is who's embezzling hundreds of millions of dollars from the Biggus Diggus is perfectly within his rights."

"His or her rights, Dad," Patricia said. "We learned it in preschool."

"I stand corrected, and hereby apologize to the legions of corrupt female construction magnates. Perfectly within his or her rights. An enterprise like this takes the old rusty elevated roads of our great city and does the only thing you can do with them: erases them from the collective eye. If a little money gets grafted in the process of giving us back our waterfront, there's nothing un-American about it!"

"You'd make out fine on Beacon Hill," Janet said. She was trying hard to join in the fun, but it seemed to take a huge effort for her to get the sentence out. Between words she made a couple of small grunting noises I'd never heard.

"I intend to run for public office," Gerard told her. "Who was it who said, 'If nominated I will not run; if elected I will not serve'? Bush?"

"Lyndon Johnson."

"Well, I say: If nominated I will run, if running I will serve!"

Gerard went on and on with his nonsense, making faces for the girls' amusement, turning to my mother with his most serious expression and scaring her half to death by shouting, "Read my lips! I did not have relations with that woman!"

Everything went along smoothly, if crazily, for a while. Soon we were drugged by the sheer volume of food. The adults ate in straight lines; Patricia and Alicia circled and wandered. They were at the age where they fidgeted a lot, getting up and down to check on their new dolls, dropping food, giggling, finding something remarkable in a mushroom cap or a blossom of cauliflower. Gerard oohed and aahed and spewed compliments in several languages. Janet's mother encouraged and spooned and found reasons to go back and forth to the kitchen. My mother had always had a good appetite and she seemed to be following the conversation in a fairly alert and congenial way. And then, as if the fog in which she lived suddenly blew clear of the best-trained part of her mind, she realized, when the second round of plates was being removed, that Janet was sick.

Janet had been coughing. She'd left the table a couple of times for bathroom runs, for oxygen. She had eaten almost nothing. Twice I saw her set her fork down and sit very still. The second time she did this she looked up at the top of the wall and took a series of short quick breaths with a shadow of fear over her eyes. It was the shadow that caught my mother's attention. I saw her stop eating and look across the table. "What's wrong, dear?" she asked.

"Nothing." Janet took a few slightly longer breaths, grunted, and gasped out, "I'm fine."

The girls sat still for once, turning up their pea-green eyes.

"She's alright, Mum."

"No, Ellory, she isn't."

Gerard said, "Mrs. E., what I want to know is why you haven't come out to see the gorgeous addition we're building in Cambridge. Don't you love me anymore?"

But my mother's attention was locked on Janet and she didn't answer.

"What's wrong, Papa?" one of the twins said.

Mrs. Rossi brought something into the kitchen that didn't need to be brought there.

"What is it, dear?" my mother asked.

"I have lung trouble," Janet told her, almost in a whisper.

"Is Janet going to die, Papa?"

"Die? What are you talking about, Lishie?"

Patricia was clutching her rag-headed doll in a stranglehold.

"What is it?" my mother persisted. She started to get out of her seat and I put a hand on her arm.

"Janet has cystic fibrosis, Mum."

"What is that, Papa? Uncle Jake?"

"It's a sickness," Janet gasped. "I'll be alright."

But alright wasn't written on her face. Amelia was standing in the doorway now, behind Janet, watching my mother over the table.

"She was a doctor," I explained.

My mother's eyes had not moved. "How did you live so long?" she asked Janet.

"Just lucky," Janet answered.

My mother kept staring, the girls sat stone still. Amelia had not moved from the doorway, but she'd started to cry again. She had her right hand wrapped tightly around her left wrist, and her left hand was squeezing open and closed in a quick, unconscious rhythm. Her pretty, oval face had completely changed and was painted in a shade of hope, a terrible species of tearstained hope, that I had never seen before and never want to see again. Over the top of her daughter's head she was looking fixedly at my mother as if, there, hidden in the shadowed valleys of her brain, might lie one treatment or medicine or procedure or idea that none of Janet's doctors had thought of.

She knew my mother was not in full possession of her faculties, but the word "doctor" seemed to have had some magical effect on her. I'd seen this before in my life, many times. It was part of the reason I'd dropped out of med school.

All of this was compressed into maybe three seconds, but they were an unbearable three seconds.

I said, "There are new treatments now."

It was absurd. I'd meant it as an answer to my mother's question, but it came out sounding as if I had good news to share, a latest development snatched from the Cystic Fibrosis Foundation website just that morning. Janet's mother turned the beam of her terrible hope on me, and it was like a sweeping searchlight that stops on you, picking you out of the anonymous blackness, freezing you there, blinding you. Janet fixed me with a look that was worse than that. She frowned and made a small shake of her head. But I could not stop myself. "She's on the list for a lung transplant," I announced stupidly.

Amelia was wringing her hands in that odd way, blinking and blinking, waiting for the news. I could not meet Janet's eyes.

"What is that, Papa?"

Gerard started to explain, and my mother searched around in a buried history of a million lessons and terms and hospital rounds and patients and the families of patients, plucked one word out of her memory, and spoke it—"Cadaveric"—just as Janet started to cough. The cough was something monstrous and drawn out. It was half roar. She kept coughing and couldn't catch her breath. All her concentration was focused on the act of coughing and then breathing a small gasp of a breath, coughing again, reaching for a bit of breath. Her eyes were down, but I knew she knew it was frightening the girls, and she pushed hard against the table and stood up, accidentally tugging on the tablecloth enough to topple her wineglass. The glass fell and cracked open against the platter of meatballs, splashing them with shards and Riesling. Janet was standing, turning away. Gerard took hold of her arm, but she shook free and made for the back bedroom. We heard the cough going on in there, a hideous animal sound. I waited for it to stop but it didn't stop. My mother had lapsed into silence. Patricia and Alicia had both started to cry. Janet's mother went into the room with her. Gerard said, "Tricia, Lishie, it's alright. We'll have cake."

When I went into the room, Janet was "tripoding," leaning straight-armed on the bed with the clear tubes clipped on underneath her nostrils, but the booming cough wouldn't let her go. I knelt down in front of her on one knee so I could look into her face. She was making small shaking motions with her head. I thought she wanted me to leave, but when I stood up to leave she took hold of the fingers of my left hand and squeezed so hard that I winced. She shot her eyes up at me.

"Call an ambulance," I said to her mother. "Now." And I watched to see if Janet would make some gesture—No—but she only roared out another swampy cough and kept squeezing.

I T T O O K S I X minutes for the ambulance to come, another four minutes for the attendants to have Janet out the door, strapped to the gurney, the oxygen mask on and something injected in her arm that had immediately started to calm the panic reflex in the muscles of her chest.

Strange, what you remember. For those ten minutes I was concentrating on nothing but keeping Janet alive—making sure the clear tubing didn't slip from its place, keeping a hand or both hands on her body to calm her—but the image that has planted itself in my mind is the image of Gerard scooping ice cream onto wedges of cake for his two girls as we followed the attendants along the six-foot hallway and down the stairs. My mother had gotten up from the table and was resting one hand on the railing of the stairs. Janet's mother stayed three-quarters of an inch behind the ambulance attendants as they were carrying her daughter— feet first—down toward the door. I was a step behind, watching Janet's chest. But what I remember most clearly is one glimpse of Gerard. He had two forks in his mouth and was waggling his big black eyebrows and at the same time spooning out huge scoops of chocolate ice cream and twitching the forks this way and that way in his lips—anything to tease a smile from his twins, anything to scrub the terror from their faces. Later, with the help of his daughters, he would clear the table, pack away all the uneaten

food except for a kind of picnic plate for Janet, which she would
never eat, wash and dry the dishes, sweep the kitchen floor, and
leave a note for Janet's mother telling her what a wonderful cook
she was.

My friend, *el macho.*

Before they slid the gurney into the back of the blinking
ambulance, with half the neighborhood out on their front steps,
watching, I put my hand on Janet's thigh. She flapped her fingers
around, caught my hand and squeezed. She boomed out a cough,
the mask jumped, and the vein in the side of her neck bulged. Her
mother climbed in, the doors closed, the siren startled us.

With my mother belted securely into the pickup's passenger seat, puzzled still, mute, pondering, I sped along the holiday-
empty streets, and back over the bridge into Boston. At the
hospital I parked with two wheels up on a curb not far from the
emergency-room entrance.

By the time they let me in to see Janet, she had already been
given a breathing treatment and was coughing less violently,
exhausted and asleep. She lay on a stretcher in the emergency
room, pale and gaunt and alive, the pulse monitor reading 121,
antibiotics dripping into her arm, a hemoglobin saturation monitor there, too. Nurses, doctors, and phlebotomists walked calmly
here and there, checking digital readouts, unwrapping sterile
needles, their running shoes squeaking on worn linoleum. And
that was the horror of it: this was routine to them—people choking their way back and forth across the border between life and
death, people with their stomachs blown open by gunshots and
their necks broken in car crashes and their babies' faces burned
with hot oil. Routine as could be. And for everyone else it was a
hideous nightmare.

I have always believed that, conscious or not, people know if someone they care about is beside their bed. So I stood there for a long while with both hands on Janet's left arm, watching her face and her chest as it moved up and down in quick flexes. Her mother—drugged a bit herself—stood at her other shoulder. My mother was behind Janet's mother, swinging her eyes right and left. The scene was vaguely familiar to her, a face from the distant past, a painting that hints at something you're sure you recognize, just hints at it, just suggests it, but leaves you to puzzle it clear.

AFTER AN HOUR and a half, Janet was moved upstairs to a semiprivate room. There was no one in the other bed. Her aunt Lucy arrived, a small, dark-haired woman with the same kindly toughness that radiated from Janet's mother, and from Janet, too.

We all slipped into hospital time, that strange, slow wash of quarter-hours where you feel cut off from the rhythm of the rest of the world, trapped in a sterile, off-white room with the faces of the nurses changing at three o'clock. We took turns standing next to Janet's bed. We touched her on the arm or leg, adjusted the blanket, looked at the machines, and then walked away past the empty bed to the window and stared down at the gray city. My mother sat in an orange armchair and watched a college football game on the TV, looking up at me from time to time with a cloud of daftness over her eyes.

At some point late in the afternoon, after we'd been standing there for several hours watching Janet sleep, Lucy persuaded Janet's mother to go home. Janet was going to be alright for now, there was nothing we could do to help. I told Amelia I'd stay and talk to the doctors, and call to give her the report, and she squeezed me and kissed me again, and cried against my chest and went reluctantly out the door, clutching her sister's arm.

Not long after they left—half an hour, an hour and a half—

a tall, slightly stooped man with an unfriendly mouth—Doctor Wilbraham—came in and introduced himself. We had spoken more than once during Janet's last hospital visit, her "tune-up," but he did not remember me. Janet said he was a big supporter of the governor, a yachtsman and a perfectly competent pulmonologist, with the bedside manner of a tuna fish. "She's in no immediate danger," Doctor Wilbraham said, in a rumbling, Charlton Hestonesque voice.

"We thought she was going to die."

"Yes," he said, meeting my eyes briefly.

My mother had gotten up out of her chair and sidled over and was listening in.

"What about the transplant?" I asked.

"She's on the list."

"I know she's on the list."

He looked at me with the smallest wrinkle of irritation on his lips. His face was almost a perfect rectangle, straight gray eyebrows, straight brown and gray hair brushed straight back. His eyes traveled down to my work boots and back up to my face, as if what I was wearing would dictate the type of answer he ought to give. As if he spoke several languages and was trying to choose one I might actually be able to understand.

"Will she live long enough to make it to the top of the list?"

"We can never say. There is a continual ratio of approximately five potential recipients to each available pair of lungs."

"How much longer is she going to live?"

"We can't possibly say."

"A month? A year? When you see people like this, with her lung function numbers, how much longer do they usually live?"

"It varies."

"Between what and what?"

He took a breath and sighed. "Between a day or a few days and perhaps a few months, depending."

"On what?"

"Many factors."

"Can we change any of those factors?"

"We're giving her powerful drugs," he said, in a tone you might use to describe the Dewey decimal system to a four-year-old. "Drugs called ceftazidime and gentamicin." I thought for a minute that he was going to spell them out very slowly. G—E—N—T . . . Beside me, my mother was nodding. "We had to take an arterial blood gas reading, which is quite uncomfortable. If that reading is not too bad and if she gets no new infections—"

"So you'll want her to stay in the hospital."

"Probably, yes."

"Until when?"

"Until compatible lungs become available." He reached out and patted me on the shoulder, already leaning toward the door. "You can call us with more questions if you think of them."

I stayed as long as I felt my mother could stand it, going down to the cafeteria once with her, for sandwiches and coffee, and then coming back up. Darkness had fallen long ago. My mother had given up on the football and on the TV, and had taken to walking back and forth along the length of the room, talking to herself in a quiet voice. I knew her well, of course, every wrinkle around her eyes, every spot on her hands, every lilt and dip of her high, warbling voice. But I had never spent that much time with her in a hospital, and I could see another woman stirring and rising up. I waited for her to click back into her doctor-self, but that did not happen.

At eight o'clock I kissed Janet twice on the ear, and whispered something there, then I walked with my mother down to the elevator and out through the quiet lobby. She hooked one arm inside my elbow.

"A ticket," my mother said, when we were close enough to the truck to see. Cold gusts were whistling off the river in the darkness, twirling up eddies of grit and brittle leaves.

I stood next to the truck in the cold with the parking ticket in my hand and my back to the hospital and my mother. Cars and trucks bunched up on Storrow Drive, then the light changed and the lines of traffic moved forward, a holiday pulse of steel, smoke, and glass. I looked out over the lanes of cars, at the arc of lights on the bridge that ran past the science museum and into Cambridge. It seemed to me then that there certainly had to be a God. But that He or She or It was a mean-hearted trickster God, a God of impossible coincidences and patterns, a God who let you walk along the levee for a while on a sunny winter day and then shoved you off into the icy water. God of men and women leaning out of a broken window on the 103rd floor with a thousand-degree jet fuel fire below them and their kids in elementary school; God of the screaming businesswoman going through the sky in an upside-down aluminum tube, and the man she shouldn't have been sleeping with beside her; God of the choking and the suffocating and of their mothers and aunts and lovers. How could Ellory believe the way he believed? How had my own mother lived with seeing so much suffering all those years and not thrown herself off a bridge?

I tore the ticket in half and then in half again and then in twenty bright orange pieces and tossed the pieces up into the wind and turned so as to have the satisfaction of watching them scatter. Some of the pieces caught in my mother's golden-dyed hair. She was watching my little performance without blinking—sadly, it seemed to me—as if she had expected more from her son the doctor. She hadn't said two audible words in two hours. I could see that she was working hard at something: the muscles near her eyes were pinched and she would periodically run the side of her right index finger across the corner of her eyebrow. Everything was a puzzle, and the puzzle had a billion scattered pieces, and she was searching through them to find just two that fit, just two, a starting place, a handhold.

I picked the orange scraps out of her hair, helped her into the cab of the truck, and drove her back to Apple Meadow. Ellory had told me once that the wise monks of the third century had come up with the idea that suffering was grace. It was absurd. The hot desert sun had done them in. "Suffering is grace, Mum," I said bitterly. She said nothing.

At the Meadow, I walked her up the path through the cold wind, and then past the receptionist and down the salmon-walled hallway to her neat, too-warm room. While I was helping her off with her winter coat she became agitated, moving her head quickly from side to side and twisting around, something I had never seen her do. When the coat was finally off her shoulders she blurted out three words with a strange note of triumph in her voice. I hung the coat in her closet, straightened out the dresses and blouses there, closed the door. I turned back to look at her, to say good-bye, and she said the words again the same way: "Living low bar." She was looking happily and expectantly at me, waiting for us to have one of our medical conversations, to make contact in that place again. But I was worn down by the day, and the words meant nothing. I only nodded and told her I loved her, and that my brother Jake loved her, and Lizbeth loved her, too, as I always did just before I left.

NEXT MORNING I drove to the hospital and parked in the pay garage. Janet was sitting up against the raised back of the mattress. The nurses had brushed her hair, and it lay smooth and black and without luster on the pillowcase and on her thin shoulders. The skin beneath her eyes was as dark as if she'd been punched. The oxygen machine hummed. The ceftazidime and gentamicin dripped into both arms. Really, the only parts of her face that looked right were the almost-black irises, which she turned on me the second I stepped through the door.

"I'm the orgasm counter from the *Guinness Book of World Records,*" I said, because the room smelled like death to me, and I did not want that to show on my face. "We understand you've made a claim."

She gave me a frail smile and turned her eyes to a little half-hidden alcove where the door to the bathroom was, and where her mother was standing.

I said, "Good morning, world's greatest cook," and drew a second flimsy smile before Amelia went through the door and we heard the lock's loud click.

"Nice going," Janet said. Her voice was very hoarse.

"I love the taste of shoe leather in the morning. How are you?"

She shrugged and turned away. Her eyes filled up.

I stood next to the bed, took hold of her fingers, and looked at her hair on the creases in the pillow, then swung my eyes around the room—at the plastic bag that had been put into the wastebasket as a lining, at the empty second bed with its yellowish curtain, at the clear plastic box on the wall for used needles. Everything in the room was perfectly clean but slightly worn and plain, all ready for the next person who would come through, the next routine catastrophe.

"Mom and I have been having a little spat," Janet said, without turning her head back to me. Her lips were dry and cracked.

We heard the toilet flush, and then her mother struggling momentarily with the door latch.

"About what?"

Janet didn't answer. Before her mother came out of the bathroom she said, still not looking at me, "What would I have to pay you to get me out of here?"

"A full body massage and eighteen percent of your next check," I said, and then her mother was with us, asking me to tell her what the doctors had said. I had gone home from Apple Meadow and sulked and dabbed paint on a canvas in a lazy, useless way, and only remembered about calling her at around one-thirty in the morning. I had dreamt a repeating dream in which I was driving a tractor-trailer truck for the first time and having to navigate impossible corners on narrow streets, steer it indoors between a table and chairs, reach my foot down for a brake that wouldn't work; I had eaten three eggs and sausages and a bran muffin at Flash's with the early morning crowd; I had waltzed into her daughter's hospital room making sex jokes. And all that time she had been waiting to hear some piece of news on which she could set down, for a few minutes, her impossible cargo of worry.

I said, "The doctor told me we'd have to wait and see how the medicine worked."

Even that piece of non-news sparked little wildfires of hope on Amelia's cheeks. She sat on a chair next to the IV pole and looked at her daughter with her eyebrows up and her lips compressed. It was a "see, I told you" look.

Janet was not in the mood for "see, I told you" looks. "Could we stop playing this game, Ma?" she said. "Please."

"Don't you dare give up," her mother said. "It's a sin to give up. And you know it is. Don't you dare do that to me." And so on.

From where I stood on the other side of the bed I thought I could see a line of history running between them, a string of mother-daughter quarreling that stretched back to how much *Sesame Street* her daughter was allowed to watch.

"Ma, I'm just tired of fighting."

"You fight. I don't care how tired you feel. You fight, Janet Rossi."

"You didn't have anything jammed down your throat before breakfast, Ma."

"I *don't care!*"

Ma Rossi had a string of pale blue glass rosary beads in her left hand, and as she shot these bursts of words at her daughter, she choked the beads between her thumb and the side of her index finger.

"You say you believe in the afterlife, Ma."

"Afterlife, afterlife. *This* is the life you have now. Don't you dare do to me what your father did."

"I'll go get us some coffee now," I said.

"Jake, stay." Janet stopped and coughed, breathed in some pure oxygen, coughed some more, then swung her eyes back to her mother's face. "Ma, it's not the same. I just can't bear to have you pretend, that's all. It's a kind of lie. It makes it harder for me."

"Who's pretending?" her mother almost shouted. "You don't think I know how sick you are? I'm not smart enough to know?"

As she said the last two words, Janet's mother exploded into tears, just absolutely exploded. Doctor Wilbraham marched into the room as if on cue. He glanced for a tenth of a second at Mrs. Rossi, a hundredth of a second at me, then took up a confident position at the foot of the bed with his hands lightly resting on the metal rail there. I pictured him at the wheel of his boat.

"You should be breathing easier, " he said.

There was something machinelike about him. He gave you the feeling that only his brain was talking, and the words weren't coming through any filter of personality or emotion. He walked in, opened up a little door in the side of his head, let information out, let a question in, let more information out, patted his patient twice on the nearest neutral body part, then turned on his heel.

"A little."

"Bowels move?"

Janet shook her head.

"We'll start on some GoLYTELY."

Janet twisted her lips down and looked away. "I can do that at home, can't I?"

"We'd rather have you here."

"I'd rather be home. Would it be so awful for me to leave when the IV comes out?"

"You'd increase the risk of relapse. We can't have that now."

"Why?"

"So we can get you back on your feet, young lady."

"Can we stop pretending, PLEASE!" Janet shouted, in the

breaking, hoarse voice. The effort sent her into another long stretch of coughing and spitting. Her mother held a crescent-shaped aluminum basin up to her mouth, wiped her face carefully with tissue, and glared at Doctor Wilbraham. Doctor Wilbraham flipped through the pages of Janet's chart. When Janet finished coughing and spitting, she fixed him with a look that could have drilled two holes in a fiberglass hull. "I'm dying," she said. "Can we use that word? It doesn't matter anymore if I have a goddamned relapse and you know that as well as I do. I want to go home to die. I want to go out in the air a few more times before I die. I want to see things other than the things in this room. Is that something you can understand?"

"Of course, of course," Doctor Wilbraham said. "But what you may not understand is that we have the ability to make you comfortable here, and we don't have that ability at your home."

"Stop pretending," Janet said, in a fierce whisper. "Stop avoiding the words!"

"I'm not pretending in the slightest," he said. "You're being melodramatic. This course of antibiotics can get you up on your feet again. You can move around the ward. You'll be able to—"

"I want to leave the hospital!"

"You have the legal right to do that. But I'd prefer that you didn't."

"Why?"

"We can give you better care here."

"Better care for what?"

"She's giving up," Mrs. Rossi said to the doctor, and he nodded at her, happy to have an ally.

"She wants to get out for a little while, that's all," I said. "That's not hard to understand. That's not going to—" I was looking at Doctor Wilbraham's square head, and I was about to say, *That's not going to kill her,* which is just an expression people use. But I caught myself and said, "That's not going to make her any sicker than she already is, is it?"

"It very well might."

"Fine," Janet said, but I had the feeling she was saying it only because she was running out of strength, and didn't want to argue with him that way, gasping for words while he watched.

"Very good," Doctor Wilbraham said, but he was offended. His eyes went ricocheting angrily around from the chart in his hands to Janet's face, and after a few seconds of that he couldn't seem to find a way to say good-bye, so he just gave a stiff nod and marched out.

We watched him go.

"Could you get us some coffee now, Ma?" Janet said.

Her mother looked hard at her and started to say something, but Janet turned over her wrist, stretched out her fingers, and caught her mother's hand. "Ma, please? I love you . . . please."

When her mother was gone, a nurse came in with a milk-shake-sized can and poured it into a tall plastic glass. "Chocolate ice cream soda," she chirped. "You know the drill, sweetheart." She watched until Janet started to drink, touched her on top of the head, and left us.

"I want two things," Janet said to me when we were alone. She was tired and weak but all fire.

"Ask."

She coughed and coughed and I held the crescent-shaped pan up to her mouth so she could spit. "When this IV is done tomorrow," she said, as I was washing the pan out in her sink, "I want you to take me for a ride, as long a ride as I can manage. I don't care if you have to lower me down out of the window and into the bed of the pickup, or wheel me out in a goddamned wheelchair."

"Not a problem," I said. I went back to the bed and faced her.

"That's the easy thing."

"Alright."

"The hard thing is, I want you to take a sip of this."

"What is it?"

"GoLYTELY. The name says it all. I have an intestinal blockage. Try it."

I took one sip—salty pineapple soup—and made a face that drew a laugh out of her.

OVER THE NEXT TWO DAYS, Janet and I had a couple of short stretches of being alone, and two phone conversations. I was not comfortable with the idea of her leaving the hospital, but that was not something I could say. I understood why she wanted to. I understood it a little better every time we talked, but I was nervous about it. We decided it would be simpler for her just to slip out of the building, rather than be officially discharged. That way she could walk back in and take up where she'd left off if she had to, and we both knew she would have to.

Except for some psychiatric wards, it is not very hard to sneak out of a hospital. Janet had been in that particular hospital so many times that she knew the schedule of the doctors and nurses, when they made their rounds and when they took their breaks. And she'd been a patient on that floor so often that she knew which nurse would be least likely to pay attention to her when she walked down to the reading room at the end of the hall for a little exercise once the IV was done. The reading room is open to visitors. It's a simple matter to have someone put a change of clothes in a tote bag and leave it just inside the leg of the sofa there. A simple matter to take the tote bag into the corridor bathroom, change, and then walk out and down the stairwell in street clothes. Sunday mornings are a little easier than other times to try this.

The antibiotics had, as Doctor Wilbraham promised,

made Janet feel stronger, and she left a note for her favorite nurse so there would be no panic when they discovered she had gone. At nine-fifteen on Sunday morning she walked out of the building on her own, dressed in jeans, a wool sweater, and cowboy boots.

I was waiting in my truck by the main entrance. I had her winter coat and hat and gloves in the cab, and three portable oxygen tanks wrapped in their narrow blue backpacks with gold trim. When she was on the seat and warmly dressed and we were driving away from the building, she clipped the oxygen on under her nostrils, but left it there for only a few breaths.

"Where to?" I asked her.

"Manhattan. I want one night in a nice hotel. And don't expect any gymnastic lovemaking."

"The rings," I said. "The parallel bars."

She reached over and put a hand on top of my leg.

"Your mum's going to be upset."

"She's at Mass. I called and left a message on her machine."

"Doctor Wilbraham isn't going to like it."

Janet didn't answer.

At that hour on a Sunday there was almost no traffic. After I asked her if she was hungry and she said no, I found the expressway on-ramp and we headed south. We drove for a long while without saying anything. The landscape there is mostly flat, and bleak at that time of year: patches of maples and oaks with a few brown leaves clinging to the branches, clusters of strip malls, and then frozen fields with the occasional sagging white Colonial presiding, the farmland waiting to be bulldozed and built on. And then, sometimes, like a surprise, an old New England town with slate-roofed houses, a mill, and church spires. I looked over at Janet occasionally as we went along. She seemed to be studying everything, drinking it, searching the American landscape for some hidden meaning that she'd missed in the last twenty-seven years. Somewhere near the Rhode Island line I asked her where she was on the transplant list.

And she said, "Stop it, Jake." Not in any kind of an angry way, but in a plain, even tone, the way someone who knew you well might ask you to turn off a radio. So I didn't try to start any conversation after that, figuring she ought to have everything the way she wanted it for those twenty-four hours: the place she wanted, and the food, silence if she wanted silence. I decided that if I was worth anything as a person, I ought to be able to let her be with what it was she had to be with then: not urge her to fight it if she was tired of fighting, not ply her with hope, not make her think about who might be upset or worried, not ask anything of her, nothing, just be alive with her while she was alive.

Somewhere in the southwestern part of Connecticut, just before we passed into New York State, after she'd been sucking on the oxygen for a while and quiet for a long time, she started to talk, without looking at me. "It's so odd," she said, and if, when we'd first met, her voice had been coming up through a wet barrel, then on that ride it was coming up through an echoing, rain-filled quarry. "It's so odd. I think about my father all the time now. I wake up in the middle of the night thinking about him. He wasn't an educated man, but he could imagine his way into the future in more detail than most people. He saw this, what I'm like now, he saw it twenty years ago. That's all. When I was a girl everyone else said I looked fine, I was going to be fine, they were going to find a cure, and if I'd been born fifteen years later that would have been true probably, but . . . year by year he saw that that was just a hopeful lie and it slowly made him crazy. He was shaky to begin with, my mother says—his father went out on the streets a few years after he was married. 'There's a gene for quitting in them,' my mother said once or twice, in her worst moments. From the day I was diagnosed—I was six weeks old—he started calling up doctors and asking them what would happen to me, and when. He never stopped pestering them. He was a big, strong, simple man, a union mason who specialized in heights, working high up. You would have loved him. If the doctors were evasive with him, he'd start to yell. He used to tell my mother about it while she was cooking dinner. I'd be in the living room watching cartoons or something and he'd be pacing back and forth in that tiny kitchen, all upset. 'They think I don't understand, Amelia!' he'd yell. 'But I understand better than they do! I understand fine! Perfect! Better than they do!' Now my mother says the same thing."

She stopped and put the oxygen up to her nose, and I held the pickup in the middle lane of the highway, flying past the little harbor at Westport, where most of the sailboats were wrapped up and drydocked for winter.

"Once, when I was eleven, he went to the office of the CEO of a huge drug company. He took a day off from work and dressed up in one of the two suits he owned—one for cold-weather funerals and one for warm-weather funerals, he used to say—and he drove his six-year-old Chevy down to some corporate headquarters somewhere in New Jersey, uninvited, without an appointment, and he sat in the waiting room of the president or the CEO. All day. Of course, the man wouldn't see him. He waited and waited there in his suit as if he was going to sell them something. Finally, at five o'clock he just lost it and he went right in past the secretary and burst into the guy's office and pounded both his huge fists on the desk and demanded to know how the guy could live with the fact that kids were dying of this disease and his company was spending exactly zero dollars on research for drugs to cure it."

All of this didn't come out at once. She'd speak in long, monotone, wet-quarry bursts, then take another few minutes of oxygen, then say another few sentences. I drove and listened.

"Know what the CEO said to him?"

"What?"

"My mother told me all this after he died. He said, 'I'm sorry about your daughter, Mr. Rossi, but it's pure mathematics.'"

"Meaning what?"

"Meaning thirty thousand people have the disease in America, and you don't make enough profit selling thirty thousand of anything to justify spending millions of research dollars. My father couldn't wrap his mind around thinking like that. He accidentally woke me up when he came home that night, he was yelling so loud. 'Pure mathematics!' he was shouting in the kitchen. 'That bastard! That son of a bitch!'"

She had started breathing more heavily, so she stopped talking for a while. We hurtled along I-95, past the knot of glass-walled buildings that is downtown Stamford, all the confidence and optimism there, all the shine. I tried to remember if I had ever heard my father shout, in the house or anywhere besides at a Red Sox game. He arranged deals for businesses and managed money for people in an office in a thirty-four-story building downtown. He advised clients on the best kind of investments to choose so they would be as comfortable as possible when they grew old.

"They sent me to a camp for CF children when I was four-

teen, because they thought it would be nice for me to be around
other kids with the same sickness. But it turned out that we all
ended up giving our germs to each other. They don't do CF camps
anymore because of that. The camp was where I got the *cepacia,*
and when my father found out about it, and heard what it was,
and what usually happens to people who get it . . . that's when he
jumped. My mother says he gave up, that he just couldn't take it
finally, that he quit. She had to go to work selling shoes at Jordan's
when he died. She's bitter, she has a right to be—she had to sell
our car and never even had another one until I bought her one,
four years ago. And probably he did give up. He had problems. I
remember some days he wouldn't go to work and would just lie in
his room pretending to sleep . . . But the thing I remember most
about him is . . . I can almost reach inside myself and put my hand
on that feeling, even now . . . he loved me more than anything,
Jake . . . he . . . I don't think everybody has that kind of warmth in
their lives."

"Not many people have it," I said.

"I never told anybody this, not even my mother, but he
appeared to me the day after he died. I had a vision of him. There
were a lot of people in the house and I went outside alone for some
reason, into the back yard, and he was there. He didn't say anything to me, but he was there and looking at me, and I could feel
that love. Really . . . You think I'm crazy, Jake?"

"No."

"Or that I was temporarily crazy, or not breathing right or
something?"

I shook my head. "How old were you again?"

"Fourteen."

"It's a lousy age to lose a parent."

"But the reason ... the thing I want to say is ..." She stopped and rested. We crossed into New York State. "After I saw him there, I was never afraid of dying. I've seen four friends die of CF, three in the hospital and one at home. Three of them died pretty calmly, but I was holding my friend Celia's hand when she died. I was seventeen. It was horrible. She was making horrible noises, like a dog that had been hit by a car, huge, drawn-out moans that started in her throat and rattled her whole head. Her hair was on the pillow—I remember this—and it was shaking there as if a wind were blowing through it. Her mother was hysterical, slapping Celia's feet and legs so hard to try to keep her alive that the nurses had to restrain her. It was horrible. I worry about the pain of dying like that and I get panicky when I'm out of breath, but I never worry about being dead. Whatever else happens, it will mean I'll just be free of this body. I won't have to work to breathe."

She stopped and rested again. She coughed, looked away from me. "Until I met you, I never even cared about living very much. I'd had so much time to get ready for the idea of being dead, you know. And being stuck in this body was not exactly a picnic."

I started to say something, but she waved at me not to.

"When you jumped in the river that time after I fell in, and you came up sputtering and slicked your hair back and it was all standing straight up, at that minute I started to care. I wanted to have some fun with you. I wanted to see if ... I've never had that much real luck with men. I mean, I had boyfriends I liked, I had enough sex. But I always felt there had to be some deeper level of intimacy that I could get to, some truer connection I could feel ... So now I know I was right about that, and I know what it feels like, and I want a few more years of it. That's what makes it shitty." She flung one hand, palm-inward, toward the window. "But I can deal with everything else, the fear and the mess and all the ugliness and everything. I just wanted to tell you that. I just want you to be able to deal with it, too."

1 4

WE MADE IT TO New York City by 2:00 p.m. and checked into the Waldorf-Astoria, two toothbrushes and the portable oxygen machines for luggage. I had been there once before, with my parents, when we'd gone down to New York for my sister's sixteenth birthday, and I'd been there once with Giselle. I love the lobby of that hotel, with its tile floor mosaics, and the stupendous bouquet of flowers in a vase there on a mahogany table. I feel religious in old hotels, an urge to believe, to worship. I don't know why. I mentioned that to Ellory once, and, without even having to think about it, he said that the whole purpose of prayer and fasting and meditation and the monk's life was to make you stop taking everything for granted, make you actually *see* a table or a tree or a person, instead of worrying about survival and pleasure all the time. If you can just do that, he said, then you're all set, as far as God goes.

So I guess I was all set then, in the Waldorf-Astoria, because when I walked into the lobby from the street, holding Janet's hand, I was seeing everything clear-eyed.

When we got up to the room, Janet wrapped herself in the thin chenille spread and fell asleep with her clothes on. I stood at the window and looked down on Fiftieth Street and everything was a little bit shocking to me in a way that I'd almost forgotten things could be—the tar rooftops and rust-stained water towers, the windows across the way with their pigeons sitting on stone sills; down below, Christmas lights, and yellow cabs angling across traffic lanes; crowds of people on the sidewalk, so many histories there, so many different worries and loves and connections. I watched the light and color seep out of the day. I put one fingertip to the cool glass. I felt like I was linked to Janet and had been linked to her for centuries, and that we were both linked to every person in that city, and at the same time I felt a kind of warm solitariness. For a little while, everything was exactly in its place, all of it made of the thinnest porcelain. In the next breath it could all shatter and remake itself in a different form and nothing would be lost.

I ordered a twenty-dollar glass of brandy from room service, gave the young man who brought it a ten-dollar tip, and sat there sipping as the room went dark. I imagined that Janet and I had children, a boy and a girl, adopted from Vietnam for some reason. They were three or four years old, precious creatures. We were on vacation in New York with them, showing them the holiday decorations, taking them into toy stores, zipping their jackets, holding them when they threw tantrums or when they were cold. I was connected to them in the same way I was connected to everyone else, only more deeply, more warmly.

Janet said "Beethoven" in her sleep. She was a gray shape on the bed. I breathed in and let my breath slowly out, and soon I was just my ordinary self again, sitting in a hotel room with a glass in one hand, two brownish drops in the bottom of the glass, a dark night and street noise and a good soul on the bed there, near me, leaking away.

When Janet woke up I suggested a room-service dinner, but she said she was feeling strong, she wanted to go out. She was using the oxygen on and off. We called down and asked the concierge to recommend someplace exotic and not too dressy and we ended up taking a cab to a Ukrainian restaurant on Thirty-fourth Street. There we had bowls of bloodred borscht with dollops of sour cream floating in them, and then small dumplings in a thin sweet sauce. Janet ate almost none of her soup, and only two dumplings. She sipped from a cup of tea, took some hits of oxygen. I ate everything in front of me and then everything that was left over in front of her. I drank a glass of straight vodka and then two more.

"Are you getting drunk, Jake? I don't mind if you do. Are you a mean drunk?"

"Goofy."

"When's the last time you were drunk?"

I thought, immediately, of lying to her, then caught myself and said, "September 11, 2001, beginning at about four o'clock in the afternoon."

"When you knew Giselle was dead?"

I nodded.

"And then you gave up sex for a year?"

I nodded again. The couple at the next table looked over at me.

"And she wasn't the love of your life? Brutal honesty."

"No, she was not. Do you want me to say who the love of my life is?"

She smiled in a way I hadn't seen her smile in two weeks, and shook her head.

I ordered one more vodka with dessert. My head had begun to shift and shimmer—it wasn't a bad feeling. But beyond that I felt as though something, some immensely heavy grief, was being laid across my face and ears, fine thin layers of dense wet black cloth, one upon another. The waitresses wore paisley kerchiefs around their hair and short skirts, and ours came with the last vodka and the teapot on a tray beside one thin slice of four-teen-dollar white chocolate pie with a boysenberry sauce.

"Ukraine is famous for fourteen-dollar white chocolate pie slices in boysenberry sauce, you know," I said.

Janet had two small bites. Even in her best wool sweater with her hair brushed, she looked like a woman who belonged already to another world: eyes and cheeks sunken, skin ashen, shoulders thin. I reached across the table and put my hand over her hand.

She put her fork down. "I'm being melodramatic," she said, setting the oxygen aside as if she would never pick it up again. "I've been pretending it's our last day on earth."

"It isn't."

"Don't spoil my little fantasy."

The noisy room tilted, righted itself. The waitresses' legs kicked past as if they were swimming there, upright.

"I'm pretending we're in Paris."

"I've always wanted to go."

"I went once, between college and grad school. I was sitting in the Louvre when this truly ancient man sat down beside me and struck up a conversation." She coughed, swallowed, took one careful breath. "He was Paraguayan, probably four and a half feet tall. After a few minutes he said, 'I would like to paint you'—dramatic pause—'in the nude.'"

"Hope springs eternal," I said. A fresh wave of drunkenness rolled over me.

She nodded.

"He had nothing to lose. He thought he'd give it a shot."

She nodded again. "I said no three times. He kept asking."

"His mother told him never ever to give up," I said, and her eyes filled right up, and my eyes filled right up, and I couldn't get a sound out then, though I tried and tried. *Don't,* I wanted to say. *Not yet.* But every time I tried, another little squirt of juice came up in my eyes and we were looking into two different blank middle distances, southern and western Ukraine, twin epicenters of the universe of suffering, the remains of a slice of cake between us.

WE TOOK A CAB most of the way back, then got out and walked, holding hands, along half a block of cold Manhattan night, me with my head spinning, Janet wheezing away and refusing to use the oxygen, and a circus of Christmas lights and window decorations all around us.

Up in the hotel room it was clear there would be no lovemaking that night—she barely had the strength to take off her sweater and clip the plastic tube under her nose—but we left the light off anyway, as if to remind each other of the pleasure we had taken from each other's bodies, or to pretend we might take pleasure like that again. I drank three glasses of water and swallowed two ibuprofen. We took turns pissing and brushing our teeth in the dark, then climbed into the luxurious bed. She squeezed my hand once and fell asleep.

It wasn't completely dark in the room. A thin yellow-gray light leaked in around the sides of the window drapes. The bed spun gently. When I knew Janet was asleep, I slipped my arm out from underneath her, but I lay on my back against her bare warm skin, listening to her breathe. Without meaning to, without wanting to, I started thinking about Giselle. She had tried to call me from the plane. When I came home that Tuesday afternoon, I was already just about sure she was dead—I'd called her parents. I was a big bursting bag of feelings; everyone was, that day. I hadn't eaten since breakfast. I walked into the apartment and saw the red message light on the phone machine blinking. Eight calls. The second message was full of static and commotion, and my name spoken twice in a panicky whisper: "Jake . . . Jake?" I listened to it over and over and over, thirty times probably, then I went out the door and walked to the nearest bar, sat there with the television going and got stupefyingly drunk.

I put my hand on Janet's bare leg. Sirens wailed in the street. I thought of my father, who had loved his work, loved the process of solving problems, "the business of business" he used to call it, the satisfaction of matching up investors and entrepreneurs. He smoked a pipe, he sat out on the patio, he loved to talk about it with me once I'd gotten past the stupidities of my early teenage years. "Jakie," he said more than once, "the mistake some fellows make is they see a problem—let's say it's a bad problem, an almost unsolvable problem, a client over-valuing his business, let's say—they see this problem and they either throw up their hands and surrender, and walk away from it, or they rush in like novice firemen with hoses spraying every which way. Sometimes, though, the thing to do is to sit back, hold back. You watch for a little while—sometimes it's only sixty seconds in a heated meeting, sometimes it's a day, a week, a year—you ponder. Occasionally it is a truly unsolvable trouble and you have to be mature enough to accept that. But usually, if you just let your mind scamper around outside the fences for a while, you see one small action you might take—a word, a shift in tactics. You tug on the knotted-up ball of string, once, here, and things begin to loosen."

THE NEXT DAY the sky was perfectly blue between the skyscrapers, and Janet was exhausted, but glad that we'd come. I took three more ibuprofen at breakfast and pondered and waited. We drove as close as we could get to the Trade Center, down there in the tight, cluttered streets of lower Manhattan. I waited. I watched the city she loved. And then, in the truck going north, I decided to say one thing to her. I said, "I'm a big fan of doctors, you know, but I think Doctor Wilbraham is a cold, worthless, stick-up-the-ass piece of horse manure."

She nodded, almost laughed. That's all we said on the subject. She slept most of the way back, waking only when she coughed very hard, or to adjust the clip of the oxygen cylinder. We stopped for soup and ice cream in Providence. She coughed and coughed and slumped back in her chair and ate almost nothing.

But when we got back to the hospital and she was in the bed again, and Doctor Wilbraham came marching in and started to lecture her, she held up her hand and made him stop. "I don't want you as my physician anymore," she said. "I don't care if it means being transferred to another hospital, or if it means I just go home and die, I want a different doctor now."

He puffed and huffed but she didn't stop looking at him. I could see the steel behind her eyes. After a while, even Doctor Wilbraham could see it.

Book Four

December

1

F OR A WHILE THEN, during the last week of November and the first week or so of December, Janet's body went into a resting mode, as if preparing for some great private exertion. I had been writing to my brother about her every few weeks, and somewhere near the start of December I sent Ellory a note saying she was not getting better and asking him to pray for her—not the kind of thing I had ever done. Janet's new doctor was a very small, coffee-skinned, tight-mouthed fellow named Ronald Ouajiballah. He was from Fiji or the Solomon Islands, I could not remember which, and he was as different from Eric Wilbraham as two people in the same profession can be. Even the way he touched Janet was different. I never saw him at her bedside when he didn't have a hand on her shoulder or arm or foot, and it was a personal, not a professional hand, the touch of a cousin with a medical degree. He switched around her medicines, beefing up the Albuterol inhaler with another steroid, adding into the IV mix an antibiotic cocktail called Zithromax, which was used for bronchitis and sinus infections, and usually prescribed for CF patients with less lung damage. He discovered she had some kind of allergy called ABPA, and prescribed prednisone. All of this seemed to help her breathe more easily.

What helped her most was just that, without pretending everything was fine, *il dottore,* as we called him, didn't stop trying, and didn't seem to have built up a wall to protect himself from his patients' pain and discomfort. When the flesh around the shunt in Janet's right arm became inflamed he had the nurses move it right away; when the pain of the strenuous coughing overwhelmed her, he was there with Valium or Oxycodone—she did not have to whimper and scream to make it real to him.

For those two weeks we fell into a routine: I stopped in to see Janet before work—usually with a raspberry muffin from a place she liked, though she had very little appetite—and spent three or four hours there at night. I brought her newspapers and political magazines. Her mother, who believed in the healing powers of red meat, brought meatball and roast beef sandwiches that Janet took one look at and set aside. If she could talk we talked about everything around the edges of us—the weather, the world, the strenuous craziness of the early Christmas season. Gerard visited a few times and made her laugh with his Bob Dylan imitations (for which he was locally famous), singing "Train of Love" so loud at one point that the nurses came in to ask him to cool it. We were at the tail end of Jacqueline's addition—hanging interior doors, grouting bathroom tile—and she was pleased, and we had our priorities straight, and so, on those early December days, we didn't worry about cutting ourselves a little slack.

Janet was still eleventh on the transplant list, and no one was talking about her leaving the hospital anymore. But for those short, cold days we all pretended things could go on like that indefinitely. It was a kind of trick, a wishful self-hypnosis, and I suppose we all knew it—Janet's mother, me, the orderlies and good nurses who emptied her bedpans and rubbed her back and changed her IV—but we needed a stretch of relative peace then, and for fourteen or fifteen days we had it.

And then, on the second Sunday of the month, the trick
stopped working. That day I took my mother out for a nice Yankee
pot roast lunch and an ice cream sundae and spent a little time
watching TV with her in the community room at Apple Meadow.
I hoped she would remember the Thanksgiving dinner at Amelia's
house—the first good hour at least—but it seemed to have left
no mark on her memory. Janet had skidded off her radar screen.
She went on and on about Lauren, a sometime friend who lived
down the hall and who, my mother seemed to think, was constantly chasing the men residents who were rumored to be still
capable of having sex. "Your father and I enjoy it as much as the
next person," she told me, in a voice right out of the high school
hallways. "Probably more than the next person, if you want to
know. But we are discreet about it, Ellory. Why, just last week we
were in Aruba, and you children were asleep in your rooms and
they have these beaches there, you know, not far from the hotel,
and we sneaked out on the beach and he started to—"

"Mum, you don't want to keep watching football, do
you?" I said.

And so on.

When I got back to my apartment the light on the phone
machine was blinking, and Janet's mother's voice was on the tape.
"Jake, Jake, Jake. Come right away when you get this. Come right
away."

Janet was all bones and sallow skin, eyelids slowly fluttering, incommunicado. Her left lung was working like an old,
worn-down bellows that had been mostly filled up with sand, and
her right lung was not working at all.

I sat there with her and her mother for several hours, watching her, touching her, sinking inch by inch in a cold quicksand.

Amelia was making the rosary beads go through her fingers faster and faster, and would not eat, and would not leave the room. I stayed until ten o'clock, then left the hospital and just drove aimlessly back and forth on the long east-west avenues of the Back Bay: Beacon to Marlborough to Boylston to Commonwealth, just staring out at the holiday lights, just shifting gears, just going from brake to gas to brake and slamming in the clutch. Snow was falling, large indifferent flakes twirling and skidding through the headlight beams. Eventually, I turned west onto Commonwealth and kept going as if headed home, and then, because I was near Betty's, I stopped and bought two coffees and half a dozen doughnuts—Carmine wasn't there—and took them over to Gerard's.

Gerard rented the top floor of a maroon and gold Victorian in North Cambridge, not far from where Anastasia and the girls lived. Two small bedrooms, a room for his books, computer, and bicycles, a kitchen and bath—the place suited him well enough, though the ceilings slanted down in a way that made for a lot of bruised foreheads. "It has encouraged me to begin dating short women," he liked to joke.

I told him about the change in Janet's condition. We drank the coffee and went through all the doughnuts—unusual for him—and then we sat at his fifties-style Formica-topped table, which was the one piece of furniture Anastasia had let him take from the house, and looked out different windows. I called my apartment four times and the hospital twice. I did not want to go home. At last I said, "Let me look at the computer, will you?"

I brought up the search engine and plugged in the same thing I always plugged in: *cystic fibrosis* and *lung transplants*. The same 239 pages came up. I started to flip down through them, looking for something new, but Gerard was standing at my shoulder. "Try something else, will you?" he said impatiently. "That's not the way to do research."

"Something else like what?"

"I don't know. Anything. *Last ditch* or something. Don't just hit the same stupid nail in over and over again. Refine the search. What's wrong with you?"

I typed in *cystic fibrosis, transplants, last ditch,* without much hope, and got forty-seven pages. I'd seen most of them before: stories of fifteen-year-olds whose lives had been saved, or prolonged, by a cadaveric transplant; professional papers so filled with medical terminology that you needed a translator to understand one-tenth of them; statistics on survival rates with various bacteria, in various hospitals, in various countries. I tapped the down arrow without much enthusiasm. When I hit the eleventh page I saw *Living Lobar Transplantation in Cystic Fibrosis Patients,* and I stopped there. I almost moved on, but something was making me keep looking at those words, and then a little faint bell sounded, a little blink of light.

"What?" Gerard leaned down closer.

I opened the page and we read it.

What it said was that, for cystic fibrosis patients, a lung transplant was the treatment of last resort. I knew that already. It went on to say that the number of people who wanted new lungs far exceeded the number of lungs available at any given time. I knew that, too. But in the next paragraph there was something about a surgeon in California who had been the first to try what was called a "living lobar transplant," in 1993, removing a lobe each from two healthy donors and sewing them into a patient whose lungs had been destroyed by the same bacteria Janet had. The patient had lived three years. The operation was riskier and more complicated and more expensive than the usual cadaveric transplant, and so it was done only about a dozen times a year in America, but some recipients were still alive and doing well seven years after they'd received the new lobes.

There were six or eight more paragraphs, having to do with complications and problems, but I did not want to know about that then. "My mother mentioned this," I told Gerard.

"Your mother mentions it," he said over my shoulder, in the tone of voice he reserved for the courts and the IRS and the big multilingual corporations. "She's got sixty-three brain cells left, she mentions it. Nobody else says a word."

Before he was finished with that sentence, I was offline and on the phone to the hospital, asking for Doctor Ouajiballah. But it was one o'clock in the morning. Doctor Ouajiballah, the nurse on duty told me, would not start rounds again until eight.

When I hung up, Gerard said, "I'll doan."

"What?"

"I'll doan. You need a donor, I'll doan. I'll give her one of my lobes."

"You wouldn't be able to race anymore."

"Get your priorities straight," he said. "It would be a way of getting inside her body without actually betraying my best friend. You gonna compare bike racing with that, Colonel?"

"No."

"Good. You're still in the general vicinity of sane, then. Go home and let me sleep."

2

I DROVE HOME and went to bed for a while and then got up and put my clothes back on. I went into the painting room and walked in circles. I looked at the unfinished paintings in one of my racks, paced some more, stood at the window. Usually if I leave a canvas alone for a month or two, I come back to it with a fresh eye. I see everything that's wrong and I think I see how to try to make it right. It's something like looking back on your own life and being able to change part of it—things you blurted out, people you should have been kinder to, or blunter with—except that your life is cut in stone and your painting mistakes are only blots of colored oil pressed onto linen. Those patches of color show the deep patterns of your mind, though, which is why it seems so important to get them exactly right.

The painting of Janet in her sea-green pajamas was sitting in one of the racks I'd built. When I took it out and set it up on the easel I could see how little I had known her when I did it. She looked smart and pretty, when in fact she was smart and pretty and almost unbelievably brave. Every morning when I walked into her room at the hospital I could see that bravery in her because all through the night she had been a step or two this side of suffocation. Every day she coughed up and spit out as much as a quart of green and bloody mucus—not pleasant to think about, excuse me. But she did that, lived that. Not once, not just one awful time, but night after night. Not one sip of GoLYTELY, but glass after glass. Not one annual invasive procedure, but dozens of them—bronchoscopies, enemas, throat cultures, sinus irrigations, shunts, IVs, pinpricks, blood tests, intestinal surgeries—from the time she was old enough to hold her head up without help. And she woke up day after day and went about her life, trying to be pleasant, wanting to be normal, working, cleaning her apartment, facing everything she had to face without making a big fuss about it. There was no way to measure bravery like that. There were no medals given for it. Instead of calling you a hero and making a fuss over you on TV or in the magazines, people heard the wet cough and shot you nasty looks, moved away from you in subway cars, made remarks in movie theaters. Natural enough from their point of view, maybe. But a kind of second-degree torture for Janet. I had not understood all that when I tried to put her on a canvas.

So I mixed white and red and brown in different amounts on different places on my glass-topped table until I had a shade of skin that seemed right, then I wiped almost all the paint from the brush and ran the tip of the bristles diagonally in under her cheek-bones, one stroke each side. I cut a sixteenth of an inch from her smile, one stroke each side. Each of her irises got one more spark of light. I tried to make it so you could see the tiny hairs on the veins on the backs of her elegant hands, and I made her hair shinier than it had been in months. In all, I put maybe ten touches of paint on the canvas.

And then, just before going to bed, I ran some lighter gray here and there into the background, because the first time around I had made it one shade too dark.

3

IN THE MORNING I brought Janet flowers with the raspberry muffin, but I did not say anything about what I'd seen on the computer the night before. It was not easy to do that, and I was not sure it was the right thing to do. But hope is an almost-tame lion—gorgeous to look at and capable of turning on you in a nanosecond. According to the nurses on duty, she'd had a miserable night and couldn't eat or talk, and I didn't want anything else that could hurt her to be in the room then. I stood or sat by the bed and held her long fingers. I pulled the blanket up an inch higher on her chest. I wiped away the saliva that dribbled down her chin. A little bit after eight o'clock she moaned and slowly woke up. We made eye contact, she squeezed my hand, and I almost told her. There was just about nothing left of her—the beating heart, a few weak puffs of air, the movement of her eyes, enough strength to say, "Hi, Joe Date," in a voice that was like three scratches from a broken violin. I opened the get-well cards from her cousins and coworkers, one from the governor himself. I read them to her and turned them so she could see what people had written: how much they missed her and were praying for her; how they knew everything would be fine. When I couldn't stand to be there anymore, I kissed her eyelids, said I would be back that night, and went out of the room as if I were only headed off to work.

Doctor Ouajiballah weighed maybe a hundred and forty pounds. I nearly knocked him flat going fast around a corner of the hospital corridor, looking for him. I didn't even say I was sorry, or good morning. I said, "Living lobar transplant."

He lifted his coffee-brown eyes to me and said, in his soft, lilting, Pacific Island voice, "Yes?"

"Why didn't anyone tell us about a living lobar transplant?"

"I assumed Doctor Wilbraham had done so."

"He didn't."

"I assumed you knew it was one option."

"We didn't. *Is* it an option?"

He pinched his lips together and tilted his head sideways. "It's not commonly done, sir. You would need two donors."

"We have them."

"They would have to match blood type or be O-positive."

"I'm O-positive."

"The other donor would have to be. And be of a certain size. Each lobe would have to be large enough to take up much of the space left by the removal of a whole adult lung. The body abhors a vacuum, sir."

"He's an inch shorter than me. He's a champion bicycle racer."

"You cannot be a smoker, or an asthmatic. You will have to be in excellent cardiovascular condition. The psychological motivation must be appropriate."

I looked at him.

"There are many factors," he added weakly.

I said, "The insurance company won't pay for it, am I right?"

He pinched the skin over his Adam's apple and shifted his eyes to the back of a passing nurse.

"Will they pay for something like that or not, at this point?"

"It's a quarter of a million dollars, at a minimum."

"Will they, or not?"

"They do not like to, not in general. In the case of the types of bacteria Janet harbors—one bacterium in particular—the data on survival after such a procedure is not encouraging. Many hospitals will not do it."

"Has this hospital ever done it?"

"Yes."

"On somebody with that bacterium?"

"Yes. In fact, twice that I am aware of."

"And the people lived?"

"Yes, at first. One is still alive."

"Will you recommend it for Janet, officially, in writing?"

"Many surgeons will not do it."

"Is there a surgeon here who does it?"

"There was. The very finest surgeon. He retired three weeks ago, unfortunately. If he were here I would recommend it. But, if we were to do it now, without him, we would have to go to New York. *If* the donors are qualified. *If* the insurance company will pay. *If* the patient is strong enough to endure traveling, and to survive the procedure itself."

There was a bustle of traffic in the hallway. Someone rolled an empty gurney past us and we moved aside. A doctor came hurrying in the opposite direction and nodded at Ouajiballah. He nodded back at her.

"I want one thing from you," I said, when no one could hear. "I want the home address of the surgeon."

"His name is Leicus Vaskis. His address, home address, is in Dover, Massachusetts, I believe. I could perhaps find it for you, though it would be highly irregular for me to give that information out."

"This seems like a good time for highly irregular, don't you think?"

He looked at me. He raised and lowered his eyebrows.

"I want your word that if he agrees to do it, you'll recommend that the insurance company pay for it."

He raised his eyebrows a second time. It was some kind of island code for yes. He said, "If all other factors are in order, I would surely consider doing that."

"Why didn't you consider doing it before?"

"Because the chances of success at this point are exceedingly slim, sir. Because I wasn't her doctor. Because it should rightly have been tried two weeks ago if we were going to try it."

"How much time do we have before . . . before it would be too late to try?"

"At the minimum, two days. At the maximum, I would guess, ten days."

I asked *il dottore* another handful of questions, yanking the information out of him, short melodies of polite and beautifully cadenced speech, and then I thanked him three times and nearly crushed his hand in mine, and, instead of waiting for the elevator, I ran down the four flights of stairs.

From a pay phone in the lobby I called Gerard's cell. I knew he would be at the job site, and I guessed he'd be putting hardware on the louvered bifold doors in the professor's new bedroom. Every couple of weeks he changed the way he answered his phone: sometimes it would be a quote from Anna Akhmatova, or a scrap of T. S. Eliot; because he had a fondness for Chinese women, he'd ask a waiter at a Chinese restaurant how to say, "I know you love me," in Mandarin, and then practice it until he believed he'd gotten it right. Anything but a simple "hello." It was funny sometimes; other times it made you crazy.

"Nixon residence. Gerard the plumber," he said when he picked up.

"Gerard."

"Speaking."

"I talked to Ouajiballah, and it's a possibility."

"That's what we like to hear!" he said. "What's Janet's blood type?"

"O-positive, like me."

"I can't doan, then. I'm AB-negative. I stayed up until three last night doing research."

"Alright." I kicked the base of the telephone, hard. "Alright, we'll find somebody. Do you know how to get to Dover?"

"Of course. I go there regularly. My bookie lives there."

"Forget the closet hardware for now. And forget the damn jokes, will you please? Meet me at my place at nine-fifteen."

"Yes, Mister Liddy," he said, and hung up.

I swung by Doctor Ouajiballah's office, which was in a building next to the hospital. When I told his secretary my name, she handed me a manila envelope, which I opened in the hallway. Inside was a piece of paper with the logo of a pharmaceuticals company on it and beneath the logo: "1339 Madison Road."

4

A T THAT POINT in my painting career, I'd had three solo
shows, all at the same small gallery between Newbury and
Boylston Streets. In order to get my paintings there—physically
move them there, I mean—I'd built a wooden box that just fit
between the wheel bays in the bed of the pickup, and a balsa-
wood rack (the same light, strong wood that racing shells used to
be made from) that could be slid neatly into the box. I'd wrap the
canvases loosely in plastic and bubble wrap and slide them into
the rack so they were standing up on one edge. A piece of quarter-
inch-thick red rubber glued to the top of the box kept the rain and
snow out.

I screeched up in front of the apartment and double-
parked there, flashers on. Gerard was waiting. He and I cleaned
some wood scraps and a sawhorse out of the bed and threw them
on the frozen mini-lawn. We carried the rubber-topped box
down from my apartment and bolted it in place with freezing fingertips. I ran back up, checked the portrait of Janet to make sure
the new paint had dried, then wrapped it as if I were taking it to
the gallery to be shown. I carried the painting, Gerard carried the
rack. We slid everything into place in the box in the truck bed,
closed and bolted the box, slammed the tailgate, and headed off.

"Sorry about the blood type," Gerard said, when we were
on our way.

"We'll find somebody."

"What about your brother?"

"My brother smokes."

"We'll broadcast an appeal. I dated a woman at WCVB, she'll—"

"The hospital won't allow any publicity."

"Screw the hospital. What can they do?"

"They'll refuse to do the operation. Ouajiballah told me. They don't want some shithead coming in and saying he'll be more than happy to give a lobe of his lung . . . for fifty thousand bucks or something."

"Or her firstborn."

"Right. Nice."

"Sorry."

"The first step is getting this guy to agree to do it. Ouajiballah says he's an odd duck. He'd never even ever speak a single word to the person he put the lungs into, never even see them when they were conscious. He refused to talk to the press. He'd just come into the hospital in a kind of zone, go into the operating room, stand there for six hours, do something that about ten other people on earth can do, and go home."

"A psycho."

"Right. Psycho-genius."

"I can relate. Why the painting?"

"He retired three weeks ago. The painting is the best bribe I could think of on short notice."

"Ah," Gerard said. "Something for the man who has everything."

5

I AM A VERY CALM PERSON. I inherited that from both sides
of the family. It wasn't unusual for my mother or father to receive
an urgent phone call at home, a nurse saying a patient had taken a
sudden turn for the worse, or a client panicking about oil futures.
Under my parents I'd served a kind of apprenticeship of calm.

But as we drove out of Boston into the picket-fence suburbs,
I could feel a sort of salty panic rising like a tide in the cab of the
truck. The sky was a woolly gray and the air outside cold and hard
as metal. I had a feeling that Janet was going to die on that day. I
had given Amelia the number of Gerard's cell phone, and I kept
expecting it to ring, and to have Gerard hand it to me across the
seat, and to hear Amelia's voice on the line, shaking with terror.

But the phone didn't ring. The premonition about Janet
built up in me. The nice houses we drove past turned into nicer
houses, until, by the time we crossed the Dover line, "house" wasn't
even the right word anymore.

We could not find a single restaurant or public building in
Dover. Finally we saw a library, and stopped there to ask how to
get to Madison Road. Even after we found Madison Road, we had
to drive the entire length of it—about two miles—three times
before we could be sure which long, unmarked driveway corre-
sponded to the address Ouajiballah had given me.

"And I thought *you* grew up in a fancy neighborhood,"
Gerard said.

We turned in between two shoulder-high fieldstone pillars with stone lions sitting regally on top. The driveway was hard-packed gray gravel, and at first, to either side, we saw only hardwood trees with red brambles on the lower tier, the bare cold branches and trunks running the whole spectrum of grays and blacks and browns. A quarter-mile in, the terrain to the left of us opened into pastureland with white rail fencing enclosing it, and what might have been mistaken for a hotel—gray-shingled, many-windowed, three-floored—in the distance. A Thorough-bred horse cantered riderless toward the house, as if hurrying to announce our arrival.

"Wise of you to drop out of med school," Gerard said.

But I had grown up around doctors. Doctors didn't live like this.

Gravel crackled under the truck tires. When we reached a high spot in the driveway, about halfway between the street and the house, I could see two people jogging in front of us, climbing a long, gentle slope that crested just ahead of them and then flattened as it approached the front door. A few more seconds and I could tell that the runners were a man and a woman. They were dressed in blue sweat suits, the woman's long straight black hair floating up and then bouncing down against her back, the man wearing a dark wool winter cap.

They were running fairly hard. They must have heard the truck wheels on the gravel because they moved to their left when we approached. As we passed I gave them as much room as I could, and slowed down and lifted my left forearm in a casual greeting, without looking at them. The way any deliveryman would.

We pulled up just beyond the path to the front steps, and got out. The man and the woman were probably seventy-five feet behind us, sprinting now, we could hear their running shoes scuffing and slapping the dirt, and then the sound of labored breathing.

I lowered the tailgate. Gerard and I started to loosen the wing nuts at the four corners of the box, but it was slow going in the cold, and by the time we had the wooden cover off and had set it in the pickup bed, the runners had reached their finish line—which seemed to be about even with the back end of the truck—and were trotting in loose circles and breathing hard, then walking with hands on hips. Ducking beneath the ladder rack, we tugged the bubble-wrapped painting out of its box, and balanced it on the tailgate. Gerard hopped down, then held it steady while I hopped down. When we started to loosen the outer covering of bubble wrap, I could not keep myself from glancing at the man and the woman again. The doctor was lanky and wide-shouldered, sharp-featured, sixtyish, breath spewing out of him in big clouds. I had told myself that I'd be able to guess our odds as soon as I had a good look at his face, but I'd been wrong about that. My hands were working the masking tape, and I didn't want eye contact yet, and just as I started to glance away the woman turned toward me, breathing hard, and I saw in that second that she was young and healthy-looking and very beautiful. A little squirt of bitterness went through my mind—irrational, idiotic. I looked away.

We let the bubble wrap and the plastic sheeting fall to the ground and rested the bottom edge of the frame on it, facing us. It wasn't exactly the way real delivery people would have done it. By that point the man and the woman were moving toward us, not breathing as hard as they had been. I realized I had not shaved that morning. Try as he did, Gerard could never completely erase a certain tough-guy pentimento from his face—the heavy eyebrows, the rough mouth and chin—and it occurred to me that it would not take any great leap of imagination for the doctor and his girlfriend to see us as thieves. Or worse.

The doctor was two inches taller than me, his eyes steady, an unnaturally pale blue, not particularly friendly.

I made my face pleasant and unthreatening. "Doctor Vaskis?"

He nodded curtly. He was not happy to see us. The gorgeous woman—thirty years his junior—had come up close to him and now pulled a foot up behind her, stretching her quadriceps and holding his elbow with her other hand for balance.

"We have a gift delivery for you," I said, and though, by then, my voice was starting to wobble like the voice of an unpracticed liar, the word "gift" caught them. Everyone likes to be given a gift. The woman tilted her head slightly, as if she might change her angle of vision and see through the back of the canvas, and, in spite of himself it seemed, Doctor Vaskis let his features soften in expectation, too, the way you do on the morning of your birthday when someone is about to give you something and you want to assure them you like it. I had more or less prepared things to that point, and then decided I would just ad-lib. But no ad-lib was coming to me. The Thoroughbred had trotted up to the end of the pasture nearest us, and was snorting and fuffing his lips over the top rail, and when he was finished, a bad, cold silence started to creep up around us.

"We're the delivery guys from Entwhistle Fine Arts," Gerard ad-libbed.

The doctor and the woman looked at each other, and then at me. I took a breath, as if I had something else to say, but I didn't, and the doctor seemed to sense then that things were not what they seemed. His face turned hard in the way of people with money or power when they are afraid. Another second and he would have thrown us off the property, or taken out his cell phone and called the Dover police, who would not have been kind to us. I saw it. Gerard saw it, too, and turned the painting around to face them. The woman studied the canvas, then bent her lips in between her teeth. She looked up at me, and then at the doctor.

"Who is it?"

"Janet Rossi," I said. "She has cystic fibrosis and maybe a week to live."

The woman moved her eyes back to the canvas. The doctor's hard gaze flicked across it for a second, and then came to rest on me. I knew I could have been wrong, but it seemed to me then that, if you could judge by the good doctor's expression at that moment, he was not a warm man. An exquisite mechanic, brave maybe; maybe as disciplined as the gods. Surely he had done more good for the world than a million people like me, but it was as if, in order to do what he did, he'd had to guard himself against the softening effects of sorrow and failure, against his own humanity, his own death. There's a certain price you pay for that, and I thought I could read that price in the hard line of his lips.

"How did you get this address?"

"I hired a private detective," I ad-libbed. "The hospital wouldn't give it out. All the hospital would say is that there is one chance for her—a living lobar transplant—and there is one surgeon in New England who can do the operation."

"She has *cepacia*?"

"Yes." I watched him. "As of yesterday afternoon she's tenth on the list for a cadaveric, she won't come close to living long enough to get one."

"I'm retired," he said. "Sorry."

"The only other surgeon who could do it is in New York. Janet won't survive a trip to New York." I looked at the woman, but if there was any well of sympathy in her, she wasn't letting me near the pump. She avoided my eyes, studied the painting for another little while, and then she said, "I'm going in to shower, Leski. It's nice, though, isn't it?" He nodded. She did not look at us, and walked up the path and up the stairs and through the front door.

"I know you're retired. And I know there'll always be one more and one more you could do, but this woman has been fighting her whole life. From about the age of six weeks she's been through things that most people—"

"I know the disease, thank you."

"I know you know it, but—"

"You two are the potential donors, I suppose."

Gerard said, "Yes."

"Blood relatives?"

"Friends. A fiancé and a friend."

"You're the fiancé?"

"Yes," I said. "It's my painting. I paint. I'm a painter. We want to have children. Adopt. Look, I'm sorry we came to your house. We're not criminals and we're not crazy, and you can keep the painting either way, yes or no, because of what you've done for other . . . you know . . . I swear to God you'll never see either of us again."

He just watched me from beneath the dark wool hat, blue eyes close-set beside a sharp nose. He said, "The procedure ties up three operating rooms, three teams of surgeons at two different hospitals. It puts at risk the lives of two healthy individuals. It costs between a quarter of a million and a million dollars, not counting the follow-up care. She'll have to take antirejection drugs for the rest of her life and the potential side effects from those drugs are manifold—renal failure, tremors, bruising, digestive troubles, weight gain, bone loss, diabetes, risk of opportunistic infection."

"I know all that," I said.

"And I suppose you also know the survival rate for *cepacia* patients?"

"Forty percent are alive after two years," Gerard said. "But the data sample is small."

"And do you know how fondly the insurance companies look upon those kind of numbers?"

"Your survival rates are better," Gerard said.

"How do you know?"

"I did some research."

I looked at Gerard then. Every drop of his usual abrasive and needy goofiness had disappeared. He was like a fact, standing there, a challenge incarnate. He wasn't blinking.

"Doctor Ouajiballah said he'd go to bat with the insurance company if you're the surgeon," I put in.

"Ouajiballah said that?"

"Gave me his word."

"Gave you this address, too, if I'm not mistaken?"

"Yes."

He smirked. His horse nickered. "No private detective, then?"

"No."

"Any other falsehoods involved here?"

"None. Except I'm Entwhistle Fine Arts."

He looked out past the horse to the expanse of frozen pasture. He should have been chilled by then, standing there in the cold air after a hard run, but there was an odd stillness about him. You couldn't imagine him being chilled, or afraid, or making a mistake, or admitting to having made a mistake. Exactly the kind of guy you wanted if you or someone you loved were about to be cut open. For probably a full thirty seconds he didn't speak to us or move, and then, without looking at us, he said, "I'll take the painting—my wife liked it—and I'll call you within twenty-four hours with an answer."

"Fine," I said, and he cut me off when I started to thank him.

"I will tell you I'm leaning toward no."

"Why?" Gerard said.

The doctor turned his head and sent Gerard a look that was lined with ugliness, and I could see the pride in his pale eyes as clearly as if it had slithered up his spine and out through the front of his pupils.

"Oops, sorry," Gerard said, not very sincerely. I saw something in my friend then, some old bad energy from the streets where he had been brought up. I did not know if the doctor could see it. "We're sure you have your reasons. Look, let me carry this into the house for you while Jake closes up the box and cleans up this mess. And then you'll never see either of us again unless you decide to cut us open."

"I wouldn't cut you open," the doctor said. "Someone else does that. I cut *her* open."

That's comforting, I almost said. In fact, I came within an absolute whisker of saying it, because I had just given away a painting that meant everything to me, and was going to get nothing in return, and because, by then, I felt I was in the presence of a thin slice of something almost hideous between two pieces of remarkable talent. Gerard felt it, too, I knew that. We had our own proud serpents pressing out through our eyeballs. I thought of Janet pursing her lips. I said, "Again, our apologies. I know we've intruded and I appreciate it that you're even willing to think it over. My mother was a doctor—Judith Entwhistle—and I know she would have been pissed as hell if the friends of a patient ever came driving up to her house asking for special care."

"I appreciate it, too," Gerard said, but there was a note of disgust in his voice. He was hoisting the painting over his head, just pressing in against the outside edges with the palms of his hands, not a fingerprint anywhere, showing off his upper-body strength. He walked up the path that way, two steps ahead of the good doctor.

I picked up the bubble wrap and plastic sheeting and jammed it into my homemade crate. Threw in two of the wing nuts and bolts and twisted the other two in place. I sat in the truck with the heater on and looked at the horse in the pasture—creature of incredible grace. I had a few sketches of her at home, photographs. I could try to make another painting, though there is a difference, painting someone who is right there in front of you, alive.

Gerard stayed inside the mansion for eight or ten minutes—giving detailed hanging instructions, I guessed. At last, I heard his boots on the gravel, then the passenger door closing. I put the truck in gear and we rattled down the long driveway, onto Madison Road, back in the direction we had come, past the library, past mansion row, and then down into the upper class.

"I see sufficient reason for hope, Colonel," he said.

"Not a prayer."

"I worked him a little."

"Tell me you didn't talk to him about Giselle."

Gerard shook his head. He never mentioned Giselle's name, under any circumstances. "I complimented his horse," he said. "You should have seen his eyes light up. Then I made my face ugly—you know how I do, you know how much work it takes—and I asked him if he remembered that fabulous scene from *The Godfather,* Part One. The horse's bloody head under the sheets. His wife was watching, fresh from her shower. I said it in a happy voice, my crazy happy voice. I made my eyes just the tiniest bit crazy, like it was just a little goofy joke."

"Thanks," I said.

"No problem."

"We'll end up in jail."

WHEN WE WERE BACK in the busyness of downtown Boston, Gerard turned serious, which happens to him about once every lunar cycle. I always know when this turning-serious is coming because he has a certain way of tapping his left work boot in a slow, steady rhythm. These are the kinds of things you learn about people when you build houses with them for a lot of years, smash fingers with them, drop $650 replacement windows when they are holding the other side, find some ingenious way of making up for an architect's oversight after you've spent an hour cursing, put in a very hard week of hammering and then go out someplace and have a cranberry juice with a twist of lime and tell lame jokes.

"You know," he said, in what I think of as his "normal" voice, "I like what we do pretty well, I enjoy it. But I think if I ever come into a lot of money someday—I don't know how that could ever happen; maybe we'll buy an old triple-decker some-place and fix it up and sell it for a huge profit—then what I want to do is open a nightclub for crippled and deformed people. A place where they can go and dance and listen to music and have a drink and not worry about anyone looking at them, you know? I've had this dream since college. Handsome people, pretty people, people who can walk right—we wouldn't let them in the door. Just men and women in wheelchairs, legless people, spastics, hunch-backs. I mean it. That's my real dream, if you want to know."

"It's a good dream," I said. We drove a little ways. I thought about his dream. I said, "You don't have your girls this weekend, am I right?"

"The colonel is correct."

6

THAT AFTERNOON I called my apartment from the job site every half hour. Gerard and I were within about one full workday of finishing Jacqueline's addition, and when she came home from her afternoon class and saw how close we were, she went floating through the rooms with her arms held out like the wings of a gliding falcon. It was our turn to watch and smile. She stood at different windows, she paced off part of the sunny second-floor room where her bed would be, opening and closing a beautiful little cherry cabinet Gerard had fashioned for a corner of her new bathroom. It had been a nice project. Besides building the two stories of new rooms, we'd sort of reached into the adjacent part of the old structure and cleaned up some of the messy work there from a hundred years ago—taken out old rough-sawn, weird-dimension studs and bulging lath and plaster and replaced them with new spruce two-by-fours and Sheetrock, leveled the old floors in two rooms so they matched up evenly with the new ones, improved the insulation in the part of the wall cavity we could get to. Everything had come out smoothly, almost perfectly. But I had the cold understanding then, watching her enjoy our work, that I would always think of Janet when I drove past this place.

That afternoon I hung two interior doors and put the lock-set assemblies in—I remember it very well. Hanging doors is not a simple job, the tolerances are small. My mind would stay on the work in my hands for a few seconds at a time, then swing away. I had to take one of the doors down and put it back up again four times before I got it right. Gerard did not make one joke.

When I came home at the end of the day, there was one message on the machine—Jeremy Stearns, who owned the gallery where I showed my paintings. He did not know anything about Janet. He was calling to tell me that he was using one of my paintings in a half-page ad in *Art in America,* something he'd been promising he'd do for the past two and a half years. When I called him back, I tried to sound pleased.

I showered and changed and drove across town to the hospital. Janet lay on her side, raking in one shallow breath after another, occasionally lifting the oxygen mask to ask for water, for help turning onto her other side, or for her mother or me to hold the metal pan up to her mouth so she could spit. I wanted in a terrible way to tell her about our trip to Dover. Every now and then she would make eye contact with me or with her mother and it tore through me and I kept wrestling with myself about whether it was better or worse to give her hope. I pictured myself telling her, and then Vaskis saying no, and then having to tell her he had said no, or having to tell her he'd said yes but we couldn't find a second donor.

On the way home, I thought I should have done it, though, at least should have let her know we were trying everything we could try, that there was still some last little glimmer.

At a specialty shop on Harvard Avenue, I bought a bottle of white Argiolas and some bread and cheese and two Granny Smith apples. I went home and made up a plate and poured a glass and sat in the kitchen, not eating and not drinking, looking at the telephone. Gerard had promised not to call. Janet's mother wouldn't call unless it was an emergency. I took a sip of wine, carried the glass with me into the painting room, and sat on the sofa there. I got back up and paced, drank a little bit, put the food away when it was clear I wasn't going to be eating any of it. I looked out different windows, poured a little more wine. Hours passed this way. At quarter after midnight, because I knew I would not be able to sleep, and knew I couldn't paint, and knew it was too late for any good news, I wrote Ellory another note telling him what was going on, and when that was done I called my sister. She answered on the third ring.

"Lizbeth, it's Jake."

"Jake who?" she said, in a voice just absolutely dripping.

"Your brother."

"Mum alright?"

"She's the same. She asks for you every time I see her."

Lizbeth paused. I thought she might be turning down her TV or something, or talking to a client, and then she said, "Here comes the guilt trip, sailing across the sand-shit desert. Mum asking for me. You visiting, me not visiting. Same old sand-shit, snake-talk Jakie."

"I didn't mean it that way."

"Some of us have the money to fly, you know, and some of us just don't."

"I didn't mean it that way, really."

"Right. My good-boy, snake-talk brother."

"Look, if you want to come back to see her, I'll send you a ticket."

"Send me the money and let me buy my own ticket. I can get a deal here. I have friends who work in the airlines."

"I'll send a ticket tomorrow if you want. I'm not sending money."

As soon as those last four words were out of my mouth, my sister started to yell, a quick crescendo about how nothing mattered to me but money, and how all I thought about was money, and how she was sick and tired of being the only daughter and being treated like a baby because of that, and how hard she worked, and how easy I'd always had it, and just on and on and on. The four words had been a mortar round, and the mortar round had blasted a hole in the wall of a dam, and now a whole lake of bitterness was pouring out.

"Lizbeth," I said, three or four times, but the bitterness drowned me out. It was not exactly a new experience for me. My sister had been systematically destroying herself for a decade by then, and over the course of that decade I had sent money, and self-help books, and humorous cards, and I'd made well-meaning suggestions, and talked to friends of mine who were therapists, and passed on their advice, and stayed up half the night worrying about her, and fielded unpleasant phone calls from bail bondsmen, bikers, bookmakers, and casino security types. None of it had changed the trajectory of her fiery downward arc by so much as a fraction of a degree.

I knew, once she started using the word "coward," that we were close to the end, so I did my best then to try to listen beyond the words and not have bad thoughts toward her. I tried to match the notes in her voice to the notes that had been there when she was a young girl, a happy soul, joy to be around. It didn't work.

"You're a *coward* and you've always been a *coward* and you call up like the *coward* you are and you should be *ashamed* of yourself for the way you treat me . . ."

And so on for another minute or two, top volume, before she slammed the telephone down in her sad little apartment in Reno, and the dial tone droned across the lower forty-eight.

I turned out the lights and lay in bed, looking at the shapes the shadows made against the wash of street light on the ceiling, listening to the muted sounds—car engines, horns, conga drums from downstairs. There was no real possibility of going to sleep, I knew that, but I held out some hope for twenty minutes or so, and then sat up and swung my legs over the edge of the bed, thinking I would go to Betty's for a doughnut and some company, or go back to the hospital. The phone rang. I let it ring twice. Sometimes, if Lizbeth was high enough or angry enough, she would decide after stewing for a while that *I* had hung up on *her* and she'd call back with more shouting. At which point I usually pulled the phone cord out of the wall.

I answered on the third ring and heard an unfamiliar woman's voice saying my name. The bedside clock read 12:56. I thought it was the hospital calling. I was already moving toward my shoes. But the woman said: "I'm Louise. Doctor Vaskis's wife. Calling unconscionably late. He says he'll do it Monday morning if you and your friend pass all the tests you have to pass. He said to tell you he'll call the other doctor, what was his name—"

"Ouajiballah."

"Yes. He'll call him in the morning."

"What's today?" I said.

She laughed a carefree laugh. "As of about fifty minutes ago, Friday."

"Tell him for me that . . . tell him I can't find the words to thank him."

"I softened him up," she said. "So you can thank me, too. He didn't really want to retire, you know. He's been a little bit grumpy since he decided to. That was his whole life, saving people. It's not something you just give up."

"No . . . I imagine . . . Thank you. Thanks . . . I—"

"Plus, I think he thought your friend kind of threatened him."

"My friend would never do that."

"Well, there was something peculiar in the air. We both felt it. He's not an ex-convict, is he?"

"Yes, he is, actually," I said, "but he has a good heart."

I turned the conversation away from Gerard's warm heart and imaginary prison time, and rambled on, telling her to thank Doctor Vaskis again, that he was a genius, a good man, that I'd never forget him until the moment I died. When we said good-bye, I called the ex-convict and he answered the phone this way: "Your call is important to us. You'll never know how important. All our customer service associates are temporarily busy at the moment right now servicing other customers, but your call is so important to us that—"

"Vaskis said yes."

"Outstanding work!" Gerard yelled into the phone. And then: "How much time do we have to find donor number two? Behind donor number two, is—"

"Probably a day. To allow time enough for the testing."

"Donor number two likes sports, pretty women, and hospital beds!"

"Right."

"We'll cast a wide net," he said, and hung up. Which made me realize he'd had a woman there with him the whole time.

7

THE ENORMOUS DOSES of ceftazidime and gentamicin did not clear up the trouble in Janet's right lung, and overnight she had begun a slow, steady slide the doctors could not stop. That morning, when I went in to bring her the good news, she was lying on her back, propped up at a forty-five-degree angle, able to keep her eyes open for only a few seconds at a time. The oxygen machine was humming and bubbling. Antibiotics were dripping into her right arm, and some kind of liquid nourishment—she could no longer eat—into her left. The hospital gown hung from her shoulders and over her breasts as if it had been draped across sharp stones to dry, and her face, so gaunt just the day before, had started to swell. The nurses had washed her hair and tied it on top of her head in a bun, but there was no life left to it. When I came through the door, her eyes, half-closed, went to me immediately and clung to me, and I could see everything there—the pain and unbroken discomfort, the fear, the resignation, the love. She smiled with just the corners of her lips, but the pain cut her smile off almost immediately.

I leaned over the bed and rested my hand gently on her chest—she liked me to do that—and kissed her on the forehead and both closed eyes. Her mother had spent the night, and was asleep on a cot against one wall, quietly snoring. For a little while I sat with them. I'd rub Janet's arm, adjust her pillow, put water on the tip of my finger and touch it to her lips. What I'd liked was that, after the first few dates, we hadn't had to talk about certain things and could just rest in some deep agreement about the way to be in the world. We thought it was right to leave lavish tips at restaurants, to let people cut in line in traffic, to make fun of arrogance and of ourselves, to be goofy and affectionate with children, to do our work well, to be unembarrassed about our bodies, to take what we really needed and then give and give, to fight honestly and without waiting and without being ugly about it. That was a sort of foundation we hadn't even had to try to set in place, and it was solid and level, which would have made building something nice and longer-lasting on top of it just a matter of keeping mistakes small and catching them quickly.

So, after a while, there were whole areas we didn't have to talk about—Valvoline, Giselle, why I painted and banged nails instead of going back to med school, why she wanted to keep working, even though, at the end, it drained away strength she could have used to fight her illness. We did not need to say how we felt about each other. We did not think we needed to.

But that morning, sitting with her, watching the last fibers of her spirit stretch and break one by one, I was sick with the understanding that I should have put certain things into words. I could stay close and rub her arm and wipe her mouth, but I had left something important undone, I knew that. Sometimes there has to be something concrete to anchor the unspoken feelings. Two nurses came in and helped her pee into a bedpan, changed her underwear, checked the monitor. They could barely look at me.

When they were gone I leaned my mouth down to Janet's ear and I said, "I know you want to just go. It's alright. But there's one more thing we can try if you want to try it."

She turned her head half an inch.

Doctor Ouajiballah came through the door then, stopped when he saw us, and went back out.

"If two people give you a section of their lung, a lobe each, then you can get a transplant that way."

She held her eyes half open. I could see her balancing between two worlds. I could see that she could decide then to turn her back on the beast of hope once and for all and close her eyes and die. And I would never have blamed her for that, because she had had a weight put on her shoulders when she came out of her mother's body, and she had been made to walk with that weight on her for almost thirty years, and she was just tired of carrying it then, at that moment, tired to the root of her soul.

Her mother stirred and sat up on the edge of the cot.

"I can do it," I said, talking quietly into Janet's ear. "Gerard has the wrong blood type or he'd do it. My brother smokes or he'd do it. We have the surgeon. *Il dottore* will recommend it to the insurance company and the surgeon is so good he thinks they'll go for it. If you say okay, I'll find another person somehow. You'd have to stay alive until Monday morning. It's Friday today. If you want to try it squeeze my hand once, alright?"

I could barely look at her. She did not move or try to speak.

"Squeeze if you want to try," I repeated after a few seconds.

Though the clear plastic tube from the oxygen machine was in the way, I lay my face in the pillow, against her neck, the way I'd done sometimes when we were making love. I held her fingers loosely. I heard her mother get up and shuffle along the linoleum, then the sound of the hinges on the bathroom door. I could feel Janet breathing—five breaths to my one. I wanted then to let her be completely, absolutely free. I did not want to hold her on this earth. I did not want her to suffer one second more because of what I wanted, or what her mother wanted, or what the doctors or nurses thought was right.

When the toilet flushed and we heard her mother wrestling with the door handle, Janet tightened her grip on my fingers.

I kissed her so hard on the side of her face that the oxygen tube came loose. When Amelia shuffled up to the bed, Janet was crying, so she started crying, too, in solidarity. Janet moved my hand this way and that, and I bent down so that my ear was near her mouth and, in a whisper, she said, "Valvoline." Then Ouajiballah came into the room, our white-coated pal with a pen in his pocket. And I was, as Gerard would say, all over that.

8

IN THE HALL, out of range of Mrs. Rossi's hearing, Doctor Ouajiballah told me Janet might not live until Monday morning, but that he was going to recommend her for the living lobar transplant in any case, as soon as he could get a certain person from the insurance company to return his call. Doctor Vaskis had already contacted him. Ouajiballah thought that, when the certain person at the insurance company heard the name Vaskis, they would agree to pay for the operation, and would hold to their agreement as long as Janet was alive and not on life support. If she went on life support she would never come off it, and the insurance company would back away. "So then, sir, you and your friend can start the donor testing tomorrow at seven a.m. It will take as long as two full days. You should find at least one backup donor if you possibly can, because even people in good health have been known to fail these tests. They are quite rigorous."

I had to look away from him then, as I thanked him.

I called Gerard from the pay phone in the lobby and told him to call every man and woman he knew over five-foot ten inches tall and get as many O-positive nonsmokers as he could to show up at the hospital on Saturday morning at seven, people willing to spend two days being tested, then have themselves cut open, lose three or four weeks of sick time, and twenty percent of their lung capacity for life.

"We'll need a bus to get them all there," Gerard said. "We'll need a motor scooter."

"Try anyway."

"All over it, Colonel," he said.

My mind, when I hung up, went shooting off in eleven directions. I was holding the black plastic receiver in my left hand, with two fingers pressing down on the metal tongue that killed the dial tone, while the right hand fished around in my pocket for another couple of quarters, and I was trying to remember a phone number, cursing myself for getting rid of my cell phone, starting to imagine what would happen if we didn't find a second donor, knowing that, at some point very soon, I would have to tell *il dottore* the truth. And I was worried about Janet right then at that moment, and I ended up fishing out a quarter, then a dime, then another dime, and placing them carefully on the top of the black metal phone box, and then switching hands and trying the left pocket, where there were three pennies and some sawdust.

I hung up the phone and hurried across the lobby toward the gift shop, forgetting my neatly lined-up change (which Gerard's daughter Alicia used to call "monies"). Halfway to the gift shop in search of more monies I had a moment when my mind cleared and I understood something I should have understood before: Janet had been hired and promoted partly because she had some kind of intuitive understanding of how people behaved under particular circumstances, what motivated them, what drove them, where their fears and needs overlapped. That was her special talent, that was the way her mind worked . . . even two steps away from death. I changed course in mid-stride, headed for the stairwell, and sprinted up the four floors. Janet had not moved. Her mother sat by the bed, sleepily pushing the beads through her fingers. A nurse was there, switching the IV bag.

"Amelia, I need Janet's purse," I said, and I was breathing pretty hard and might have said it too loudly. "Where'd she leave it?"

Janet's mother pointed to the peach-colored metal cabinet next to her and shifted her chair over so I could open the drawer. "I have money if you want it," she said. The nurse gave me a look.

I rifled the purse, found the phone, and went out of the room without saying anything. I went down the hall to the bathroom and closed the door. It seemed to take about thirteen minutes for the phone to power up, and then another ten minutes for me to scroll down through her saved numbers until I reached the one I wanted. I went past it twice because I was looking for GOVERNOR.

When I finally figured things out, I highlighted CHARLIE, punched the call button, and sat on the toilet. Five rings and the man himself answered. "Nettie?" he said, and there was such a chord of boyish vulnerability in his voice that I winced. I closed my eyes, and leaned my head down so that my palm was wrapped around my forehead and I could focus on getting the words exactly right and not on anything else. "Janet has three or four days to live," I said, as calmly as I could.

"Who is this?"

"This is John Entwhistle, the guy who wrestled with you in Janet's office a couple months ago. Don't hang up. She's just about ready to die. A few minutes ago she asked me to come and see you and give you a message. I need two minutes of your time. It has to be today and it has to be face-to-face . . . I don't even want it, Janet wants it."

"Let her call me herself, then."

"She's the next thing to comatose, Charlie. I'm at the Mass General right now. I can be in your office in six minutes. I'll give you her message and I'll leave."

"I have an appointment with the head of Ways and Means in sixty seconds, and I'm solidly booked for the rest of the day. Say what you have to say."

"I have to say it to you in person, that's what she asked me to do."

He put his hand over the receiver. I kept my eyes closed and focused on him, on his heart, on his insides. I pretended to myself that I had some control over what went on there, though at that moment I understood very clearly that I had control over nothing. It was a hunch, that's all, an intuition that I should talk to him face-to-face. My legs were trembling from the kneecaps down, which was something that used to happen to me right before big crew races.

"I'll give you two minutes at ten past five," the governor said. "And if this is some sort of a trick, I'll have you arrested."

"Fine. Ten past five. I'll be—"

He hung up. I put the phone in my shirt pocket and splashed cold water on my face at the sink. I went and spent the rest of the day in Janet's room, but she did not wake up except when the nurses came and moved her around, or when she coughed so hard she had to spit. I tried to take Amelia down to the cafeteria for lunch, but she wouldn't move from her daughter's bedside, and wouldn't stop praying, so I stayed there, too, pacing the room, rubbing Janet's feet, watching her breathe, going into the hall every little while to get away from it.

In late afternoon I kissed Amelia on the forehead, and Janet on the eyes, and I put on my coat and went out and crossed Storrow Drive on the pedestrian bridge and walked to the river. Four o'clock on one of the shortest days of the year, and the sun had already gone behind the low hills to the west of the city. To

the left of where I stood, the sky was colored in winter pastels—
robin's-egg blue, a smoky scarlet, streaks of willowy yellow—all
of it swinging and splashing in a broken-up reflection in the deep
river basin just in front of me. Every few seconds a little more of
the color would leak out of the sky, and the water would take on
more purple, blue, and black. The wind was dying—as it did
sometimes at that time of year—just as the sun went down. It
would gust up and then calm a bit, then gust up again and calm
entirely. In the quiet between gusts you could feel the steady cold
night coming on, then there would be another, weaker gust, as if
darkness were blowing in over the city in diminishing pulses.

I don't know why I had wanted to go to the river, or why I
was thinking so much about rowing then. Maybe it was because
I'd had some times on that water when I had pushed myself so far
into the precinct of pain and shortness of breath that it almost had
no power over me anymore. A whole boatload of us had done
that, day after day, year after year, for reasons we couldn't really
understand or explain. We'd be all lined up and ready to go at the
starting line, a cool river wind blowing across the skin of our arms
and legs, hearts going, hands sweaty. The coxswain would be
telling the bow man or the number two man to just touch the
water with his oar to keep us from drifting off line. The race was
going to start in five seconds or ten seconds and then everything
would be happening at such a rate of speed that it would not be
possible to think, not be possible to do anything but react the way
we had been trained to react. If the referee waited too long to yell
out "Ready!" through his megaphone, my lower legs would start
to shake, and there was nothing I could do to stop it. "Ready all!"
he would say next. And then "Row!" and all hell would break
loose, the oarlocks clacking and the seats ripping along their

tracks, and the cold river water in your eyes and face. A minute and a half into the race your muscles would reach a point where you couldn't get oxygen to them fast enough no matter how you breathed, no matter what kind of condition you were in, and from that point until the end it would be pure focus, pure willpower, pure pain.

Our friends were smoking dope and getting laid and taking naps, and we were making our bodies hurt. Crazy thing for a college kid to do. But sometimes, doing that, you felt as though you'd gone across some line into a territory where you could will yourself to do anything, anything at all. The spring races lasted only six minutes, but if it was a longer practice piece—ten minutes, thirty minutes—the pain would creep up slowly inside you and reach you on another level. The will and the force and the strength in you and all the hard conditioning scraped up against something impossibly large and brutal, and you would remember that feeling long after you were done rowing hard for the day and were climbing out onto the dock. You'd remember it after you had showered and changed into street clothes and were walking across the BU Bridge to your supper. You'd be very small, but it was a magnificent smallness.

I sat beside the river for an hour, until my body started to shake from the cold, and then I walked back to my truck and drove to the State House with the heat on high. I couldn't get warm. I parked in Janet's spot. I went in past the first security check, and climbed the three flights of stairs to the governor's suite of offices, where there was a state policeman I'd never had any trouble with.

When I was past him, too, and had entered the high-ceilinged suite of rooms that surround the governor's office, the secretary saw me. She reached for the telephone. I put my hands up in a gesture of peace. I said, "Janet has a few days to live. She wants me to say one thing to the governor. I already called him, he already knows." She took her hand off the phone and glared at me. While she was glaring, the door behind her opened and the president of the senate stepped out of the corner office and walked by me, winking as if he'd just done me a favor. Then the man himself appeared.

"I'm not afraid of you," was the first thing out of his mouth.

"Good," I said.

"Janet's dying," the secretary told him, and he looked away from her and away from me and stared, tight-lipped, through one of the tall windows that faced out over Boston Common. I could have been wrong, but it seemed to me then that there was the smallest glint of satisfaction in his eyes, as if Janet's troubles were a kind of punishment that had come from not loving him, or not sleeping with him again. At that moment I hated him, there is no other word. He had done some good things from that office, but it seemed to me then that in order to run for an office like that, you had to have an ego, or a need, the size of a Macy's Thanksgiving Day float. It had to be festooned with all sorts of fine ideas about public service, with good deeds, pretty phrases, clean suits. But it had to be there; it had to be the motor and the wheels. It had to want authority and praise, that great sweet surge that comes from knowing a million people had pulled the lever beside your name. I don't know what creates an appetite like that in a person, but I saw it in him then, through the filter of my hatred, and I realized I was counting on it being there, under the neat hairdo and the clean cheeks and the excellent posture.

I tried to imagine I was speaking directly to that need and not to him. "Two minutes and you'll never see me again," I said.

The secretary was looking up at him like a puppy. For her benefit, perhaps, he struck the posture of an unafraid man, a big man. But what was hard for him was that, inside, he was tiny— not in the good way we'd felt after rowing hard, but in a frightened way, a sad, self-pitying, little-boy way—and he knew I knew it. He motioned me into the office with a sideways swing of his head.

Near his small desk was an oval conference table. He took his place at the head of it. There was a kind of steady pulse of power in the high-ceilinged room, with the portraits on the walls, the limp flags held up by spear-topped poles, the small couch and table with the pictures of his girls. I sat down across from him. He swiveled back and forth once and then looked at me over the tips of his fingers.

"Janet has three or four days to live," I said. "At the outside."

"I'm extremely pained to hear that. We sent cards, all of us. We call every day. We'd visit if we were allowed."

"She appreciates it. Her mother said to thank you. But she's tenth on the transplant list. She won't live to be ninth."

He kept his fingertips together, tapped them once. "If you've come here to ask me to put her at the top of the list, that's something I simply cannot do."

"I'm not asking that. The one thing that could save her life is something called a living lobar transplant. She needs two people to give up one lobe of a lung each. The donors have to be taller than five foot ten, nonsmokers, in good shape. We have one so far—"

"You?"

"Yes. We have probably the best transplant surgeon in the

country set to operate on her first thing Monday morning. Leicus Vaskis. The insurance is all approved."

"I know Vaskis," the governor said. He blinked twice. He lowered his forearms so that his hands hung down over the ends of the chair. He said, "And?"

"And Janet asked me to ask you to be the other donor."

He closed his eyes and let out a quiet, one-note laugh.

"No donor has ever died in surgery. You'll lose some of your lung capacity, but won't really notice it very much in the course of any ordinary day. You'll—"

"I have a state to run," he said.

I looked at him when he said that, really looked at him. I had an urge to go over to one of the windows and open it and throw all the chairs out, including the one he was sitting in. "You'd be out of commission three days," I said. "The lieutenant governor runs the state for longer than that when you're on vacation. You'd be in the hospital two weeks, tops."

"I understand that," he said. "And under different circumstances . . ." He fluttered one hand at the windows. "Under different circumstances I'd oblige you."

"It's not me you'd be obliging. It's her."

He looked out the window for a little while. I thought we were finished, but then he swung his head around so that he was facing me dead-on and spoke in a quiet, violent voice, all the politician stripped away so that, even in his suit and behind the big table he was not the governor then: "You couldn't begin to know what I felt for her. You couldn't begin to guess what was between us. I was going to marry her," he said, and it occurred to me then, in a hideous flash, that I was looking at myself in a terrible dream, talking to Brian, about Giselle. "I didn't care what it cost me, with my children or with anyone else. You couldn't begin to know what it was like to see her day after day after day and not touch her, not talk to her except about business, to feel her drifting away from me."

By then the trembling I'd had in my legs earlier, talking to him on the cell phone, had started again, and moved into my arms and hands. It occurred to me that maybe Janet had a residue of love for the governor, some secret feeling she hadn't wanted me to know about. In my mind I had been making him out to be pure ego. Naturally, it was my own ego, my own anger, my own jealousy, my own smallness, that had been doing that.

I said, "She asked me to ask you if you'd do it. She could barely speak. She said your name."

He slammed one fist down on the wood. "I have a *state* to run!" he yelled.

I said, "Fine."

His face was shaking. Jealousy funhouse mirrors.

I said, "I asked you to give me two minutes and that's about two minutes. My name is John Entwhistle. In case you change your mind, I'm in the phone book in Boston. Or you could just be at the Mass General Hospital pulmonary lab at seven o'clock tomorrow morning. For testing, you know."

I stood up. He was breathing hard. I thought, for one second, that if I made the wrong kind of move or said the wrong kind of thing, he was going to charge at me, and we were going to end up wrestling around on the floor again. I wanted him to do that. I waited two seconds, hoping, then I made a quick turn toward the door, so quick I accidentally bumped my thigh on the arm of the chair. And then I turned back to him and said, with almost no bitterness, "I'll tell Janet you sent your best. I'll tell her you said you'll be praying for her."

The governor did not stand up.

At the door I turned around again. "I was envisioning the headlines, though, you know? GOVERNOR DONATES PART OF LUNG. SAVES STAFFER'S LIFE. A person could go a long way on publicity like that."

He looked as if he would spit. I closed the door quietly, smiled a trembling crazy smile at the secretary, and went down the blurred sets of stairs and out into the cold blackness. I walked and walked along Beacon Street. At some point I stopped on a corner, took Janet's phone out of my pocket, and called my apartment like a robot—no messages—and then Gerard—no volunteers.

Eventually, I went back to the hospital. But I couldn't bring myself to go up to Janet's room, so I sat in the cafeteria sipping bad coffee and watching the nurses and doctors and orderlies on their breaks. I went and sat in the dimly lit chapel on the first floor, a perfectly nondenominational, quasi-religious place with pews and stained glass. I put my face in my hands. For a long time after Giselle died I had been angry at God, and at a lot of other things. And then one day it occurred to me that it was anger that had killed her and everyone else who'd died on that day, and I started trying to imagine my way backwards in time to where that anger had come from, a crazy-making, evil, righteous anger. And then I started to notice, firsthand, that anger was almost always righteous and crazy-making. All you had to do was turn on the radio talk shows and you could hear that plainly enough, hear the pot being stirred and heated. All you had to do was yell at somebody in traffic and you could see it in yourself. Anger began to seem wrong to me, almost always wrong, and I began to think it might be my problem, not God's. So I talked to Ellory about it. Ellory said, "You always have a choice," which made sense, and was helpful.

I tried not to be angry. I tried to pray.

Maker of cells, I said. That amount of suffering has to count for something. I'm not trying to tell you what to do or how things should be set up. I just believe that that amount of suffering has to count for something, I just believe that. It can't be just random. If it's just random, and people suffer like that, then count me out, I don't want another second of this. I'm going to go and jump—

Someone in one of the other pews was weeping quietly. I stopped trying to pray and just sat there for a while, then I left the chapel and took the elevator upstairs, where the nurses all knew me, and knew what was happening to Janet. One nurse in partic-ular—a very large, very dark-faced woman named Bethany—was such a kind, sweet soul, and cared for Janet so tenderly and patiently, that I had an urge to ask her, as I walked past, who she prayed to, how she put the words together.

I went into Janet's room, all set to lie to her and tell her Valvoline was considering it—when I knew he wasn't. But she was sleeping, her face turned sideways on the pillow, her mother asleep, too, in the chair beside the bed. Amelia woke up and lifted her tired eyes to me, all the hope in the world there.

"No news yet," I said. "Gerard's calling everyone we know."

"My sister is, too."

"We'll find somebody, don't worry."

Doctor Ouajiballah came by on his last rounds and checked the digital readouts on the various machines near Janet's bed. Pulse. Blood pressure. Oxygen level. Janet's mother gazed at him as if he'd been holding out on us, and was now going to raise her daughter up with a sweep of his hand. But he had nothing to say to Janet's mother.

I followed him out into the hall, and when he started to tell

me what to expect in the way of testing the next day, I tried to listen carefully but couldn't.

"There's a problem," I said, when he finished. "Right now
we have only one donor."

"What do you mean, sir?" Something like a smile wavered
along his thin lips. He was looking for a punch line, and when
none was forthcoming he said, "You told Doctor Vaskis you had
two donors, sir."

"I had to tell him that to get him to do it. I lied. We have
one. We're working on getting the second."

I watched the kindness on his face just evaporate.

"You lied, sir?" he said.

I nodded.

"To Doctor Vaskis and to me."

"Yes."

"And you had me call the insurance bastards and tell them
we had two donors to test, when we do not. The same bastards I
will have to call again, on someone else's behalf, in a week or a
month or a year, and ask them to underwrite a quarter-million-
dollar operation, or a lifetime of medication, based on my judg-
ment and integrity."

"I'm sorry," I said.

"You had me call the pulmonary testing lab and ask them
to put you ahead of people who already had appointments?"

"Give me one day. We'll find somebody, I'm sure we will.
Just one day. I'm sorry."

But I was only partly sorry, and he knew it. He spun
around and went striding down the hall past the nurses' station. I
went back into the room.

Janet stirred often, and coughed, and moaned loudly from

time to time. Every ten minutes I called my apartment for messages, but there was only something from a prospective customer who wanted us to bid on her apartment-house renovation, and from a painter we sometimes used, looking for indoor work, and something else from Jeremy at the gallery. It was not easy to be there with Amelia. Every time I hung up she was watching my face for the smallest twitch or sparkle of news. Every time I shook my head—nothing—it felt like I was sawing off one of her limbs. Worse, I could see that the thought of Janet dying had brought back the pain of the other big death in her past, and the same thing was happening to me. Giselle was haunting me then, not a lover but a sister, a cousin, a ghost.

Eventually, Amelia told me she had to eat something, she'd be gone twenty minutes, and would I be sure to have her paged if Janet woke up, or if something changed?

By that time I was so twisted up by the ghosts and the echoes and the pure misery of everything that I pulled my chair close to the bed and just lay my face down on the sheet over Janet's thigh, not thinking anything or hoping for anything. When Amelia came back upstairs with her sandwich in a Styrofoam box, she found me that way, and came and put her hand on my back.

Janet's aunt Lucy arrived after supper. I used that as an excuse to leave. I drove my truck around Boston for an hour, in the Friday night traffic, under a kind of evil spell. When I couldn't do that anymore, I stopped at Adam's Steak House, where Janet and I had gone a few times, and tried to eat my way into oblivion. A sixteen-ounce sirloin, two glasses of Cabernet, salad, potato, two pieces of pecan pie, coffee. I had done the same kind of thing the day after Giselle died, though I didn't remember that until I was sitting there with an aching stomach.

My stomach still hurt by the time I got home. The phone was ringing when I came through the door, but when I picked up, there was only a dial tone. I called Gerard, thinking it might have been him, and for once he answered by saying, "Hello?"

"Anything?"

"Jake, I'm going up to complete strangers and asking them to volunteer for major surgery on the Monday before Christmas."

"I forgot Christmas. What about friends?"

"Julie, Alex, Bob Twining—O-negative, a closet smoker, and a sympathetic-but-no, in that order."

"Did you call Coach Florent? I should have called him."

"Sympathetic, sort of, but no. And no, you shouldn't have called him. How's Janet?"

"Lousy. I told Ouajiballah we lied. He's not happy."

"We had no other option."

"He doesn't see it that way."

"What about the gov?"

"He has a state to run."

"A state to run? That's what he said? A state to run?"

"Under other circumstances he'd oblige me."

"What about Janet's family?"

"They're all too short, and the ones that aren't too short have asthma. Her aunt is still trying, though. Neighbors, friends of neighbors, cousins of cousins."

"Alright, I've got one fireman at the precinct here who was wavering a little. I'm going down to harass him. You have to get up early for the testing, yes?"

"Six."

"Good. I'll call you after midnight, then."

I put the phone in its cradle, lay back in the bed, and fell almost immediately into a deep sleep, with one spark of vivid dream in it. In the dream I was in a jewelry shop where I had once bought sapphire earrings for Giselle for her birthday, only Carmine Asalapolous was behind the counter, lifting out one beautiful ring after the next, and setting them in a neat row on the glass countertop. "Wait three days and give her this one," he said. I was struggling to tell him I couldn't wait three days, trying to find the words, trying to get the urgency of things across to him, when the telephone woke me. I rolled over to the edge of the bed and grabbed it.

"This John Entwhistle?" the voice said.

I squeezed my eyes tight and shook my head hard. "Yes."

"Governor Valvelsais. Listen, I've given it some thought and I've decided to give a lung to Janet."

I held the phone against my face.

"Are you there?"

"Here."

"Well, say something, then."

I said, "A . . . a lobe . . . you only have to give one lobe. Your right lung has three lobes and your left—."

"I'm stepping up," he said.

I was squeezing the phone hard.

"Where do I report?" he said.

"Pulmonary testing. Mass General. Seven o'clock tomorrow morning."

"I'll be there at eight."

"Good," I said, awake by then, clearheaded as could be. "You're . . . you're a good man."

"Coming from you that means so much," he said.

"Right."

"There's a condition."

He paused. A list of conditions ran through my head. He wanted Janet back. He wanted me to leave town.

He said, "When people ask, you say I volunteered without a moment's hesitation."

I could not speak.

"Clear?"

"Fine."

"That's the phrase: 'without a moment's hesitation.'"

"Got it," I said.

"I want your word."

"You have it."

"Then I'm stepping forward for her. Tomorrow, eight a.m."

"Mass General," I said, but he had hung up.

I called and left a message for Doctor Ouajiballah, and at the nurses' desk for Janet's mother. I called Gerard. I lay back on the bed in the darkness and did not go to sleep.

9

WHEN I ARRIVED there at quarter past six the next morning, the beautiful beast of hope was prowling the hospital corridors. I could see it in Amelia's sleepy face as we stood outside Janet's room, and hear it in her voice. She said that Janet was out cold then, had been awake for two hours in the middle of the night, coughing up blood, that she'd told her then about the governor's decision, and that Janet had smiled a smile to break your heart in five pieces.

"What a fine fine man he must be," Amelia said.

At the nurses' station, and at the reception desk of the pulmonary testing department, it was the same: the nurses, orderlies, and technicians knew Janet's story, knew what she'd been through. Some of them had watched for years as the bacteria with the big names did their work on her. They knew exactly what was happening, and what would happen—they'd seen the same slow sinking with a hundred other CF patients, and thousands of people with cancer and MS and ALS and diabetes and diseases they had no name for. They were lined up like foot soldiers against those diseases. All their working lives went into that war, all their tiredness and tedium. They had the smartest generals in the world and the most sophisticated weaponry, and their weeks were filled with one lost battle after the next.

So when they understood that there was a chance to save

someone they cared for, that was not a small thing to them. You could see it plainly on their faces: it was not a routine Saturday morning.

The governor and I spent all that day getting blood drawn, and more blood drawn, breathing hard into sterile tubes, peeing into sterile cups, answering questions, filling out forms. Sometimes we were in the same room; usually we weren't. We did not exchange a word. Our eyes met once when he was on a machine, blowing every last molecule of air from his lungs. He looked away immediately and blew harder, as if it were a competition, and our pulmonary function numbers would be published on the front page of the *Herald* the next day.

Fine, I thought. Knock yourself out. Break every lung record known to man, as long as you don't back away from this.

At the end of that day I went up and sat with Janet and her mother for a little while, and talked with her aunt in the hallway for a little while, and talked with Doctor Ouajiballah, who seemed to have forgiven me. Then I drove—tired by then—to the fancy mall in Chestnut Hill and found the jewelry store just before it closed, and bought a simple gold ring with little pairs of triangular notches at its edges from a salesman whose name was Dimitrios Cassas.

On Sunday, it was more of the same. Only, in the afternoon the fun was capped off with two hours in a room talking to a mustachioed psychiatrist, who worked, I guessed, not for the hospital but for the insurance company. "You are aware that you are putting your life at risk," he said.

I said that I was.

"You understand that, even if the surgery goes perfectly, you'll have a period of painful recovery."

"Yes."

"And you understand that, even if the recipient survives the surgery, she may live only a day or a month or a few months if her body should reject the new tissue."

"I understand that very well."

He went along like that for a while, giving me horror stories about transplant operations gone bad, infections, collapsed lungs, bleeding, suffocation, rejection. He showed me pictures of men and women with drainage tubes sticking out of their chests and frightened expressions on their faces, and when that was over, and I'd responded calmly and rationally to every question, he made good aggressive eye contact and he said, "Why are you doing this, Jake, really?"

And I could not help myself. I was tired from the testing, and worried because Janet had looked like a skin-draped skeleton in the bed that morning, and because more blood had come out of her overnight, and we hadn't been able to talk at all the day before. I was pretty sure the governor wasn't being grilled this way. He had, in fact, made the front page of the *Herald* that Sunday morning: GOV GIVES TILL IT HURTS superimposed over a full-page photo of his face. There was a glowing article inside, complete with a quote from John Entwhistle, who said the governor had agreed "without a moment's hesitation." And I didn't care about that. I was a little bit nervous about the operation and the recovery, but not afraid. I didn't care about the drainage tubes, or about not being able to run as hard as I liked to run, and I didn't care about whether or not Doctor Ouajiballah liked me, or Amelia thought I was a decent boyfriend for her daughter. All of that had somehow boiled away. I was just tired then, and worried we were too late. The whole thing was taking on a cold realness that seemed to echo off every square inch of the plain walls and the chipped linoleum and the lab machines.

Against that realness, I heard the psychiatrist say, "Why are you doing this, Jake?"

And so I looked back at him very calmly, and I said, "Because I'm hoping to be president one day." And he blinked and closed his notebook and went off to tell whoever he had to tell that we were a go for Monday morning.

I WENT UPSTAIRS after the testing, and walked through the doors of the ward, and Ouajiballah was right there in front of me, talking quietly to one of the nurses. When he saw me he said good-bye to the nurse, put the palm of his hand against my shoulder blade, and steered me to a two-chair waiting room at the end of the hall.

"She is sitting up and talking, sir," he said. "She is quite energetic. But this is not necessarily the best of signs. With cystic fibrosis patients, shortly before the end of their lives, we can sometimes see an unnatural burst of activity like this. We are not sure what causes it. The lungs have very little capacity remaining and are working very hard. When the body works that hard, certain other chemical processes are triggered. Perhaps that is the reason. We don't know. I did not want you to be falsely encouraged."

"Her mother is falsely encouraged, though, I bet."

"Yes."

"The governor passed?"

"Yes, both of you are extraordinarily fit. He visited with Janet briefly."

"Will she live until the operation?"

"Most likely."

I thanked him for everything he had done, then I went into Janet's room, and saw her sitting up in the bed. Her eyes were flashing. She was thin as a stick, and her face was as swollen as if someone had been pumping air into it all afternoon, but even under the oxygen mask, she was smiling.

"The governor was here!" Amelia said, and if Janet was happy, then there is no word for what Amelia was. "He passed! He passed! You passed, too! Look at Janet, look at her!"

Janet pulled the mask down off her face. When she lifted her arm, the hospital bracelet slipped all the way to her elbow. She smiled and pushed at her hair with the fingers of one hand, as if, for the first time in weeks, she cared what she looked like. She and her mother asked me some questions about the testing, and I tried to make little jokes when I answered, exaggerating things. I told them the psychiatrist looked exactly like Geraldo Rivera. I told them the doctors had made me do calculus problems to be sure Janet was getting an intelligent lobe. As a comedian, that night, I wasn't at my best.

After a while, Janet took the mask off completely and said, "Ma, I feel like a chocolate milk shake now, all of a sudden. Would you mind going downstairs and getting me one?"

"A chocolate milk shake?" Mrs. Rossi said. "I'll get you five chocolate milk shakes!"

"Just one, Ma. Or two, if Jake wants one."

Amelia came over, took my face in both hands and gave me a hard kiss straight on the lips, then marched happily out the door on her milk shake run.

"You okay?" Janet said when we were alone. She had taken hold of my right hand and was gripping and regripping it. Her eyes shone out from the puffy skin around them. She was breathing in short gulps.

"Sure. Other than the bruised lips."

"Are you okay about Charlie? Be honest."

"Honestly?"

She frowned.

"He has my vote for all eternity. I don't care what he runs for, or how many times he says he loves you."

"He does love me."

"I figured that out."

"But that street only runs one way."

"Good. We'll fix him up with somebody. We'll start a fund to keep him in escort-service babes and fried clams for life."

She started to laugh, but the laugh caught in her throat and became a cough, and she spit up a bloody mess into the pan. I took the pan to the sink and washed it clean.

"Didn't we start with this?" she said, when she'd caught her breath and wiped her face twice. "Me spitting into a bucket."

"You spit into a bucket only after an evening of gourmet sex."

"Right. I remember now. A swim in the river and gourmet sex. Under a drop cloth, wasn't it?"

"And we started with you smashing my truck, is how we started."

"My insurance company compensated you fairly."

"Blessed are the insurance companies," I said.

She stopped and looked at me long enough so that the little joking air we'd been puffing out floated away. That fast—two blinks—and we were right in the middle of the bright warm room where we never went with words. I thought, for a second, that she was going to thank me, which is not what I wanted. She was holding my fingers. "We had some fun anyway, Jakie," she said. "No matter what happens."

"Sure," I said, but I was starting to have a little trouble talking. Janet was squeezing my hand in sad, excited pulses. Her eyes were like hot black coals in a face as pale and gray as ash. I could see that she was sinking, the little burst of energy already leaking out of her. After all those years of wrestling with it, she knew her body from the inside out, and I knew she could feel the end of her life close by—or at least the end of the life those lungs had given her. It seemed to me then that she was trying to tell me she knew the transplant wasn't going to work.

I started shaking my head against that. My throat wouldn't let anything through, and I would have been afraid to say those things anyway, but what I was thinking was that there are times when you have to push back hard against what happens to you. There are times to yield, and times to push back hard, and this time I wasn't yielding, and I wasn't going to let even the smallest wisp of doubt into the warm, bright room with us. It was very strange, because I wasn't thinking that way for my own benefit, or even for hers. I was having a vision of her, healthy again, pushing two little children on swings in a park. It wasn't a sentimental feeling but a calling almost. A certainty. A vision. We were there in our little puddle of light, speckled and mottled—we were human—but there were parts of the connection between us that were as pure and perfect as threads of virgin silk. I would be thirty-one in eight more days, old enough to know how rare those threads were. Janet knew it, too. She put the mask up to her face for a few seconds, then took it away.

She was holding my left hand. I had my right hand in my pants pocket, poking just the tip of my middle finger through the ring. I wanted to do what I was going to do in a way that was movie-star cool, just taking the ring out with one hand and slipping it onto her finger without saying anything, without pulling my other hand away. I tried it. And I got the ring most of the way out of my pocket pretty well, without her noticing anything, but then, somehow, it got snagged up on the edge of the pocket, on the little double line of thread there. Snagged up pretty bad. But I still wanted to do it one-handed, so I tilted my wrist down an inch, and turned it sideways, and then somehow the ring came unsnagged all at once and as I was turning my hand palm-up, it popped out into the air. It flew up only a few inches, but it seemed to stay there for an impossibly long time, wobbling in the light. We were both looking at it. I pulled my hand out of hers and cupped my hands together and caught it, but all hope of being cool was ruined. Before she could say anything, I reached out and slid it onto her finger. She'd lost so much weight that it was like sliding a hula hoop onto a pencil. I took my hands away and the ring almost slid right off. Janet was staring at it.

I waited a few seconds, then I said, "The salesman promised it will shrink after you wash it a few times."

She looked at the ring and looked at it and then looked up at me finally, with such a gleam of joy and love on her face that it almost didn't matter to me what happened after that, whether she lived, or I lived, or whether we would ever be able to adopt children, and pour the feeling we had for each other all over them, minute by minute, year after year. The world was speckled and mottled and full of pain and evil, but during those few months we had stumbled into this little bright room together, and stayed there for a while. That was almost enough.

I said, "It doesn't matter if those old lungs get infected now, does it?"

She shook her head. She was squeezing her left hand to

keep the ring on, and her eyes were full of silvery wet light, and she was the one who couldn't talk now, and we had one quick, over-the-side-of-the-bed kiss, one little breakdown of borders. Then she held me against her with one thin weak arm around the back of my neck, no words coming out but her spirit all wide open against me, yes to yes.

BEFORE HER MOTHER could come back with the milk shakes, I went out of the room to the sound of Janet coughing, and down the stairs, and outside into the damp, cold night. The surgery on Governor Valvelsais and on me had to be done at a different hospital, four miles away, because no hospital wants to tie up all its operating rooms and all its surgeons on one patient. As I drove across town, snow began to fall, cutting diagonally through the darkness. During the testing I had heard the nurses and technicians talking about a storm, and there it was: swirls of small, icy flakes above Boston Common, and a quick dusting of white on the cars and sidewalks of Tremont Street. By the time I'd parked in the lot of the other hospital, the wind was picking up, too. People were walking out the front door with their coats wrapped tight in front of them and their faces lowered.

I checked in and went upstairs. I changed into the hospital gown and lay down in the bed. After a while two nurses came in and talked to me, took my temperature and pulse, made sure I hadn't eaten anything. They told me a little bit about what to expect and then left me alone in the darkness. I listened to the hospital sounds—nurses' shoes, announcements in the hall, the clinking of a cart going past with its load of instruments or plates. I closed my eyes but could not fall asleep for a long while.

Sometime after midnight I heard footsteps in the room. I opened my eyes to see a priest's plain black overcoat in the darkness next to the bed. I thought it was my brother Ellory. I looked up, past the collar, and saw Gerard's smiling face.

"What do we need in the way of materials for tomorrow, Colonel?" he said.

"You have a thing about disturbing my sleep, you know that? I must have lived in the apartment next to you in a past life and played my electric guitar loud all night."

"It was a violin," he said. "You were very devoted." His face was shadowed and tired, but fierce somehow. "I just came from the other hospital and I can report two things: one, members of the clergy are allowed into that ward at any hour. Two, the love of your life is coughing in her sleep."

"Outstanding work."

"I appreciate it, sir."

"Those lungs have to last seven more hours."

"It appears that they will. I will be there when she awakens from the surgery, Colonel, in my capacity as her spiritual counselor. And I shall come give you my report soon afterwards in person."

"Excellent."

"Anything to confess before you go under?'

"Impure thoughts and desires, Father."

"Describe these thoughts and desires in detail," he said. Then he shook my hand, told me he'd seen the ring on Janet's finger, said, "Don't screw it up like I did," and was gone.

I lay awake for another little while, thinking about him and about his wife and the girls.

In the morning I woke up nervous, but not afraid. Snow was still falling outside the window. A nurse came in and gave me a Valium and two sips of water, but the Valium did nothing to make things less real. I knew the governor was already in surgery by then, and Janet, too. Doctor Vaskis would be making a looping incision from her right armpit, down beneath her breast, cutting the muscle between two ribs, then sawing through the sternum, and then making another looping cut on the other side. A lobe from the governor's right lung, and a lobe from my left, would be pulled out between two of our pried-apart back ribs and sent across the city in special coolers, one by one. Time-release life gliding in ambulances through the snow. When everything was set, Vaskis would lift the top of Janet's chest cavity as if it were the hood of a car, take out the ruined right lung while the blood that should have been going through her heart was detoured through a machine at the side of the table. He'd wash and clean the chest cavity. He'd set the governor's lobe in, and then, if everything went well, he'd begin the slow process of sewing together the pulmonary vein and the pulmonary artery and the tube through which Janet's breath would pass—the bronchus.

He'd run some blood through to check the first lobe, then start in on the left side of her body, and do the same thing there, with a part of me.

Two nurses and an orderly came in to the room. They asked if I was ready. I said that I was. I climbed out of the bed and onto a gurney and we rolled off down the hall beneath a parade of ceiling tiles and fluorescent lights. In the elevator, one of the nurses rubbed my arm. When they wheeled me into the operating room, a very young doctor with sandy, boyish hair greeted me, and after they'd wheeled me up beside some machinery I did not want to look at, he said, "Now, Mister Entwhistle, we are going to insert a needle into your vein."

"The veins are the blue ones," I said.

He didn't smile. He put the needle in, and checked the tube attached to it. He said, "Now we are going to start a medicine called fentanyl, a narcotic, which will prepare you for the actual anesthesia."

"Narcotic away," I said.

In another moment the room began to spin and shift in a kaleidoscope of delight. I could feel the drug going through me, down into my arms and legs, pulsing warmly in the middle of me like a billion cells having orgasms. With the pain taken out of it, the world was a wonderful place, a perfect place, and I thought, for an instant, about my sister and brother and mother and dad. They seemed, then, like just four more drips of good matter in a singing, happy sea. I held a picture of Janet in my swirling mind.

"Now we are going to put you to sleep," the doctor said, and from the deepest part of me, the soul of my will, I struggled and struggled and tried to push some words out into the air between us.

"Just give me another few seconds of this," I wanted to say, but I could not manage it.

Conway, Massachusetts
May 3, 2003–January 20, 2005

About the Author

ROLAND MERULLO has written four previous novels and two books of nonfiction. His writing has appeared in the *New York Times, Boston Globe, Philadelphia Inquirer, Newsweek, Outside,* and *Reader's Digest*. He lives in Massachusetts with his wife and two children.

About the Type

This book was set in Granjon, a typeface designed by George William Jones in 1928 for L&M, an English branch of Mergenthaler Linotype Company. It was modeled after sixteenth-century letterforms of Claude Garamond and was named for Garamond's contemporary, Robert Granjon, who was known for his italic types.

Composition by Stratford Publishing Services
Brattleboro, Vermont

Printing and binding by Berryville Graphics
Berryville, Virginia